DEMON'S MATE

HARPER DAKOTA

Cover Design by: Artscandare

Editing by: Lori Parks

WARNING:

This book contains mature themes and is intended to be read by ages 18+. Contains some curse words, sex, knotting, tail play, paranormal creatures, magical and fated mate themes. Brief scenes of kidnapping and captivity, torture, attempted rape, and trauma flashbacks. Scenes are graphic and do go into detail.

TRADEMARK ACKNOWLEDGEMENTS:

The author acknowledges the following trademarks and trademark status of these items mentioned in the book, including: The Proposal, Nailed It, The Great British Baking Show, Twix, Reese's, Starbucks, Tylenol, Google, Gardenscapes, Costco, Target, Walmart, Uber.

To my family. I love you all. To my husband: thank you for pushing me to finally publish. I wouldn't have gotten here without you.

To the wonderful people who help make this happen: my beta reader, proofreader, formatter, and cover designer. And thank you to everyone who reads and reviews!

SYNOPSIS

Viv had her job, her best friend, and a great apartment. So what if dating had been awful lately? When her best friend finds his forever person, it turns out that all those paranormal romance books she liked to read had some truth to them. Unfortunately, she also learns that having a mate doesn't always mean happily ever after.

Mac wasn't looking for a mate, especially a human one. He's avoided humans as much as possible for hundreds of years after his first mate tried to kill him. To say he has trust issues would be an understatement. He's happy his friend found his mate and they seemed to be doing well, but no one can make him accept the one suddenly thrust into his orbit. Who knew fate would give him another mate after all these years?

Will they be able to overcome Mac's fears, or will an enemy lurking in the shadows take the choice from them?

PROLOGUE

Viv opened the apartment door, propping it open with her foot as she juggled a few bags of snacks and soups for Thomas and tried to get the keys out of the lock. He hadn't been feeling well this morning and had taken the day off. She had left him with some medicine and a bottle of water, but she knew they were out of soups and saltine crackers. She had decided to grab a few things and drop them off during her lunch break. Wiggling her key out of the lock, she looked up to find her best friend and roommate bent over the back of the couch, his boyfriend behind him gripping his hips and thrusting.

"Oh shit! Sorry!" Viv mumbled, slamming the door shut.

She stood in the hallway in shock for a minute before giggling. Okay then. That had never happened before in all their years together. Normally he was better at telling her he was having someone over. Was he even sick? Maybe D had stopped by to check in on him. Viv decided to leave the groceries outside the door and text him, in the event that he really was feeling bad. He could grab them later.

Viv climbed back into her car, knowing she was going to give him so much grief over this later. She started typing a text to Thomas, her fingers stopping suddenly. Did D have a tail and horns? She had been so shocked by seeing them having sex that she somehow missed that. But sitting here, thinking about it, she was pretty sure she had seen a tail and a pair of black horns. Maybe they were having some sexy role play?

Not her business. Viv hit send and turned the car on, only to scream at a knock on the window. Thomas stood there in his robe and bare feet. He made the rolling the window down motion.

"I'm sorry! I didn't mean to interrupt! Just ignore me and go back to...whatever. I wanted to leave you some soup and snacks," she said.

"Viv. Can you come back in? I need to talk to you," Thomas asked her, his face serious.

"I'm on my lunch break. Can we talk tonight?"

Thomas shook his head. "I really need to talk to you now," he replied.

Viv looked over her friend closely wondering why he needed to talk to her so badly. There weren't any marks on him, other than maybe a hickey, and he didn't seem like he was feeling that badly anymore. After double-checking that he was okay, she called her boss to see if she could take a half day. Her boss was great and since she rarely took off, it wasn't a problem. Hanging up the phone, she climbed back out of the car.

When they got back to their apartment, D was dressed in clothes, no sign of horns or a tail. It must have been a costume, she thought. D seemed nervous as Thomas stood next to him, grabbing hold of his hand.

"So, there are a couple of things we needed to talk to

you about," Thomas said, biting his lip, a sure sign he was nervous. "D and I were thinking of moving in together," he admitted, shifting on his feet.

Viv was shocked. She knew they had been getting along really well, even exchanging 'I love yous.' But she hadn't expected this. She liked D, she really did, but this seemed fast. Were they asking her to move out? Or move D in?

"Um...can you...expand on that?" she finally asked, knowing she could be working herself up over nothing. "Do you need your own space? I can see if there's a single bedroom apartment available in the building." She really liked the location of their building and wanted to stay close.

"No!" Thomas shouted, running over to her, and grabbing her in a hug. "I will never, ever kick you out. You're my best friend, my family. I just wanted to talk to you about options. See if D could move in here, or if you would be more comfortable with us finding our own place. He has a home out of town, but he wanted to move here permanently."

Viv nodded, feeling relieved. That was something easy enough to work with. "I'm fine with D moving in. As long as you remember to let me know if I need to go get coffee or something. Although D is incredibly nice to look at, I'd rather not walk in on you two again," she teased.

"Did you see anything weird?" Thomas asked cautiously.

Viv shook her head. "I'm fine with you role playing, or whatever. I just don't need to see it, you know? Just like I'm sure you wouldn't want to see me having sex," she pointed out.

Thomas gagged. "No, I definitely don't want to see that. Um. So. What if it wasn't role playing?"

"Thomas. We've known each other forever. I'm fine with whatever you do that makes you happy. Role play, dress up, get kinky. I don't care as long as you're safe and happy. I just don't necessarily need to see it, yeah?" Viv couldn't figure out why he was pressing this. What he wanted to do with his partner was his business. As long as it didn't cause him harm, it wasn't anyone else's concern.

"I don't know how to do this," he said, looking over at D.

"I can show her?" D offered.

"I really, really don't need to see," she protested. Viv didn't know why they would want her to see them naked again. Thomas had never been into exhibitionism before.

"Wait a sec," Thomas told D. He looked her right in the eyes and said, "Remember the types of books you like to read? The paranormal ones?"

Viv nodded, really confused now. What did her books have to do with them getting naked?

"What if it was real?"

"That would be cool," she said slowly, wondering if Thomas hit his head or something while they had been having sex. The frame on the couch was pretty hard.

"So, uh. D is a demon. But he's nice, right? He's not mean, most of them aren't. I wasn't sure if you saw his tail or horns when you came in earlier?" Thomas asked.

"I saw the costume he had on," Viv admitted.

"Did you see a headband or belt for the tail?" Thomas pointed out gently.

"No, but there are plugs," Viv replied, her face bright red, knowing that tail plugs were a thing.

D laughed, shaking his head. "No plugs for me," he said.

Thomas grabbed her hand, looking at her intently. "Can

you listen to me please, and not freak out? You're my friend and I don't want to lose you over this."

"You'll never lose me," she protested.

"Okay. Just breathe and watch D," Thomas told her, still holding on to her hand.

Viv watched as D took his shirt off. She made a noise of protest when he started unzipping his pants, but Thomas shushed her.

"Just wait."

D shoved his pants down, stepping out of them, keeping his underwear on. There was a pressure in the air and Viv's world changed. She knew her mouth was hanging open, her eyes wide in shock, but she was in no way in control of her reaction at this point. D had suddenly sprouted horns on the top of his head, a tail snaking out behind him. The horns were black and tipped in red, his tail a dark, deep, almost black-red color with black swirling designs. The tip was lightly pointed, almost arrow-shaped but with rounded edges. He had grown all over, both gaining a few inches in height, but also bulking up in muscles.

As she stared at him, D reached out his hand, now tipped in black curved nails. "You can touch," he offered, his voice deeper, a little rougher.

Viv slowly reached out, lightly touching his hand. His skin felt different, a little tougher, more textured. The claws were real, and she jumped when the tail wrapped around Thomas' waist. Viv sat down suddenly on the floor as her legs gave out on her. Her mind racing. There was no way a plug would allow D to move the tail like that. What the fuck?

Thomas sat next to her and started to explain that he had wanted her to know the truth. He didn't want to keep anything from her, especially something so big in his life. Her brain felt fuzzy and a little lightheaded, but she was determined to get over it. D moved off to the side, coming back a minute or so later, his clothes back on. Viv briefly wondered if they made special pants with tail holes.

"Okay. I think I'm ready. Let me move to the couch first. I'm too old to sit on the floor for long."

"We're not old!" Thomas protested.

"Tell that to my butt," she muttered, her left cheek starting to go numb. Viv shakily stood up, shaking her leg a bit to encourage circulation before sitting on the couch.

Thomas sat in D's lap in the chair across from her. "I did meet D at a club. He was hot and could dance and was funny. He made sure I drank enough water, got something to eat. Just made me feel safe and cared for. Which is all I've ever wanted. I thought it would be a hookup or maybe I could convince him to go on a few dates, but D made it clear he was looking for something long term. We didn't do anything more than kiss that night, maybe a few close dances. *(More like grinding together, she thought, knowing how her friend danced with someone he was into.)* We went on a date the next day and it was perfect, but D still didn't put out," Thomas teased his boyfriend.

"You know why," D protested, his face pink.

"I know," Thomas said softly, pressing a kiss to his cheek. "Anyway, I felt connected to him, super fast. I know I have an issue of falling quickly and was worried I was repeating this cycle again, so I was actually happy that D was taking it slow, even if I teased him about it. It wasn't until about a week into our dating that D had to go out of town for work. He ended up popping in my room one night, looking like he had gotten into a fight. You were already asleep," he said.

"I was going to say, I don't remember the doorbell going off at all," she replied.

"It didn't," Thomas said. "He literally just appeared. Apparently, they can create portals to places, although it's to places they've already been or to a specific person. That night, he had ported to where I was. He had gotten in a fight, but it was work related," Thomas said, looking at D.

D cleared his throat. "I guess that it's my turn. So. Uh. Demons do live in the Underworld, Hell, whatever you want to call it. We call it Netherworld. We have jobs, houses, and families just like everyone else. There are angels too. We're not really like Christianity portrays us at all. That was made up to keep humans in line by churches. There is a heaven and a hell, as it were, but we help keep the balance. Angels work for and guard heaven, or Arlysium, demons work for and guard the underworld. Lucifer and God are like CEOs of different companies. We help keep evil souls from coming back into the world, either as spirits or as reincarnations or possessions. Angels help good souls find peace, whether that's hanging out in heaven, floating along as a spirit, or being reincarnated. Trust me, angels aren't all purity and virtue," he said with a smirk. "They're just as naughty as anyone. Demons aren't all bad, although we tend to be a bit more mischievous, maybe more promiscuous than most humans. We live a long time, and sex isn't really associated with love like humans do. We do have mates though, same with angels and other kinds of nonhumans."

"Mates? Like fated mates in the romance books?"

"Similar. We can recognize them by scent, although perfumes and colognes can block someone's natural scent and make it hard for us to realize it. There's a connection, but we still have to work at making a relationship, it's not an easy give-me. I've known mates who have separated or gotten the equivalent to a divorce. Just because you are chemically compatible doesn't mean that it's going to work out. When it's two nonhumans, it's a little easier because we know what that connection means. When it's with a human, it's harder because we need to woo you a little more, plus explain everything and hope the person is understanding and accepting."

"What happens if they're not? Like what if you get paired with someone who hates anything not normal?" Like a bigot or ultra-conservative religious person. She didn't imagine a pairing with a demon would go over well.

"There's an emergency number to call," he admitted. "They would have their memory erased. The nonhuman would continue on with their life, hoping that eventually they might be granted another mate."

"Do you get more than one?" she asked, surprised.

"Sometimes. There's been a few cases where a mate has been rejected, or one of them dies, and they've been granted another one. Sometimes the mate's been reincarnated and this time they match."

"Are you immortal?"

D shook his head. "No. We live a long time though. Thousands of years. We can choose to stay in hell as a spirit or be reincarnated in a new body. Our mate's soul would stay the same, so we generally try to figure out what happened to them first. If they went to heaven then we could remain a spirt and stay with them. We're not confined to hell, and heaven is just another plane just like hell is. If they're in the queue to be reincarnated, then usually the nonhuman tries to be reincarnated around the same time."

"What if you had a mate, they died or rejected you, and

you were granted another one? How would that work when you all die?" Viv asked.

D grinned. "One big happy family. Usually, it ends up in a throuple and they all match to each other."

"Huh." Alrighty then. "Thomas is human. Will you have to watch him age and wait for him to reincarnate?" Viv knew it was rather personal, but she wanted to know.

"In cases like ours, with a human and a nonhuman, when we bond, the human's lifespan will match. If I were to die though, Thomas would die as well if he's older than a normal human. If I would die when he's fifty or sixty and he doesn't have any underlying health problems that would have killed him if he was a typical human, then he would live out the rest of his natural lifespan. If I would die when he's a hundred and fifty, then he would die as well since my lifespan was what was keeping him alive. From what I've seen in other couples, it's like the human stops aging and then suddenly dies one day."

"You'd have to move away," Viv said sadly, thinking of him outliving her and seeing her get old. She had thought they would grow old together with their respective partners. She was still happy for her friend, but sad for herself.

"Maybe eventually. D says there may be something that could conceal my age, something that would make me look like I was aging to most people. If we needed to move, you could always come with us," Thomas offered sincerely.

She shook her head. She didn't want to be the third wheel for the rest of her life. "We'll see what happens," she replied vaguely.

"If I freaked out, what would have happened?" she asked suddenly.

"Mind erase," Thomas admitted, chewing on his bottom lip again, watching her nervously.

Viv reached over and smacked his arm. "Jerk."

"I knew it would be fine!" he protested.

"There's more than angels and demons, I assume?" she said, looking at D.

He nodded. "Shapeshifters, vampires, Fae, djinn, Shadows."

"Are they all like you? Jobs, regular life?"

"Most. Think of it like being a different race. Even us demons and the angels have a human form we take to go out on Earth. Same with the shapeshifters. Older vampires go out in the day, newer ones have an allergy to the sun. It doesn't kill them, but it does make them weaker, making them pretty much human. Shadows have it the roughest; they generally don't have a solid form. It takes a lot of effort to make one. If they have a mate, it's easier for some reason."

"Where do you live? Or work?" she asked, realizing that D had been vague and changed the subject whenever she asked.

"I have a home in Netherworld. I work more of an office job; I sort the souls as they come in. Most of the time they belong there, but every so often we get one that was lost and sent in by mistake. I send them back where they belong. The others who belong there, I sort and send to different areas. For those souls, it's not a fun place to be. There is punishment for what they've done. I help decide the level of punishment they deserve and send them there. There are others who administer the punishments. Not everyone there works with the souls though. There's the same type of jobs humans have; garbage collection, cleaning, food service, shop keepers, creatives. My dad works in punishments, my mom is a painter. She has her art in galleries both in Netherworld and on Earth."

"How did you get in a fight at work, if you have an office job?" she asked. Were office jobs more violent in the underworld?

"There was a particularly strong soul that didn't want to be there. He had been brought in by an Enforcer after terrorizing Earth. He had escaped custody a couple of years ago when they first tried to bring him in and had been haunting and possessing people since then. He jumped around a lot, which made him harder to catch. He tried fighting his way out when he was brought to me."

Wow. Okay then. Office jobs there could be more dangerous. Although if she thought of it more like a jail, she imagined people who worked in human law enforcement dealt with similar situations.

"Why would you move here? Is Thomas not allowed in Netherworld?"

"You're here," D said simply, hugging Thomas tighter.

Viv looked at Thomas wanting more of an explanation.

"You're here," he repeated. "I could go there since I'm D's mate, but you can't. Humans aren't allowed unless they're mates. They go mad, like crazy. We'll vacation or take date nights there, but I'm not missing any time with you," he said, tears in his eyes.

Because she would die before him, she realized. She held her breath and counted slowly to three, keeping her own tears in. How horrible would it be for her friend to watch her age and die? She didn't want to waste any time with him either, but that didn't seem like something that would be good for him.

"Nope. Don't even think about it," Thomas said firmly when she opened her mouth. "I'm a grown-assed man and I've made up my mind. I am not leaving you. I don't care if I have to change your diapers when you're old, I'm not giving you up until I have to."

Viv surprised herself when a laugh escaped. "Ew. Just hire someone at that point. I don't need you touching my bits."

"Good point. Don't make me give you up, okay?" Thomas pleaded, giving her teary puppy eyes.

She never could say no to those eyes which is why they had gotten into trouble at school so many times. "Fine," she huffed, not really angry but trying to tease him. "Are you really okay with moving in here?" she asked D. She didn't want him to give up everything just to make Thomas happy either. There was a compromise somewhere.

"I am. You guys are a pair, I've known that from the moment I met him. If it gets to be too tight or awkward, we can talk about other options. I've been thinking about it a lot. If need be, we can buy a larger-sized house close to both of your jobs. I can port from anywhere to work."

"That would work," she agreed. She didn't need a repeat of today. Or even a two-family house might work.

Viv nodded, feeling touched that they wanted to still keep her close, but also at the end of her ability to keep the tears in. "Is there anything else I need to know right now?" she asked. It had been a lot, and she was feeling wiped out and ready for a nap. Not to mention a cry.

D shook his head. "I think everything else can wait. It's not something you can talk about with anyone else," he cautioned.

"Oh! There is something else I have to show you!" Thomas shouted as he jumped up. He threw his robe off, thankfully wearing underwear. "Look!" he said, thrusting his arm in front of her face.

He now had a tattoo around his arm. It looked similar to

the ones D had. D pulled his sleeves up, showing off his new band too. This one was more stylized than the others. It looked like there was a cursive script as well, but she didn't recognize the language.

"When did you get a tattoo?" she asked, surprised. Thomas had never expressed an interest in getting ink before, probably because he had a low pain tolerance.

"They're not tattoos! When we mated and accepted each other, it showed up. Pretty cool, huh? It looks badass and it didn't really hurt much."

"What's the language?" she asked, curious.

"Netherkin and Entiretium. Netherkin is the demon language, Entiretium is the universal nonhuman language. It shows I'm mated. Mine says Mate of Thomas, and Thomas' says Mate of D, although it is my entire name which is hard to translate to English. Most nonhumans have something similar in their language and in Entiretium. Shapeshifters and vampires also have bite marks."

"That's pretty cool. Do the rest of your tattoos mean something?" she asked, incredibly curious.

D nodded. "Family line, job and level," he pointed out. "Sometimes there are others, like for children, or those we take under our protection."

Viv didn't want to get into what that meant right now. She just wanted to escape to her room and to let her brain digest everything.

"I'm so happy you guys found each other, and I can't wait for you to move in, D. That means I get your lasagna more often," she teased. "My brain is exhausted though, so I'm going to go take a nap. Be warned; I'm going to have a ton of questions later." She gave them both a hug before going to her room.

Climbing on her bed, she grabbed a pillow, thinking over everything. How did they get here? Thomas was her family, her best friend, her brother from different parents. They had always been together. They grew up just a few houses apart, attended the same high school, even dormed together in college. She had been there when he came out to his parents in high school. To be fair, she thought that everyone had known since he was younger but had waited to say something until he did. There were a few assholes in their school, but in general Thomas was liked and it had gone as well as she could have hoped for her friend.

After college, they both stayed local. Viv worked as a librarian, having worked there in college part-time and then hired on full-time after graduation. Thomas was a grade school teacher and they had found an apartment to share that was close to both their jobs. She enjoyed her work; she viewed being a librarian as someone who helped others. She had free rein on what books to stock, and made sure to have a wide variety, including self-help, banned, and LGBTQ+ books. She loved sharing her knowledge and love of reading with others.

The paranormal romance book section had always been her favorite. She adored the fated mate book trope. How awesome would it be to have someone just know you were perfect for them? To know they would always be faithful to you? She had thought it was a nice fairy tale until today. When Thomas had met D a few months ago, he had raved about him the next day. She had been wary, especially after finding her last boyfriend in bed with someone else. Thomas tended to see the good in people and he had been screwed over several times with his trusting nature. But then he had brought D to meet her. He had been extremely handsome; tall, towering over both of them at six foot six inches, dark auburn hair that looked like it was on fire when the sunlight hit it, piercing green eyes. D had actually taken the time to get to know her, and at this point she considered him a good friend as well. He wasn't threatened by her and Thomas' friendship. He took excellent care of Thomas and was everything she could have asked for in a partner for him.

She had always known that someday one or both of them would find their significant other and had hoped that they could still stay close to each other. Viv was happy that Thomas had found his person, while at the same time feeling sad and like she was left behind. Which was ridiculous since Thomas made it clear he wasn't going anywhere. But he would outlive her by thousands of years. He would watch her age, getting slowly more frail and sickly until one day she died. How was that fair or good for him? But if it was reversed, she wouldn't want to give him up either. The undeniable heartbreak would be worth having many more years together. Viv covered her face with a pillow as she let the tears flow, not wanting him to hear her cry.

1

"Viv! Come here!" Thomas whisper-shouted.

"Wha'?" she came out of her bathroom, toothbrush still in her mouth.

"Look outside!"

She wandered over to the window to stand next to him. They didn't have the best view, it was mostly of the parking lot, but at least it let in a lot of sunlight. It wasn't raining, no major craziness going on, and it was too late for a pretty sunrise.

"Wha' am I lookin' at," she mumbled around her toothbrush.

"Down there! Look at the hottie," Thomas said, grabbing her head and turning her to look at where his partner was standing with another guy.

"Oh," Viv said, the toothbrush forgotten in her mouth. The guy was gorgeous, at least from up here. He was a little taller than D, his hair dark. She couldn't tell what color his eyes were from so far away. He was built like a brick house: solid, wide, trim waist, large biceps. He had a slightly rounded ass, his thighs thick. He was huge and muscular. Yum.

"Who is that?" she asked.

"Don't know. One of D's friends. Did you know you're drooling?" Thomas asked, laughing.

Which meant that was the exact moment the mystery man chose to look up at them. She hurriedly wiped her face, her hand now coated in toothpaste and saliva. Lovely. That was sure to make a good impression. His eyes bored into hers and she swore she felt a connection, but he sharply turned away, putting his back to them. For some reason that made her heart ache a bit.

"Thanks for that," she said dryly, ignoring the way it hurt when he turned away. It didn't make any sense.

"Anytime," Thomas replied cheerfully.

"I'm going to finish getting ready," she said, walking back to her bathroom. She did her best to put the man out of her head. She had things she needed to get done today. The library was going to be busy. There were several book clubs meeting, a delivery was due this afternoon which would mean inputting and cataloguing everything into the system, and then there was also story time and a tutoring event after school.

She shouted goodbye to Thomas, who was in the other bathroom when she was leaving. As she walked out of the building, she passed close to D and his friend. They were standing within ten feet of her car, so it wasn't like she was being a creeper trying to get a better look.

"See you later, D! Bye," she called out. As much as she wanted to go over and introduce herself, she worried that it would seem weird. She was going to be late to work as it was if she didn't leave now.

The wind blew past her, making her shiver. As it hit the

men, the mystery guy stiffened, his head whipping around to stare at her. Weird. She smiled and waved at them. D waved back, but his friend didn't. He just stared. Alrighty then. She didn't get creeper vibes, so she would find a way to ask D about it tonight.

Pulling into her spot, she was excited to go to work. Her boss had been giving her more responsibilities the longer she was there. She thought that maybe he was grooming her to take his spot when he retired. It would be amazing to be in charge of her own library. The only thing that might top that would be owning her own bookstore. Either way, she was going to be able to help people learn to love reading and would books that would help everyone in her jurisdiction. She firmly believed that the mission of a librarian was to help; whether that was to provide self-help books, help them research a school paper, get them in touch with a tutor, or just listen when they came to the desk.

"You live with a human?" Mac asked, trying to keep the derision out of his voice.

"Two of them actually. My mate is human, remember? Viv is his best friend. If you can have platonic soulmates, that would be them. I knew when I met Thomas that they were a packaged pair."

"And you're fine living in this place?" Oops, that sounded more condescending than he wanted it to. But come on, instead of the nice house in the Netherworld that was what was expected of a demon of D's level and job, he was choosing to live here. In an apartment. In a shared apartment. When he had a perfectly good house back home.

"I am. It's a nice enough apartment, but I'm looking at buying a house close to Thomas' work. I think I found one, but it needs some renovation, so I may buy it and then have it worked on before I tell him. If he doesn't like it, I can always sell it. It's a good investment either way."

"It would be good for you to have your own place," Mac agreed. The less humans nearby the better, in his opinion.

"No, Viv would live with us too, if she wanted. The place I'm looking at would give each of us our own spaces, with a communal kitchen and living room area. Thomas doesn't want to give up his friend."

"She's just going to get old and die," Mac muttered.

"She is," D agreed. "Until that time, she's part of our family," he said firmly, a warning in his voice. "They're human, Mac, but they're not bad. They both accepted me right away. Viv even made sure it wouldn't be too hard for me to live here. They're not anything like your past. Those people exist, but Viv and Thomas are the complete opposite. I want you to give them a chance."

"We're friends. I'll be nice to your mate," he said. He didn't want anything to do with the other one.

D started to respond but then looked up and snorted. Mac turned around and saw two humans standing in an upper window looking at them. Based on the besotted look on his friend's face, the male must be his mate. Which left the female as the friend slash roommate. He wrinkled his nose in disgust as a line of used toothpaste goop trailed out of her mouth. He turned away, not wanting to see more. In his experience, nothing good ever came from being near humans. Just standing near the apartment complex that housed so many of them made his skin itch.

"Mac," D started.

"Nope. I will be nice to your mate. You cannot make me be nice to his friend. I'm not going to be near her often anyway. I'll be polite if I have to, but I will not befriend her. Don't ask this of me," he said, trying for demanding, but he had a feeling it sounded more pleading.

"Fine," D sighed. "But no being a dick, or I'll never hear the end of it. Tell me about work. Do you have another assignment, or did they give you a break?"

"There's a rumor of a Shadow turning bad. It sounds a lot like a haunting, but the few witness reports list a dark shadowy mist, which makes me think it's a Shadow. He's been escalating for a long time if the rumors are right. From what I've been able to piece together, he started with lighter offenses, and I've found connections to newer more serious offenses. If I can nab him, he's going to be meeting you. He definitely belongs in the punishments, but I'll keep you informed," Mac promised.

"Be careful," D said. He had faith in Mac's abilities, but he knew it only took a second of inattention for things to go badly.

"I will."

"See you later, D! Bye," a light cheerful female voice called out. His demon stirred, looking for the source of the noise.

Mac kept his back turned to the parking lot, not wanting to encourage her to come over. A gust of wind blew toward them, carrying a scent on the air. Mac whipped around to see where it came from. There was only one person in the parking lot. The female from the window. She didn't have toothpaste on her now. She was much shorter than him, probably about five foot four, if he had to guess. Her brown hair was slightly wavy, her blue eyes bright and cheery. She was average weight, he would guess, though she had thick thighs. No thigh gap there, he thought. His favorite kind.

His demon roared in his head, his nostrils flaring as he breathed in her scent. Mac made certain to keep his face bland, not giving D any clues that something was wrong. D waved at her, but he kept his hands firmly at his sides. He couldn't bring himself to turn away though. It wasn't until her car turned out of the parking lot that he could tear his gaze away.

D was looking at him concerned.

"No. I'm not in the mood," Mac said. "I've gotta go. See you later." He ported out, back to his home in Netherworld. As he stood in his kitchen, his demon side trying to tear out of him, he screamed, letting lose all the anger and frustration he had inside. When he was done, he felt empty. How could the higher-ups be so cruel? He had already been betrayed by a mate, one who had tried to kill him. Breaking that bond had nearly killed him in the process, something that not even D knew. How could they have given him another human mate?

2

It was time to go, she realized as her alarm went off. She was supposed to be meeting Thomas at the coffee shop. He had been in Netherworld with D for some alone time, aka being able to be loud during sex. At this point, it didn't even seem awkward sharing the apartment with them. D had become like another brother and he was a great chef; she had been treated to many wonderful dinners that she didn't have to make. Which was a nice change because Thomas had a hard time making even plain pasta. Half the time it was still crunchy, the other half mushy. It was nice having someone else who could help in the kitchen.

Although there was no set schedule, it seemed like once a month they had a group date. Date wasn't the right word, but they all hung out together. D made sure that she and Thomas still had their Friday nights to themselves. They had always kept Fridays for each other since high school, and D made sure they kept that tradition. It was very sweet of him, and Viv tried to make sure he knew how much he meant to her too. She made his favorite cookies every week and he was always so excited to get them. Poor guy had such a sweet tooth and his mate couldn't make him any. To be fair, Thomas had tried when they first got together. The cookies had turned into hockey pucks. D had been so nice about it and had even tried to eat one, but it had almost broken his tooth.

Pulling into the lot, she saw Thomas, D, and D's friend sitting at a table. She wondered if today was going to be the day she finally officially met the handsome guy. He always seemed to disappear when she was around. As she pulled open the door, his eyes met hers and a bolt of awareness ran through her. His eyes just pulled her in each time she saw them.

"Gotta go, D. I'll let you know if anything comes up," he said.

D sighed. "Bye, Mac. Be careful. This guy is getting more reckless."

He nodded and left. As he walked by her, she caught a whiff of his cologne. God, he smelled amazing. She wanted to roll in the scent. Shaking it off, she walked to the counter to order her coffee. She got a refill for Thomas and D as well. It looked like their cups were almost empty.

"Hey, you. I missed you," Thomas said, coming up next to her in line.

"I missed you too," she said, turning to give him a hug. "How was your time away?"

Thomas blushed, but he grinned. "Delicious. Ten out of ten, would recommend."

Viv shook her head but had to smile. "Good. I'm glad. Mac couldn't stay again?" she tried to ask casually.

"He's been busy with this case. He only dropped in to update D. I guess if he can bring the guy in, D's the one that would be dealing with him."

"What does Mac do?"

"He's an Enforcer. I know he tracks down the bad guys, but I'm not sure if he works for Lucifer or if he works for both Netherworld and Arlysium. He's always polite enough when he's near me, but he's not very talkative."

Viv nodded and grabbed the drinks when they were placed on the counter.

"Oh! I bought you something!" Thomas said, bending down to dig in his backpack as they sat down. "Here," he said, handing over a small jewelry-sized box.

"Thank you," she said, smiling. "It's not even my birthday." Opening the box, she saw a beautiful necklace, a silver pendant hanging from the chain.

"It will let you call me when I'm out of town," he explained.

It took her a second. Out of town? Oh, to call down to Netherworld. Right now, her cell phone couldn't call him when he was there.

"Thank you! It's so pretty," she said, as she slipped it over her head.

"I miss talking to you when I'm gone and I worry sometimes since you can't reach me," Thomas said.

"I am a grown-up," she pointed out. "But I miss talking to you too." This was the thing that had driven a lot of boyfriends away. On her side, they didn't understand how they could be so close and not be in a relationship. On his side, they didn't like sharing, or something. D just smiled and seemed happy to have her around. She couldn't be the third wheel all of the time though and she was thinking that maybe it was time to give dating a try again. The image of Mac popped in her head, but she didn't think he was interested. He had plenty of opportunities to talk to her but usually left with maybe a head nod if she was lucky.

"What did you guys do on your trip? Besides each other," she teased.

D turned red and Thomas laughed. "Went sightseeing, some shopping. I met his parents, who turned out to be really nice. You would love his mom. She loves baking too and watches The Great British Baking Show. You guys could bond over Paul."

"It's the blue eyes."

"They are gorgeous. Not as gorgeous as green ones," Thomas assured his mate, giving him a kiss.

"What was there to sightsee?" she asked, curious.

"There were a bunch of shops in his town. Apparently, there's different towns scattered all over. Since they can get places so easily, they don't have to live close to work."

Being able to create a portal and port to different locations would make your commute a lot faster.

"I took him to see the beach nearby. It's not in town, but not far. If you drove, it would be maybe an hour or so," D added.

Thomas leaned forward. "The beaches are a little freaky. The sand is all black and the water is red. There's some funky-looking fish too. I'm not sure if I'm going swimming there anytime soon."

"You guys have sharks," D pointed out.

"I saw that fish. I think I'd prefer a shark," Thomas shot back.

"Was it that bad?" she asked.

"It was clear, like you could see all of its veins and organs. It had tusks, not teeth, but tusks, top and bottom. It had two tiny arms with even tinier hands, plus normal fish fins, a tail like a snake. The worst part was its face looked like one of those shrunken heads, complete with a few strands of hair. It gave me nightmares of being eaten."

"Love, you're too big for that fish to eat. They go after much smaller prey," D pointed out helpfully.

"Be quiet. I'm still not swimming in the water with them," Thomas said adamantly, shaking his head.

"Okay," D laughed. "You don't have to."

"Did you get any pictures?" Viv asked.

Thomas shook his head. "Pictures aren't allowed to leave there. But the good thing with the pendant, is I think we can do a video call and I can show you," he said excitedly.

"That would be cool!" That would be amazing actually. She would be able to be part of that side of his life as well in some small way. It would help that she could understand what he was talking about, since he didn't have anyone else to discuss these things with besides her and D.

"What do you guys want to do the rest of the day? Do you have laundry to catch up on?"

"We got it done before we left. I thought we could go see a movie? There's that new rom-com we talked about. It's playing in an hour, if you wanted to go?"

"That sounds perfect," she agreed.

D excused himself to run to the bathroom. While he was gone, Viv leaned forward. "What do you think of me trying out a dating app?"

Thomas frowned. "Is this because of me?"

"No, not really. What you guys have is amazing and I want to find that for myself. Even if it's with a regular old human," she teased. It was partly because of them, she felt lonely and wanted to be able to find someone to love and who loved her in return, but she didn't want him to feel bad. If he hadn't found D, she would have probably been content without putting herself out there again.

"Okay. But I reserve the right to approve your profile

and the guys. D has to meet them too. He has a good sense if people are good or bad."

"Sounds good to me," she agreed. If D could tell her which ones to avoid, that would save a lot of time.

"What sounds good?" D asked as he slid back into his seat.

"Having you clear Viv's dates," Thomas said.

D got a weird look on his face, but it cleared so quickly that she wasn't sure what she had seen. "Dates? I didn't know you were dating anyone," he said.

"I'm not. Not yet. I was just thinking of trying dating again and Thomas said you and he needed to clear my dates."

"Of course we do," D agreed. "Is there someone you're interested in?"

"I haven't met anyone who I think is interested in me," she replied, thinking of Mac again and avoiding answering with a yes or no. "I was thinking of joining an app. I'm too old to try the bar scene."

"We're not old!" came the expected response from Thomas.

Viv laughed. "I'm not a big bar person, never have been," she explained to D. "There's usually only older guys or dads who come into the library, so I don't have a lot of opportunities to meet people at work. I thought maybe joining a dating app would help."

"I definitely need to clear all your dates then. You'd be surprised how many guys from dating apps end up where I work," D said.

Maybe dating could wait awhile then, although she did want to find her person.

3

Mac was beyond frustrated. His demon was clawing at his insides trying to go see Viv. She was cute, he'd admit that, but she had the misfortune of being a human. He had vowed never to get involved with another human again, and other than when he had to deal with them for work, he had kept that vow for hundreds of years. He wasn't going to break it now. He didn't care why they had paired him with another human for a mate. He was doing pretty well avoiding her, but he didn't miss the way her eyes lingered on him when they were near the same area.

His phone started ringing.

"Hey. How's it going?" he asked, seeing D's name on the screen.

"Alright. I thought I'd check in on you. It's been a couple weeks since I've seen you. How's the case going?"

"It's not," he sighed. "It's hard enough to collect evidence left behind by a Shadow, but then there's the problem with any witnesses. As in there's none. If I talk to one or set up a meeting, they end up dead. I'm starting to wonder if he has an accomplice. I can't pinpoint anything, just this feeling I have."

"Go with your gut. It's never been wrong," D advised.

"Except for the time it was," Mac pointed out.

"The mate pull and your excitement led you to not paying attention to it. I guarantee it was there. You know now to be more cautious and to listen to it harder," D told him.

"D. I was almost killed. The person who was supposed to be my mate set a trap for me. They bound me, shot me, dosed me in salt and holy water, and she tried to stab me through the heart. The only reason I didn't die was because she was off by an inch. Those were all humans. I get that your mate is human, and he seems decent but I'm not willing to accept all humans just because of one."

"You're willing to write them all off because of one," D countered.

Mac rubbed his head, feeling a headache coming on. It was an old argument, neither side having gained ground for over a hundred years. "The most important one. The one meant to be my mate. And there were other humans there as well."

"Okay. I just worry about you. You might miss out on something wonderful if you keep hold of this hatred."

Mac snorted. "I'm fine and I'm not missing out on anything." A face popped in his mind, but he shoved it back in a box.

"I'll let it go for now. Call if you need anything, even just to talk. I've got to run. Viv has a date picking her up in a couple of minutes and I told Thomas I'd look him over to make sure he wasn't on track to show up at our jobs."

"I didn't know she was dating anyone," he said, aiming for a casual tone.

"She just started. She said she wanted to have someone special in her life too. I guess there wasn't anyone she thought was interested in her, so she joined a dating app."

"That's not safe," Mac protested. "We get a lot of those guys brought to us."

"That's what I told her! It's why I'm here to at least make sure they're not evil. Can't do much more than that, but I can at least make sure they're not killers or abusers. Gotta go, that's the doorbell. Call if you need me."

Mac sat there for a second, staring at his phone. He didn't know why the thought of Viv dating was making his stomach sour, but it was. He didn't want her, remember? he told himself. If she wanted to date other people, good. It would keep her away from him.

His demon growled, unhappy with the news. Mac blinked and somehow found himself outside of her apartment. He stayed in the shadows, using his abilities to blend and hide. The door opened and she walked out next to another human. Mac snorted. This guy couldn't fight his way out of a sack. He was scrawny, with tiny little facial hair trying to grow into a goatee. There was no way this puny human could protect his—his friend's friend. He didn't even open the doors for her. Maybe he should follow just to make sure the guy didn't try anything. He knew Viv by scent so he could follow and port wherever they went. Not that he didn't trust D, but there was a big difference between killers and rapists and the average asshole. If the guy started to become an asshole, Mac could step in, he decided. It was to help a friend of a friend, after all.

Grinning, he opened a portal and followed the car until it stopped at a restaurant. It was okay looking, nothing impressive. It was like this guy wasn't even trying. Sliding into the restaurant, cloaked in shadows, he followed them to their table. As he passed by her chair, which the guy didn't pull out for her, her head came up and she looked around the room. Did she sense him? When she didn't see anything, her shoulders drooped, but he watched as she put a cheerful smile on.

"Thanks for picking me up. Did you grow up here?" she asked.

"No. I was transferred for work. This wasn't my first choice. I'm transferring back out as soon as possible," the man complained. "I hate this town."

"Oh. What do you do?"

"Finance type of stuff. What do you do?"

"I'm a librarian," she replied.

"Really? Those still exist?"

"We do. There are many of us."

"Don't you want to do something better with your life?" her date asked, a snotty tone in his voice.

"No, I enjoy it and I think helping people is very important," Viv replied. Mac could tell she was trying not to lose her temper.

The entire dinner seemed to go that way. What a loser. Mac couldn't have been happier when the guy corrected the waiter and asked for separate checks.

"I just don't see this going anywhere. I want someone with ambition and who wants to leave this loser town. Plus, you don't seem like the type to put out on the first date, so I'm going to say no thanks." He threw a few dollar bills on the table and left. When the checks came, Viv looked at them and swore.

"He didn't even leave enough to cover all of his bill and a tip. What a douche," she muttered.

As she walked outside, she stopped suddenly. Ah. He had driven and then left her at the restaurant. Mac would make sure she got home safely and then pay the man a visit. When the Uber arrived, Mac slid into the car before her, keeping himself cloaked in the shadows. He followed her to the apartment, making sure she got inside safely. She kept checking her surroundings and he wasn't sure if she always did that or if she sensed him.

"How was your date?" he heard Thomas ask as the door opened. He stood by the door, waiting for her answer.

"Horrible. He said I had no ambition staying a librarian, he hates this town, he split the bill but didn't even leave enough money to cover his part, and then he left me there," she said. It sounded like she was crying.

"What do you mean he left you there?"

"He threw some money on the table after telling the waiter to redo the bill and split it. I didn't look like the type to put out, so he wasn't paying for me. Then he left."

"Why didn't you call me to come get you?" Thomas asked.

"I didn't want to take you away from your alone time with D. I Ubered home. I could use a glass of wine, a snuggle, and then bed."

He heard a few sniffles and ported to the man's home. He was already on the app, looking for another date. He may not want a human for a mate, but that didn't mean someone should treat her badly. Maybe it was time to teach this man some manners.

4

Viv looked around the library. It was quiet, but she swore someone was watching her. Grabbing her phone and her Taser, she decided to take a quick walk. She kept her steps light, trying not to make any sounds. She walked the entire library, looking in between the rows, checking behind tables and chairs. Nothing. She was the only one here. The shadows still seemed like they were watching her. Maybe she needed to ask D to come check out the library. She didn't feel unsafe, necessarily, but it was a strange sensation. One that kept distracting her. As crazy as it sounded, it had a familiar presence to it.

She jumped, startled as her phone buzzed in her pocket. Good grief, she was working herself up over nothing. Grabbing her phone, she looked down. It was just the dating app. She sighed. The guy was handsome enough; *not as handsome as Mac*, her brain supplied. He wanted to meet up for drinks tonight. She clicked on his profile, noticing it was a little light on the details, although it looked like he worked locally as a mechanic. She supposed she could go after work and meet him at the bar. D wouldn't have a chance to scan him, but she would let them know where she was going to be. It was a public place so it should be fine. Viv hit accept and put her phone back in her pocket. A breath of air tickled her neck and she spun around trying to find the source. Nothing. There was nothing there.

"Maybe I need this date more than I realized," she grumbled. It was close to closing; she finished up the last of her duties before shutting down the computers and locking the doors. As she climbed into the car, she sent a text to Thomas letting him know she wouldn't be home for dinner and that she had a date. She sent a screenshot of the guy and the location she would be at. They had done this for each other since college after one of their classmates had been drugged at a bar. Luckily, nothing had happened to her. After she had her drink, she had gotten into her car to drive home. She took out two mailboxes and remembered nothing when the cops found her car in her driveway the next morning, but the tox screen showed the date rape drug in her system. Since then, Viv and Thomas had decided to send pictures and locations of their dates to each other. It sounded morbid, but at least there would be something to go on if one of them had issues.

Pulling into the bar, she grimaced. It was packed, which meant that it would be loud and crowded. Not the best for getting to know someone. But maybe they could find a quieter corner or something, she thought optimistically. Pulling open the door, she saw the guy sitting at the bar, already with two drinks in hand.

"Mark?" she asked, coming up next to him.

"Viv? Hi. Have a seat! It was so busy in here; I already ordered us our first drink. I figured we didn't want to wait a long time for the bartender to be free again."

"Oh, thanks," she said, sitting down. She was torn.

Everything in her said not to drink it. That was drilled into her since she was a teenager: don't drink something without a lid or you didn't see poured, don't leave your glass unattended and come back to drink it. She didn't want to insult him either if there was nothing wrong going on. He could just be trying to be nice.

She sat, playing with the drink, but not drinking it yet, trying to decide what to do.

"Did you grow up here or move here?" she asked, trying to get the conversation started.

"I actually live about thirty minutes away. You?"

"I grew up here. I think it's a nice town to live in. You're a mechanic?"

"What do you do?" he asked, not answering her question.

"I'm a librarian. I enjoy helping people find what they need and helping kids learn to love reading."

"You're a big reader then?"

"I am," she answered. "I'd rather read than watch TV most of the time. What about you? Are you a big reader? Or do you have a favorite movie or TV show?"

"I like the real-life crime type of shows. I find them interesting."

"It is interesting to learn more about how people think," she replied.

"Do you live close by or with anyone?" Mark asked.

Viv was taken aback. It seemed like a weird thing to ask. Maybe he was hoping for a hookup.

"I have roommates. My best friend and his boyfriend," she replied.

"Ah. We can always go back to my place. How's your drink?"

"Good," she said, pretending to take a sip. "I'm just going to run to the restroom, I'll be right back."

Viv stood in line for the bathroom, sending a text to Thomas.

Date going iffy. Seems a little weird. Already had a drink ready, but maybe he was just being nice? Then he asked if I lived with anyone and suggested his place when I said yes. She typed out.

Her phone buzzed seconds later.

Don't drink it and don't go home with him. Could be innocent, but don't risk it. Do you want D to port there and take a look at him? Thomas wrote.

Viv bit her lip. She hated dragging D away from Thomas for something that could turn out to be nothing. *Not right now. If it gets weirder, I'll send you a text and he can come then. Thanks. Love ya.*

Love you too. Be safe. Thomas replied.

She took her turn in the bathroom and headed back to the bar. She hadn't realized just how loud it was until she opened the bathroom door and was hit with a wave of sound. The bar had certainly gotten more crowded, and she had to squeeze her way between bodies to reach her seat.

Her date was standing, scowling, brushing his shirt off. His shirt and pants were soaking wet. The bartender was trying to hand him a towel, but Mark was having none of it.

"What kind of idiots does this place hire? Are you retarded? How hard is it to walk by and not spill something on me? Huh? Got nothing to say for yourself? Dumbass. You fucked up; I'm never coming back here and I can't wait to tell everyone I know how shitty this place is. I should sue you for assault."

"What happened?" Viv asked.

"This moron tried to hand me another beer and

knocked over your glass, spilling it all over the floor. Then he somehow dropped my drink in my fucking lap. Guy's a loser. Let's get out of here; you can come back to my place to help me clean up."

"Uh. No, thank you. Not tonight. I'm pretty tired after work. It was nice meeting you though," she said. She understood being angry getting a drink spilled on you, but there was no reason to yell like that at the poor bartender.

"I should have known you were a cock tease," he muttered as he stormed away.

Viv kept her mouth shut. Arguing that meeting for a drink did not mean she would be putting out would be a waste of her energy.

Turning to the bartender, she said, "I'm so sorry for this. Do you need any help cleaning up?"

"No, I've got it. Thanks. You weren't even here when your boyfriend lost it, not your fault."

"Oh! No! He's not my boyfriend. This was a first date," she said. She did not want to be associated with his behavior at all.

"Bad first date," the bartender replied.

"Yeah," she agreed.

"Do you need someone to walk you to your car?" he asked.

She almost said no, but when she opened her mouth, "Yes, please," came out instead.

The bartender nodded, grabbing a walkie-talkie and said, "Need a safety escort."

"Go to the front, check in with Bob. He's the big bouncer at the front door. He'll make sure you get to your car."

"Thank you," she said gratefully. At least there were

some nice people out there still. Two out of two dates had gone poorly.

Bob was a big bald-headed man with large arms. He was dressed all in black and had the walkie-talkie clipped to his belt.

"Safety escort?" he asked.

When she nodded, he opened the door and followed her to her car. "Thank you," she told him as she climbed in.

He nodded and waited until she shut her door and locked it before he walked back to the bar's front door. He kept an eye on her as she pulled out of the lot.

That asshole. That complete waste of space. Mac was livid, his demon pushing to take his skin. Mac held on to his human form by sheer determination.

Knock it off, he told his demon side. *We're going to make sure she gets home safely first. Then we can hunt.*

Viv's dates had only impressed upon him that humans were trash. Date one had been a conceited, self-important prick. Date two was even worse. Mac had caused the drinks to fall on the man, hoping that it would end the date. He had been watching her in the library when she had gotten the date request. He had a bad feeling about it and had followed her there. The guy had had two beers sitting in front of him and had pushed one over to Viv when she sat down. Mac scoffed; he knew from D's stories that she preferred wine. He had moved closer, wanting to hear what they were talking about. The guy had clearly lied on his dating profile. Those were not the hands of someone who worked with cars. As Viv held her drink, slowly spinning it, he had caught a scent and had leaned closer.

Focusing on the drink, he took a deep breath. The low-life piece of shit! Viv's drink had something added to it, and he would bet it wasn't anything good. A human wouldn't be able to scent it, so she would have no idea. He kept a close eye on her, making sure she didn't take a drink. When she finally raised the glass, he almost smacked it out of her hand, but realized she was faking it. He grinned when she excused herself to the bathroom. It was time to end this date and protect his m—his friend's friend. Not mate. Nope. Not for him.

Keeping himself cloaked in shadows, he gleefully tipped over her drink, spilling it just so. It ran down the bar's top to fall onto the floor. It was kismet that the bartender was standing there to give the guy another beer. Mac knocked it out of the bartender's hand and directed it to fall on Mark the Prick's lap. He felt a little bad for the bartender when Mark started going off on him, but as he scanned the man, he realized this wouldn't get him fired since he was the owner. Good.

Mark kept going on his rant, belittling the bar and the bartender. Viv walked back in, her face showing shock and discomfort and a bit of disgust, he thought. He was happy when she told the guy no. He followed her and the bouncer to her car. Mac ported to the back of Viv's car, making sure she got home safely. As she walked inside the apartment, Mac decided to pay her date a visit. He had a feeling this wasn't the first time he had tried to drug someone.

He focused on the man, porting to a nice enough house. The landscaping could use some work, but it didn't scream that the guy was evil. The man was inside, sitting on his couch. Mac sneered when he saw him sitting there, watching porn, his legs spread and his tiny dick out. Looking at the screen, he realized it was dark stuff. The lady was being raped, clearly drugged. As he looked closer, he realized this was a home movie, the guy had actually filmed himself doing this crap. The cops must not know about him, because this was enough evidence to put him away. The dick was jerking off to himself and his past crimes.

Mac grinned though. He wouldn't be hurting anyone else after today. He would make sure of it. Letting his demon form take over, Mac stepped out of the shadows.

"Hello," he said, his voice deeper, his eyes burning flames.

He let his grin expand as the man pissed himself. This was going to be fun.

5

"Viv! Viv! Wake up!" Thomas shouted, banging on her door.

"What?"

Her door flew open, her former best friend standing there. "I'm tired, it's early. What's wrong?"

"Your date the other day. His name was Mark, right?" Thomas asked.

"Yeah. He turned out to be an asshole. Why?"

Thomas sat on her bed, handing her his phone. She had to blink and rub her eyes to clear them enough to read.

"Oh shit."

"A man was arrested last night after evidence was found on his computer implicating him in multiple unsolved rape cases. Mark Gessin was charged with ten counts of rape and battery. He would drug his dates, found through local dating apps, and bring them back to his house. There he would film himself raping the women. One video even shows him slipping the drugs into a woman's drink. Police are asking anyone to come forward who may have more information. If you were a victim, please reach out to the police to help put this man

away behind bars. There are medical and mental health professionals standing by to help." The screen had both a help line and the police department phone numbers listed.

"Oh my god. I thought it was weird he had a drink ready, and I didn't drink it." She looked at her friend, shaken about what could have happened.

"No more going on dates without D checking them out first, okay?" Thomas demanded. "I can't have anything happen to you."

Viv nodded her head, holding on to Thomas. She had no idea how long they sat there, holding each other. D knocked on the doorframe, holding two cups of coffee in his hand.

"You okay, Viv?" he asked gently.

"Yeah. I just. I had no idea he was that kind of person. When he lost his temper with the poor bartender, I knew I wouldn't go on any other dates with him. He was so mean to the guy. But this? I had a weird feeling with the drink, but I still didn't expect it, I guess."

"Here's your coffee. No more dates without meeting me first, huh?"

"Yeah. I know I was lucky. I'm glad I have you," she told him with a small smile. She was really lucky that she had such good friends, including a demon who could tell her if they were someone to avoid. He couldn't always tell if they were rude or an asshole, but bits of evil he definitely could sense.

"I need to head to work. Is there anything you guys need before I go?" D asked. When they both shook their heads, he came over to give Thomas a kiss goodbye. Before he ported out, he switched to his demon form, the leather pants and black silk shirt filling out as his body bulked up.

"Hmm," Thomas said appreciatively, giving his mate a

heated look-over. "Need another kiss," he said, tilting his head up.

"I've got to go or I'm going to be late. Call if you need anything," D said before porting out.

"We're both off today. What do you want to do? Movies, blankets, and junk food?" Thomas offered.

"That sounds perfect," she admitted. Part of her wondered if she should tell the police about her date last night, but nothing had happened and she had no proof that her drink had been tampered with, so she really had nothing to add that could help them.

Sitting on the couch with her coffee, she grabbed the remote to turn on a rom-com movie, something cheery. She finally decided on *The Proposal*. They had both seen it, but it sounded like a great one to watch again. Thomas climbed in next to her, covering them both in a blanket before handing her a bowl of mini donuts.

"I didn't know we had donuts," she said.

"D ran out to get some this morning," Thomas replied. "I figured I could talk you into relaxing today. I need to spend some time with you, so I know you're okay," he admitted.

"I'm fine," she said, bumping his shoulder with hers. "D can clear all my future dates. Maybe the third time's the charm?"

"I hope so. I love spending time with you, so does D, but I know you want to find your own person."

They made it through three rom-coms before deciding to order lunch. They had an extra cheese pizza delivered, her mouth watering at the smell of their favorite pizza place. As they ate their lunch, she looked at her friend, wondering if she should ask. She was super curious though, especially after seeing D in his demon form this morning.

"What? I can hear you thinking," Thomas said, taking a bite of pizza.

"Is there a dating app for nonhumans?"

"I'm not really sure. I can ask D about it later. Why?"

"Just curious. If they could have humans as mates if they used human dating apps or if they just wandered through life hoping to run into them. You guys met in a bar, so I was just curious if they dated the same way humans did."

"Huh. I'll have to ask him. I don't know," Thomas admitted.

"I'm feeling a little like veal," Viv confessed. "Do you want to walk down and grab a coffee?"

"Sure, let me throw some real pants on. Give me a couple of minutes."

Viv also ran to her room, throwing on something besides her pajamas. She grabbed her phone, keys, and wallet. It would feel nice to move around and see the sky. As they left the apartment's parking lot, Viv could almost feel the shadows following her.

D's phone rang, the ringtone for work. He put his fork down, grabbing his phone. "I need to get this," he said getting up from the table.

"Hello? Yeah? You found him? Do you need help?" he asked, his voice getting fainter as he walked out of the kitchen.

Viv looked over at Thomas.

He shrugged. "My best guess is Mac. He's been working

on tracking a Shadow. The guy has been getting bolder in his kills and has been giving them grief trying to find him."

"Does Mac have backup?" she asked. She had no idea how the demon system worked.

"Normally he works alone, but I'm sure there are others he can call for help if he needs it. He's not the only Enforcer."

D came running back into the kitchen. "I've got to go. Mac finally got him. We're going to get him processed before he has a chance to escape again."

"Be safe. Call me and let me know when he's locked up," Thomas demanded, standing to give D a kiss.

After he had gone, Thomas picked at his food. "I'm not really hungry anymore. I'm too worried about D."

"He'll be fine. He's a high-level demon, he's good at his job, plus Mac will be there. If he already escaped once, I bet they have a lot of support people there to make sure it doesn't happen again," Viv said, trying to sound calm and assured. "Go find us a show to watch. I'll be right there."

She put the rest of dinner away and pulled out ice cream from the freezer. She had bought a double chocolate with pieces of brownies and nuts earlier this week and had hidden it in the back of the freezer. There was whipped cream and cherries in the fridge, so she went about making them both a sundae. Thomas' comfort food had always been ice cream. She put a new pot of coffee on, not sure how long it would take D to process the criminal, but knowing Thomas would want to wait up until he got home.

"*Nailed It*? That sounds perfect," she said when she saw the baking competition show on. It was something light-hearted and they groaned over some of the creations.

"I don't think she added the right amount of sugar," Thomas pointed out.

"I think that was salt," Viv said, squinting at the container and trying to read the label.

"Oh, that's going to be nasty. I'm glad I don't have to eat it," Thomas laughed.

They cheered when their favorite contestant won, a grandma who was atrocious at decorating, but her cakes had tasted nice. Viv pressed the 'watch next episode' button, not wanting Thomas to tense up again.

They got caught up on *Nailed It* and then switched to *The Great British Baking Show.*

"Spotted dick just sounds gross. Like some type of STI," Thomas pointed out.

"It really does. I get the spotted part, but why dick? It doesn't look like a dick," Viv said staring at the screen.

"What's suet?" Thomas asked.

Viv grabbed her phone. "Fat, I think. Let me double-check. Yup, animal fat found near the kidneys. Cow is the most popular, it seems."

"Doesn't sound as tasty that way. Let's make some steamed dick dessert with kidney fat," Thomas laughed.

"Ew." Viv laughed with him. It did sound awful when you said it that way.

The Star Baker had just been announced when D ported back in. He looked exhausted and had a black eye. Thomas jumped up, rushing to his mate.

"What happened?"

"He really didn't want to go to punishment. There were so many more crimes he's committed that we didn't know about. He's been sent to the worst level there is, no chance for reincarnation, no release."

"Can he escape from there?" Thomas asked.

D shook his head. "No. There are safeguards. If a soul tries to escape, they're destroyed."

"How did you end up with a black eye?" Thomas asked.

Viv started to quietly clean up, wanting to give them a minute alone. She would grab the frozen peas from the freezer for D's eye.

"He tried to escape. We had him surrounded in the office, but he still tried. I stepped in to stop him from going after Mac again."

"Is Mac okay?" she called out, unable to help herself.

"He's a little banged up. He took a couple of good hits in the office and the guy had stabbed his leg when he was trying to subdue him to bring him in. He was at the doctor's getting stitched up when I left. I'm grabbing a shower and then I'll head back in to check on him. I wanted to let you guys know what had happened first," D replied.

Stabbed? Viv was horrified that someone she knew had been stabbed. Well, kind of knew. Knew by association. What did she have that she could send over when D went back? Chicken soup! She had made some earlier in the week and froze it for emergency meals. She had a big bowl of it. She had made soda bread for dinner, but D had been called out right before they had really started eating and it hadn't been cut into yet. She could add that. Viv wondered if she had enough time to throw together some cookies. When she saw Thomas follow D into their room, she smiled, knowing that it would be a long shower, giving her enough time to make cookies. Maybe a half batch of chocolate chip cookies and half of snickerdoodles? She wasn't sure what kind of cookie Mac liked. Looking into the pantry, she changed her mind. She would make her Everything Cook- ies. Everyone seemed to like them, and they were both sweet and a little salty with pretzel pieces, chocolate chips, and caramel bits. She was pulling them out of the oven when she heard the shower shut off and she hurriedly grabbed the frozen soup, writing out a quick note on the best way to reheat it, wrapping up the bread, and sticking the cookies in a basket. They were still too hot to seal up in a container.

"D! Before you go, can you grab this?" she called out, not wanting him to leave without the food.

He came into the kitchen, dressed down in a pair of sweatpants and a t-shirt. "Sure, what did you need?"

"Can you give this to Mac? There's nothing worse than having to make yourself food when you don't feel well," she said. Or you know, when you've been stabbed, either way. "I remembered you saying he doesn't have a lot of family, so I thought I could send this. I can make more if he needs it." Thomas gave her a look, letting her know that they were going to be talking about this later.

"Oh, that's nice. I'm sure he'll love it," D said.

"He should. Viv's chicken soup is amazing. And those are my favorite cookies," Thomas said.

"I'll make you your own batch. I still have enough ingredients left," she replied.

"Thanks," D said, giving her a hug before grabbing the food and porting out.

Thomas spun to face her. "What was that?"

"What?"

"You know what."

"I just thought it would be nice for him to have a home-made meal when he's injured. It sucks being on your own and not having anyone help you."

"Uh huh. That doesn't explain the babbling," Thomas pointed out.

"I don't know," she sighed. "I've only seen him a few times, never even really talked to him, but I'm attracted to him. Like if he asked me on a date, I would totally say yes.

I," she paused. "It doesn't make sense, right? But I feel drawn to him."

"He's hot," Thomas agreed.

"Yeah." It wasn't just that, she thought. She had met lots of attractive people, but she felt drawn to him in a way that she hadn't experienced before. However, she knew it wouldn't go anywhere. He seemed to leave as soon as she showed up. She had a feeling he was either uncomfortable around humans or didn't like them.

6

Mac sat on his couch, his leg stretched out in front of him. He was thirsty and was due to take an antibiotic. Probably the pain pill too, but he generally didn't take those. They always made him feel nauseous. The doctor gave him one just in case, but he wasn't going to take it unless he had to. They had given him a little of the healing potion, but he had been cranky and left before they brought another one over. His stupid thigh would take a while to heal; the Shadow had used a large serrated knife and twisted, making sure to tear up muscle and ligaments.

He sensed a portal opening and sat up straighter. His wards only let a few people into his house, so whoever was coming was friendly.

"Hi. I'm glad to see you're actually sitting down," D said as he came in. He had a bunch of stuff in his arms.

"I am. Figured the laundry could wait another day," he joked. "Whatcha got?"

"Food. Viv sent some of her chicken soup, bread, and cookies."

"Oh yeah?" Mac said, trying to keep from smiling. His ma—friend's friend had thought of him.

"Thomas was very put out that you got his favorite cookies, so she was going to make him his own batch. I'm missing out on the bread though. This was supposed to be for our dinner."

"I'll share," Mac offered.

"I'll heat up some soup for you. Here's the note she sent and the cookies," D said, handing him a basket of still warm cookies and a piece of notebook paper. It looked like it had been ripped out in a hurry, the little tabs still hanging on.

I'm sorry you were hurt tonight. I hope you feel better soon. Tell D if you need anything else, and I'll send it through him. ~Viv Below that were reheating instructions for the soup.

He glanced quickly at the kitchen, seeing D with his back to him standing at the stove. Mac brought the note up to his face, sniffing, trying to catch the scent of Viv. It was there, mixed with the smells of D and Thomas.

"Care to tell me what that's about?"

Mac jumped. Damn man was awfully quiet when he wanted to be.

"What? Just reading the note," he answered.

"I didn't know you read by sniffing," D said dryly.

"Eat a cookie and shut up," Mac muttered, shoving the basket of cookies at his friend.

They munched away on the cookies in quiet until the timer went off for the soup. D brought him a bowl and a slice of the buttered bread. Mac was hopeful that D had forgotten about him sniffing the note.

"She's your mate, isn't she?"

At least he waited until he was done eating. The soup had been perfect, his demon practically purring that they were eating a meal provided by their mate. No, not mate.

"Can we not talk about this?"

"I think we need to at least once. She's extremely nice. Hence your dinner. It's not like you've gone out of your way to be nice or even say hi to her, but she still rushed to make you fresh cookies and sent you food."

"Probably because we're friends," Mac pointed out.

"I don't think so. She asked about you. Her eyes always go straight to you if you're nearby. She feels the pull, doesn't she? That's why she worded her answer the way she did when I asked if there was anyone she was interested in dating. She didn't say no, she said there wasn't anyone she thought was interested in her."

"Let it go, D."

"Just tell me."

"Yes, she's my mate. But it's not going anywhere. It can't."

"Why? She's not like—"

"No. We're not going there. The answer is no. I'm not going to take her for my mate. She can keep on dating and find some human that will work well enough. I'm fine alone. I swore no more humans, and I'm keeping that promise to myself."

"Does she know?"

"I've never talked to her, D, so I really doubt it. It wouldn't change anything if she did. Can we talk about this case now?" he asked, getting angry.

"Fine."

He knew D was angry with him, but he was still here because he was a good friend. Mac knew this was the best for both of them. He was an angry asshole who hated most people, especially humans. Viv was not. She always had a smile for people.

"There's evidence of someone helping him, but I

haven't been able to find anything. He's refused to talk," Mac said, frustrated with this case. He had caught the Shadow. There was plenty of evidence linking him to the killings, much less the fact that when Mac had finally caught up to him, he was about to kill another. They had him for so many crimes; part of his and D's abilities were able to sense evil and the crimes a person committed. Unfortunately, it didn't extend into reading someone's mind and learning if they had help.

"Maybe some time spent in punishment will loosen his tongue. We can try interrogating him in a few days and see if anything changes."

"Maybe. I just know there's someone else involved. Maybe drawing the victims out, selecting them, clean up. Something. Maybe they just watched. I don't know, but I know there was someone else and it's driving me nuts not being able to get them too," Mac vented.

"I'll keep an ear out. If I hear anything, I'll let you know," D promised. "You need anything before I leave?"

"Can you help me up? I've got to hit the bathroom before I go to bed, but getting up is challenging."

D pulled him up easily, making sure he was steady on his feet before loading the bowls and plates in his dishwasher.

"I'm heading out!" D called out. "Call if you need anything."

7

Viv stared at her phone. She had another request for a date. This guy was drop-dead gorgeous. She had no idea why he was on a dating app, there was no way he had trouble getting dates.

"What are you looking at?" Thomas asked, popping up next to her.

"Another date request," she said, tilting her phone so Thomas could see it.

"He's sexy. Are you ready to try another date after the last one?" he asked, worried.

"I don't know. Maybe. It's not like I'm getting any younger," she joked. "I'll make sure it's public; I'll meet him there, and maybe D can drop by to scan him?"

"Why don't you have it at a restaurant and we can run into you? We can eat at a different table and keep an eye on you?"

"Is that weird?" she worried.

"Your last date was with a serial rapist. I think it's fine," Thomas replied.

"Okay. I'll say yes and set up the reservations. That way

we can make sure you guys can get a table there at the same time," she said, typing out a response. "What are you in the mood for?"

"Steak's always good. Most steakhouses will have a salad or chicken too, depending on what he likes to eat."

"He doesn't list any food restrictions," she said, looking over his profile again. She found a local steakhouse and set up two different reservations. Now she just had to wait for three more days.

As she got ready for her date, she made sure her hair was tamed enough. Her black dress was simple, but she had added some bling and a pop of color with her necklace and earrings. Thomas had given them to her for her birthday years ago and they were one of her favorites. She slipped into her heels and gave herself one last look before meeting her friends in the living room.

"I'm off. I'll see you there," she said, grabbing her purse.

"Are you sure you don't want me to drop you off?" D asked.

She shook her head. "It's not far and they have a good-sized parking lot. I'm good driving." D could only transport one other person when he used a portal. It didn't make sense to have him make multiple trips. And if the night went well and she ended up with plans for after dinner, she would have her car.

Driving to the restaurant, she sat in the car after she parked. Pulling down the visor, she opened the mirror, applying a layer of lip gloss. "This could be fun," she encouraged herself. "He's hot. Maybe he's not a douchebag." The shadows were getting longer, and she got out of the car before she would be late. Instead of anticipation, she felt...blah, not excited. He was waiting by the door, and he was as handsome in person as he had been online. Maybe even more, she thought when he smiled. It still did nothing for her; no spark of interest, no excitement, just a general 'he's nice-looking' type of thought. Mac's grumpy face flashed in her mind, but she pushed it away. He clearly wasn't into her; he sent back a verbal thanks through D for the food, but that was it. Her heart needed to get the memo that the mysterious man wasn't going to suddenly want her, and she needed to find love elsewhere.

Roland was a gentleman and opened the door for her, his hand on the small of her back as they made their way through the restaurant following the maître d'. He even pulled the chair out for her.

"It's so nice to meet you in person," Roland said, his voice a nice bass.

"You too," she replied. The waiter came over, filling their water glasses and dropping off a warm loaf of bread.

Roland held the basket out for her first before taking a piece for himself. "What do you do for work?" he asked.

"I'm a librarian."

"Really? That's amazing. I love libraries, especially the older ones. They have so much character. I remember when we used to have to use the card catalogues to find books. Does that make me old?" he laughed.

"I love those! I wish I had bought them when the library was selling theirs. I was in college though and didn't have that much extra cash lying around. I should have just eaten rice and noodles and bought one. They're hard to find now. What do you do?"

"I'm in sales," he replied, adding butter to his bread before taking a bite.

Viv waited until he swallowed before talking to him again. "What kind of sales? Do you like it?"

"Right now, I'm a pharmacy rep. I've done a few other things, but that's it for now. I do enjoy it. I get to meet all kinds of people, even travel a little bit. What kind of books do you read?"

"Mostly romance. All different subgenres and tropes, but usually romance. Are you a big reader?" she asked.

"I would say I'm more of a medium reader. I like to when I have the time."

"What do you like to read?" Viv asked. At least this date seemed to be going better than the other two had. Of course, it didn't take much to top those.

"Suspense and mystery mostly, with a few biographies thrown in."

They ordered their meals and were talking about their favorite TV shows when Thomas showed up.

"Viv! You look amazing," he said, dragging D over behind him. "I can't believe we ran into each other. Who's handsome?"

Viv had to keep from laughing. Thomas was really playing it up. But it was another good test. If someone couldn't handle her bestie, then they weren't going to work out anyway.

"Hi, I'm Roland. Nice to meet you," he said, standing up to shake Thomas' hand.

"I'm Thomas and this is my boyfriend D," Thomas introduced himself.

Roland shook Thomas' hand easily enough, although he did pause when he saw D. Their waitress was still waiting there to seat them at their table.

"We better go. It was nice to see you," D said, leading Thomas away.

"They seem nice," Roland said.

"They are. Thomas is my best friend," Viv replied.

Her phone buzzed and she discreetly pulled it out, seeing it was a message from Thomas.

Meet me at the bathrooms.

"I'm going to run to the restroom before our food comes. I'll be right back," she said, grabbing her purse as she stood up. She saw Thomas was already gone from his table, although D gave her a smile. It must not be too bad then.

"We need to talk about some things," Thomas told her, dragging her down the hallway.

"Last time we did that, I learned your boyfriend was a demon. Is this guy bad news? A serial killer? Puppy torturer?"

"What? No. I would have called you for that and gotten you out right away. D says he's good on that front."

"Then what is it?" she asked, a little perturbed because this date had been going well so far and he could have just texted the all clear.

"Sex," Thomas said, his cheeks red.

"Yes, sex. I'm hoping to have some someday, hence the date. Which you seem to be cockblocking."

"Okay, but see, this guy is a nonhuman. D thinks he's an incubus. Now, they're not bad like the stories. But they do like sex. A lot of sex. They get energy from having sex and they're not always monogamous unless it's their mate. I thought you should know what you're dealing with before the date ends. He's hot and seems nice, but if you're not his mate then he's probably not going to be around long term."

"Thanks for letting me know. Maybe a hookup is what I

need to take my mind off of...someone," she suggested, even as her stomach churned with the thought.

"You're not the hookup type. Never have been. I think it's a bad call. But just in case, you should get a quick nonhuman sex ed rundown. Sex with a paranormal is different. They're uh, larger usually. Tails come into play sometimes. But their dicks are the biggest difference. Depending on who you're with, there's barbs if you're with a cat shifter, or ridges if you're with a wolf. Demons tend to be extra-large, have ridges, are uncut, and they have a, um, a knot."

"Knot? Like in the romance books?" she asked incredulously.

Thomas nodded. "That's why I couldn't chase you down right away when you walked in on us," he admitted. "Of course, being walked in on made it go down quicker than normal, but we were still stuck together for a few minutes. He can control it popping out, but we thought we were going to be alone, so we went for it."

"And you decided to have sex bent over the couch knowing that? That seems like it would be uncomfortable," she said, looking at her best friend.

"Maybe, but it was totally worth it," he replied with a grin. "I don't know about incubuses. D said they're rumored to be great lovers."

"I could try dating him for a while even if I know it won't be forever," she suggested. She knew she was reaching. He was a nice guy, but her body seemed to not be interested.

"Do you really think that's a great idea? That's settling and not what you want," he pointed out.

"I don't know. I'm lonely, I think. If we both know going into it that it's not forever, it's not hurting anyone."

"You're not made that way. You would catch feelings," Thomas warned her.

Viv shrugged. It's not like the current object of her affection was returning said interest.

"Don't jump into anything yet. Think about it a little more," Thomas advised. "You should get back out there, or he's going to wonder where you are."

As she walked back to the table, she swore she saw a pair of black eyes staring at her, the shadows watching. She chided herself. Mac wasn't here. He was at home healing. Plus, he never stayed where she was, so it clearly wasn't him.

Roland was at the table, his face a little paler than when she had left.

"Are you okay?" she asked, concerned.

"I am. I need to leave but didn't want to abandon you before you came back."

"Oh, I'm sorry. Is everything alright?"

"Just something at work. I already paid the bill. It was so wonderful meeting you. I think we could be great friends, if you're interested," he said earnestly.

"Sure. Friends would be nice," she replied. He gave her a hug before he left.

"What happened?" Thomas asked as he stormed over.

"Work, I guess. He thought we'd be great friends," she said.

Thomas winced.

"Yeah. At least he was polite and paid for dinner," she murmured. She flagged down the waiter to get her food boxed up. She wasn't going to eat alone. "I'll see you back home. You guys should stay and have a date," she said, finding a smile for her friend.

Sitting on the couch, eating her perfectly cooked steak, she had to wonder. Was she really that undatable?

Mac gritted his teeth against the pain in his leg. D had called to tell him he would bring dinner over later. Viv had a date and they were going to supervise after the last one. It was at a steak place, so he would order a meal to go and bring it over when they were done.

Mac sat at home fuming, stewing in his own anger. Anger at his case, anger over the pain in his leg, anger at his pouting demon. He finally pulled a portal and stood in the back of the restaurant where he could watch Viv.

Her date was better than the last ones; both better looking and better behaved. When Mac slid closer, he realized her date was a damned incubus. There was no way she was his mate, so the guy was just looking for sex. Not that there was anything wrong with sex, he'd had plenty of hookups in his life, but the guy didn't need to be looking at his Viv for one.

He debated what to do when the perfect opportunity presented itself when she went to the bathroom. Thomas was gone too, so he would guess he had a few minutes before she came back. Keeping himself mostly cloaked in the shadows, he stood by the man's chair.

"What do you think you're doing?" he asked, keeping his voice low. He didn't want D to realize he was here.

"What the—?"

"Shh," Mac hissed. "What are you doing with Viv?"

"We're on a date. Why do you care?"

"She's my mate," Mac told him, his voice harsh.

"Shit, man. I didn't know. She didn't say anything. I never would poach on a mate."

"She doesn't know."

"What?"

"It doesn't matter. I'm not claiming her as my mate, but that doesn't mean that I want an incubus playing with her either. She's looking for love and commitment. Not a one-night stand."

"Why don't you claim her? She's beautiful and funny. She's smart. You're a fool if you don't claim her," Roland scolded.

"It's my business."

"You can't have her, so no one else can? What kind of life is that for her?" Roland asked.

"She can find love with another human. If she's not your mate, then you're not sticking around for the long haul. Say something came up with work or some other excuse to end the date but do it nicely. She doesn't deserve to have another shitty date."

"She doesn't deserve having a coward for a mate who scares off other potential matches," Roland countered.

"End the date or I'll cut off your dick," Mac threatened, grabbing his knife and making sure the incubus could feel its point through his pants.

"Fine. She's a wonderful girl and you're a horrible mate," Roland told him, sweat breaking out over his forehead.

Mac saw Viv walking back from the bathroom and withdrew the knife. "Remember what I said," he threatened as he pulled back fully into the shadows.

He was pleased when Roland followed directions and

ended the date. He followed Viv home, making sure she got inside before heading back to his house.

It was about forty-five minutes later when D popped in.

"I'm surprised to see you here. I thought you'd be lurking outside the apartment still," D said, his face stony.

"What are you talking about?" Mac said, feigning ignorance.

"You forget that I've known you for a really long time. I could sense you at the restaurant tonight. Maybe no one else could have, but you're my family. I know when you're nearby."

Mac sat there, not willing to admit to his behavior quite yet. He knew it wasn't rational, but he also had no plans on stopping.

"I can wait all night," D threatened.

Mac looked at his oldest friend, not surprised to find disappointment on his face.

"I'm looking out for her," he justified. "I saved her from the last date. The guy had laced her drink, and she would have been another one of his victims. I let the police know where to look, and now the bastard's rotting in jail."

"That was good, but what about tonight?"

"He wasn't good enough for her. He was an incubus. She's not his mate, so he would only be using her for sex."

"Maybe she wanted to have sex. I don't think she's had any in all the time that I've known her."

"She's not the hookup type, and you know it. She would get attached to the stupid incubus and then one day he'd move on, and she'd get her heart broken."

"I think that was up to her to decide. Thomas was telling her about Roland. She had the right to make her own decision. I know you're not listening, so I'm just going to leave your food. I'll see you later."

Mac sat there in the silence, eating. He was going to keep his mate safe, even if he never claimed her. It was the only way to keep his demon side in check.

8

Viv pulled a batch of snickerdoodles out of the oven. She'd only had a few hours of work this morning and had stopped on the way home to pick up some last-minute items. She swore her watching shadows followed her to the store, but they were gone when she pulled into the apartment's parking lot. There was a surprise party for Thomas at the nearby park in a little bit. D wanted to propose. He asked for her help with ring ideas a few weeks ago and they had finally decided on the perfect ring. She was so excited to see her friend's reaction. They were gathering a few different people to meet at the park; D's parents, Thomas' family, some of his coworkers and their other friends. Her part was to get Thomas to the park. She was using the cookies as a bribe.

"Cookies! You do love me," Thomas said happily as he tried to sneak a cookie.

"Leave those alone. They're for later," she said.

"What's later?"

"I thought we could do a picnic at the park today. It's supposed to be a gorgeous day."

"We haven't done that in a while. That sounds fun," Thomas replied. "What can I do to help?"

"I have almost everything ready, just waiting on the last of the cookies to cool down so I can pack them up."

"Alright. I'm going to go put on sunscreen and I'll be ready to go. This is going to be a great day," he said.

Viv grinned, knowing it was going to get better. She drove them to the park, carrying the basket. She didn't want him to feel how light it was, as the cookies were the only thing in there. D was getting food brought in, along with a cake. But it was hard to ask someone to go on a picnic without bringing food along.

"Are we going to one of the shelters?" Thomas asked as they headed away from their usual spot.

"I thought we'd give it a try. Gives us some shade from the sun if it gets too hot," she replied.

They turned the corner and Thomas jumped as everyone shouted "Surprise!"

He turned to look at her, shock on his face. "What is this? It's not my birthday."

Viv tilted her head toward D, who was walking toward them. He was wearing a pair of leather pants and a tight black t-shirt. Viv had pointed out it was going to be hot, but he said he wanted to wear Thomas' favorite outfit.

Stopping in front of them, D took one of Thomas' hands. Viv scooted off to the side, not wanting to be in the way. She had done her part. She pulled out her phone so she could get a picture of the proposal.

"Thomas. You entered my life, bringing joy and laughter, and brightness. I love you, now and always. Forever. Would you do me the honor of becoming my husband?" D asked, sinking to one knee, holding the ring in his other hand.

"Yes! Yes, yes, yes." Thomas knelt down in front of him, holding his face in his hands, pulling him in for a kiss. D slid the ring on Thomas' hand. Viv couldn't stop grinning. She looked around the crowd, seeing lots of smiles and a few teary eyes. Her gaze stopped on one grumpy face in the background. Mac was here.

Six foot seven, dark pitch-black hair, eyes so dark they looked black. If you went outside on a night without stars or moonlight, those were his eyes. They were vast and deep, and she would love to get lost in them. He was staring at her, but abruptly cut off eye contact. When she moved to walk over to him, he walked into the woods. She knew he wouldn't be there if she followed. Maybe it was just her he didn't like, although how he could dislike her so much when he never talked to her was beyond her. Why she had a crush on him was another mystery. She had hoped dating would bring someone she could become close to, but so far they had all been duds. Roland still sent her a few messages, all very friendly, but clearly not interested in more. He could become a good friend at least, she thought.

"I can't believe you knew and didn't say anything!" Thomas exclaimed as he wrapped her in a hug.

"It's not a surprise if I said anything," she pointed out, laughing.

"True. You did good. I love the ring," he said smiling, looking down at his hand. It looked like the perfect fit, so she was pleased. "Where's my cookies?"

Viv laughed. "You don't want cake?"

"I can have cake too! It's my engagement day and I want my cookies."

Viv shook her head, but pulled the cookies out of the basket, letting him grab a couple before placing the rest on the table. She grabbed a piece of cake and a sandwich.

There were cute little tea sandwiches, with a few of the roll-up kind as well. It was quite the spread with fruit salad, a veggie tray, drinks, and the cake. D had done well.

She looked into the woods, sensing the shadows watching her. At this point she had gotten used to the sensation. It made her feel safe now instead of just being stared at. It didn't feel threatening, so she hadn't said anything to D or Thomas. Plus, D was there, along with his parents. If there was danger, one of them would have said something. She settled back, watching contently as her friend enjoyed his day.

The party wound down and Viv started to help clean up. It was nice to meet D's parents. They seemed like really nice people. They would make great in-laws for Thomas. It was nice to see that they had even gotten along with Thomas' parents. She wasn't sure if they would ever tell them about nonhumans though. That might be hard for them to come to terms with. Thomas was a very late in life baby and his parents were older. They were like another set of parents to her, so when Thomas had to move because he wasn't aging, she would be there to help take care of them. They were in their seventies now, so he might be able to stay here through the rest of their lives.

She shook off the morose thoughts, putting a smile on her face. This was a happy day.

"Thank you for my party," Thomas said, coming up to hug her.

"I didn't do much," she protested. "D did most of it."

"Well thank you for what you did. I had an amazing day. I even saw Mac was here for a hot minute."

"Hmhm," she agreed. She didn't want to talk and have him hear her tone.

"Did you finally get a chance to talk to him?" Thomas asked.

Looked like she wasn't getting out of this one.

"No. I started walking over to him and he ported out. I should have known better than to move in his direction. He never stays long when I'm there and I can never get close to him. Do I smell weird or something?" she asked sadly.

Thomas wrapped her in a hug. "Nope. I think you smell nice. D would have said something by now if you smelled bad. I don't know Mac's story; he doesn't even talk to me much and D is his best friend. I think he might not be comfortable around humans?" he said, hesitantly.

"Or he doesn't like humans," she pointed out. Or just me, she added silently.

"I don't know. Mac is the one thing D doesn't talk about with me very much," Thomas admitted. "He was mad at Mac after your date with Roland over something, but he said he was trying to stay out of it. Not sure if it's work or what."

"It's fine. Not everyone has to like me, right?"

"Viv," Thomas started.

"Hey! Did you get pictures of you and D with your ring? We should get some before the light starts to go," she said, pulling him to stand next to his fiancé. She took a lot of pictures, the parents taking some with her in them.

Her friend smiled happily up at his mate, and she snapped the picture. That one was perfect to go on their wall.

9

Viv pulled the chicken out of the oven. It was a nice simple recipe, but one she loved. She had gotten home from work and threw it together. It was really only three ingredients: chicken, parmesan cheese, and mayo. It kept the chicken moist while it baked. It had been a long day, several kids had gotten sick in the library, someone had poured water into the book return so she had to lay out the books to dry, and a shipment of books had gone missing. Her watching shadows hadn't been there at all today and she actually missed them. She wondered at what point she should be worried that she was going crazy. If she told Thomas that it sometimes felt like the shadows were watching her and it made her feel safe, he would probably (and maybe rightfully so) be worried. So she kept that little secret for now.

But now the chicken was finished and the broccoli was ready to drain.

"Will you grab D and let him know dinner is done? I'll drain the broccoli and finish setting the table," Thomas asked.

"Sure." Viv took the oven gloves off and headed out to the front door. She had seen D in the living room earlier. The door was open and she heard raised voices in the hallway. She walked closer, trying to decide if she needed to call for help or not. That's Mac's voice, she thought with relief. At least it wasn't someone trying to attack D. Her heart broke when she could make out what they were talking about.

"I don't want her," Mac said angrily.

"Mac, you're hurting both of you. She keeps wondering why her dates are never good enough. You keep getting angrier. Your demon is furious. I can feel it. How long are you going to let this go on?"

"Fate got it wrong. I don't know what else to tell you. I'm not taking her as my mate. You and my demon and everyone else can go fuck yourselves," he shouted.

"Keep it down," D growled.

"What? Now you're worried about someone hearing? You probably should have thought about that before."

"Viv? Are you there?" D asked, hesitantly.

She sucked in a breath; she had been coming to tell him it was time for dinner and had heard raised voices. She hadn't been trying to eavesdrop.

"Yeah, it's me. I was coming to tell you dinner is ready," she said, walking around the corner to face them. "Hi, Mac. Are you eating with us? I can go set another place." She tried to act like she hadn't heard them arguing.

"I'm going to say this once because D doesn't want to listen, so I'm going to tell you directly. I don't fuck humans. Not interested," Mac said, making sure his voice was hard and full of derision. He hated being the cause of the hurt on her face and the tears he could see in her eyes. His demon was raging inside him, trying to take control and comfort their mate. He couldn't let it happen. Mac opened a portal, his heart feeling like he had ripped it out and stomped on it himself. He ported out, deciding that he wouldn't let her see him again. He would still hang around to protect her, but he would do so only from the shadows. Hopefully he could figure out how to salvage his friendship with D later.

Viv tried to hold in her pain, not wanting D to see how much Mac's words had hurt. "Thomas is waiting for you," she reminded him.

She walked inside, keeping her steps even, not running even though she wanted to.

"Hey! Where are you going?" Thomas called out when she walked past.

"I think I'm going to grab a shower. I feel gross from today. Just go ahead and get started," she said. Shutting her door, she slid to the ground, her heart in pain and her soul screaming. Mac was her mate, that's why she felt so drawn to him, why she hadn't been very excited to go on a date with a handsome man. Her body must have recognized its mate. A mate that didn't want her. A mate who had flat out avoided her at all costs and then rejected her to her face. At least she now had a reason why he never talked to her. She had no idea how long she sat there, but she felt the coolness of the floor seep into her bones.

"You're going to be okay," she heard a voice tell her. Looking up, she saw Thomas crouched in front of her. "Come on, up on the bed. The air vent was blowing right on you and you're freezing."

She tried to get up, but her muscles didn't want to work. D came in and picked her up, laying her down. Thomas covered her with a blanket before climbing in to lie on his side facing her.

"You have horrible taste in men," Thomas pointed out,

trying to make a joke. She could hear the tears in his voice though. "At least this one isn't really your fault. Fate kind of fucked you over."

D came to sit behind Thomas, both of her friends trying to support her.

"Was it me, D? What did I do to him to make him hate me so much?" Viv asked quietly. She wasn't sure her heart could take much more, but she needed to know.

"I truly believe it's not you specifically. I think he would love you if he gave himself a chance," D said, pausing for a minute. "Mac had a mate before. A human. This was hundreds of years ago. He thought he could trust her; she didn't seem to freak out when he told her who he really was. After he confessed what he was, they had a date set up. He went to pick her up for a walk in the park, but when he got there, he was attacked. He was shot, bound by chains, holy water dumped on him. A priest was there trying to expel him. Of course, it didn't work. He's not evil and those things were made up by humans. She walked over to him, spat on him and told him she had no desire to be associated with filth. The final thing that sent him over the edge was when she stabbed him with a cross. He was lucky that it missed his heart. He had been hopeful until then that it was a mistake, that someone had overheard him and set up the ambush. But no, it was all her doing. He ported home and managed to get to a doctor. He healed physically, but he didn't leave Netherworld for a long time."

Viv remembered D telling them that mates were reincarnated and given another chance sometimes. "Am I the reincarnated version of that bitch?" Viv asked, horrified.

"No! No. Mac had that bond permanently dissolved. It's rare, but it can be done. You're your own person, nothing to do with the other mate."

"He could dissolve our bond?" she asked quietly.

D took a minute to answer, sympathy and pity on his face. "He could, but there has to be a really good reason for the higher-ups to do that. It really is rare. I don't think his bigotry and unwillingness to bend would be looked upon favorably. My best guess is that he will just avoid you from now on."

"I think that's what he has been doing," she admitted. "He worked awfully hard at leaving as soon as I came near him. Thomas and I thought it might be because he didn't trust or like humans. But when I first saw him that day in the parking lot, the wind blew from behind me and he looked over, so maybe he's known this whole time. At least that explains why I was crushing so hard and not knowing why," she said with a sad smile. "I think I'm going to just go to sleep," she said.

"I'll stay with you until you do," Thomas told her, holding her hand just like when they were kids and she was upset. She squeezed his hand, grateful she had him in her life.

"I don't want him anywhere near her," Thomas said angrily. He was trying to keep his voice down, but it had woken her up.

"I don't think he's going to be coming around anymore," D pointed out.

"Ever. He is never going to be welcome in my house. I understand that you're friends, and I'm not going to come between that. I know how much history you guys have. But even after she's...gone," Thomas' voice hiccupped, "he's not welcome in my house. She is my best friend, my family, and she deserves to be treated better. Your Fates screwed up on this one."

"I understand, love. I don't know why he's being this stubborn. I honestly don't," D said, his voice sounding sad.

They walked away from her door, their voices fading. At least she knew why he hated her and why no other man seemed as appealing. She couldn't see herself venturing into the dating pool again anytime soon. Even though he didn't want her, it felt a bit like cheating now that she knew. Which was ridiculous. Maybe she could adopt a dog.

10

Viv walked through the library giving it one more pass before shutting the doors for the night. The shadows still kept watch over her and she still hadn't told her friends. At this point, she simply said good night and left. They never seemed to follow her home. Maybe the library was haunted. She'd have to ask D if ghosts were real too. She couldn't believe that she hadn't asked before now. Of course, maybe it was just because Halloween was tonight. If it was a ghost, they didn't seem like the type to cause problems. They made a good listener though; she often found herself talking to the shadows when the library was empty. There was the possibility that she was desperate for company, but she really did feel like sometimes the shadows were sentient and other times they were simply dark spots and normal shadows.

She walked to her car, thinking about how much candy they had and if they would need to buy more. There had been a few new families who had moved into the apartment complex in the last couple of months. Her primal brain suddenly screamed at her to run and her head spun around, trying to find the danger. She had her pepper spray in one hand, her keys in the other. There had been a few attacks recently that had her on edge. The shadows in front of her seemed sinister, nothing like the shadows in her library. She felt a gust of air come from the direction of the library behind her and the other sensation disappeared.

Viv shook her head at herself. Too many scary movies at night maybe; Thomas had convinced her to watch a few jump-scare and horror movies over the past week. She locked her doors as soon as she got in the car, eager to get home where it was warm. The temperatures had taken a dramatic turn toward winter. Cranking up the heat and the music, she headed home. She loved her relatively short commute. Fifteen minutes later, she was in her warm apartment getting the candy ready to hand out.

"I've got to run into work," D said.

"Everything okay?" Thomas asked.

"I think so. There was a lead on the Shadow's accomplice. Someone came in to confess and they want me and M—me there to make sure he's the one we want. Stay safe. Stay in the apartment until I'm home? I might not have great reception, depending on where in Netherworld I am even with the booster."

"We'll be fine. We'll stay here and hand out candy," Thomas promised. "You need to be safe too."

"I will. Call if there's anything weird," D said, giving Thomas a kiss before porting out.

"Ready for candy?" Thomas asked, holding out the cauldron.

Viv grabbed a Twix. "Yup. I've got the coffee going, I have my Halloween socks and hat on. Spooky music is already on my phone."

Thomas grabbed a Reese's. He had little horns and a tail

pinned to his pants, a nod at his mate. Viv had on a witch's hat. It was kind of lame, but an easy enough costume. It was cold, so they were both in long sleeves. And black. She had on black jeans and a billowy type of long-sleeve pirate shirt. Thomas had on leather pants and a black dress shirt. They had both worked today and didn't feel like cooking, so they had ordered a pizza instead. When the doorbell rang, Thomas jumped up. "Pizza!" he cheered.

Viv laughed, going to the fridge to get their drinks ready. She poured the peppermint mocha-flavored creamer in her coffee cup.

"Did you want the peppermint or plain creamer in your coffee?" she called out.

There was no answer. "Thomas?" she yelled louder. Still no answer. Looking around, she groaned when she realized she had left her phone on the coffee table. Grabbing the marble rolling pin, she crept into the living room. A female demon stood there, holding Thomas, her hand over his mouth.

"You both stink of him. Which one of you is his mate?" she demanded.

"Who? Who are you?" Viv asked.

"D. He sentenced my mate to punishment. There's no way out for him. He took my mate, I'm going to take his."

"Who's your mate?" Viv asked, trying to slide closer to her phone.

"My Shadow. They took my Shadow, so I'm going to take his human."

Viv ran for her phone. She managed to open her contacts before she was picked up and thrown against the wall. Ouch. All the air rushed from her lungs as she collapsed to the floor. Thomas ran for his, but the woman ported in front of him, throwing him into the coffee table.

Viv dragged herself up, standing in front of Thomas until he could get up on his own. Her phone was close if she could just reach it. She still had the rolling pin gripped in her hands. How she hadn't dropped it when she hit the wall, she didn't know. She felt wetness on the back of her head and figured she must have been cut from the wall.

"You can back the fuck off, crazy," Viv warned, brandishing the rolling pin.

The demoness laughed at her, lunging for her throat. Viv cracked the marble against her skull but it didn't seem to slow her down. She tripped over Thomas but caught herself on the couch. Seeing her phone on the floor, she dove for it and managed to get 9 1 dialed. A foot stomped on her hand, and she screamed as the stiletto pushed its way through her hand. The shock of pain caused her to lose control of her fingers and she dropped the phone. Thomas groaned, trying to crawl toward her, bleeding from a cut in his forehead.

"This has been fun, but I think we're going to finish playing somewhere else," the demoness said, looking at the front door. There was a knock, probably the pizza, and Viv opened her mouth to yell for help.

"Uh uh," was the last thing she heard as pain exploded in her head and everything went black.

"You're too late," the man grinned at them.

"Too late for what?" Mac demanded. His demon was screaming at him, but that was nothing new.

"Your mate. A mate for a mate, she said."

"What are you talking about?" D demanded, pulling out his phone and dialing Thomas.

"You sentenced her mate to the deepest pits. No escape or he's destroyed. He wasn't alone. But you will be. That's what she said," he giggled.

"Thomas. Call me back as soon as you get this."

"Call Viv. See if she answers," Mac ordered.

"No, neither one of them are picking up."

"Shit."

Mac called in another Enforcer, one he trusted. "He's a decoy. The real accomplice was the Shadow's mate and she's going after D's. Keep working on him, get everything out of him you can and let the rest know we might need them. I'm going with D."

They ported out, landing outside the apartment. There was a pizza box on the floor. It was cold. Opening the door, they could smell blood. The table had been overturned, a dent in the wall that looked suspiciously like the size of a human torso. Both of their phones were lying on the ground, the screens cracked.

"They're gone."

11

Mac was barely hanging on to human form. D had already changed over. He pulled out his phone, calling into work.

"Any news?" he demanded as soon as someone answered.

"Nothing yet," his boss said. "Your end?"

"They're both gone. There's sign of a struggle, blood in a few different spots. Human."

"What do you mean both?"

"D and his mate live with his mate's best friend. Who happens to be my unclaimed mate."

"You're telling me this woman has two of my demons' mates?" Lucifer asked, coldly furious.

"Yes, sir. We believe it's the mate of the Shadow I recently brought in. I knew he had an accomplice, but could never find proof of who it was," Mac admitted. He had failed. He had failed his friend and his mate.

"I'm going to go question this Shadow myself. I'll try to get you some answers, at least some clues to where she might have taken them. If D claimed his mate, he may be able to portal to them if it's not warded. Try to calm down and scent the area. See what kind of nonhuman we're dealing with," he ordered.

"Yes, sir." Mac stood there holding his phone. Lucifer had hung up on him. He would not want to be that Shadow.

"D. Snap out of it. We need to see if we can tell what kind of nonhuman was here. Lucifer is going to question the Shadow. Come on. We need to find something to help them."

Mac watched as D took a deep breath, his eyes showing the flames of the Netherworld in his fury. "I smell blood. Thomas and Viv. No nonhuman blood."

"Try again. Sniff everything," Mac ordered. He walked to the front door, leaving the pizza outside. There was a note saying the pizza had been dropped off but no one had answered the door. Since it had been paid for, they were leaving it. It had a time too, 5:50 pm. Okay, so it had to have happened before then or the delivery driver would have heard the noise. Viv left work at 5:00 pm. He had rushed out because he had sensed something in the parking lot, but there had been nothing there when he arrived. He had followed her home, no one close by that set off his alarms. But that didn't mean that the Shadow's mate couldn't have had someone watching it. Why didn't he think of that sooner? He leaned forward to smell the door. There were so many scents here it made it hard to pull out an individual smell. He went back inside where there was less to sort through.

He pressed his nose near the door, blocking out Viv, D, and Thomas. There it was, a faint smell of the Netherworld.

"D. I think we're dealing with another demon. Block out

your guys' scents, close your eyes, concentrate. What do you smell?"

"The Netherworld," he said, confused. "But I smell like that too."

Mac counted to three. D hadn't been trained like he had, so it wouldn't seem different at first sniff. "Smell yourself. Block it all out and smell yourself. It's hard, but really concentrate."

"Okay. I think I have it."

"Now compare it to the other scent."

It took several minutes, but D's eyes finally flew open. "You're right. There's a difference. So we know it's a demon. How does that help us?"

"We'll be able to identify her for one. Two, since she's a demon and interfered with a demon mating, we can dispense justice and not have to involve any other nonhuman groups."

"Good, good. What are we going to do about Thomas' and Viv's jobs? Best-case scenario, we find them in a day or two. It looks like they're going to be injured. Work is going to want an explanation," D pointed out. If they didn't show to work, their bosses may also call the police and as the roommate/boyfriend, D would be their first suspect. If D was held up by the normal police, he wouldn't be able to help search for them.

And if they didn't find them within a day or two, how would they explain it to their bosses so that they wouldn't get fired. Mac listened when Viv talked in the library. She thought she was next in line for promotion to take over the entire library when her boss retired. If she suddenly no-showed, it could cost her everything she wanted.

"Let me call a detective I know. He's a nonhuman and

will be able to help. I've worked with him on cases before," Mac said, pulling out his phone.

"Liam. It's Mac. I need you ASAP at the address I'm going to text you. Full uniform, but it's a mixed case. Thanks."

"What good is calling a detective going to do?" D asked when Mac hung up.

"We can create the paper trail that Thomas and Viv's house was broken into, and they are believed missing. If nothing else, it gets their picture out to other authorities and maybe someone will see them while they're patrolling. I'll see if Liam can't contact the school and the library and let them know. It should save their jobs; after all it was police documented that they were abducted, not their fault. Liam also has a great nose, he may be able to pick up other scents we missed." Plus, he wasn't close to this case, so he wouldn't be overwhelmed by the scent of Viv's or Thomas' blood. "If the regular human police aren't involved, then it should free up your time to help locate them as well since we know you're not a suspect."

There was a knock on the door a few minutes later. D peeked out the peep hole to see a large German Shepherd dog and a female police officer.

"Is Liam a dog?" D asked.

"He's a shifter," Mac responded, walking over to the door. He could smell him on the other side and opened the door, letting them in.

"Hey Gina, Liam. I said full uniform. What made him change?" Mac asked.

"He caught scent of something in the parking lot and realized it was leading to the apartments. He figured he'd have better luck this way."

"Gotcha. You can check everything out and I'll tell Gina the background," Mac offered.

Liam woofed and got to work, his nose going everywhere.

"Tell me," Gina said, pulling out her notebook.

"I got called onto a case. There was a Shadow causing issues. By the time I got it, he was bound for punishment. He started many years ago, small things: harassing people, stealing things. It moved to assault, no theft. He was starting to enjoy hurting people. It finally escalated into him killing. He killed four people before he was caught. And then he escaped. He lay low for a couple of months before resurfacing and killing again. This is when I came in. We finally got him; D was the one in charge of processing and punishment. The Shadow got the deepest pit, no escape option. I had a feeling he had an accomplice but couldn't find any proof. We got a call tonight saying someone had turned himself in as his accomplice. D and I both went to process and interrogate the guy. He was a decoy. He had been sent by a female, who turned out to be the Shadow's mate. A mate for a mate, is what he said. We couldn't reach Viv and Thomas on their phones and raced back here. We found it like this. She left work at five o'clock, the note on the pizza says they attempted to deliver it at five fifty. There was no answer, but since it was paid for, they left it. My best guess is it happened before the pizza guy arrived or he would have heard something. There's no way this was quiet."

"Next question. Who are Viv and Thomas?"

"Thomas is my mate," D said, his tail twitching in agitation. "Both he and Viv are human. Viv is his best friend, they grew up together and share this apartment. I moved in when we bonded. Thomas didn't want to miss any time with his friend since she would grow old and die much sooner than he would now. She's a great person. My only guess is that the demoness didn't know which one of them was my mate and she took them both."

"Do you think she'll let Viv go if she realizes she doesn't have a mate mark?"

Mac shook his head. "I think she enjoys pain. If she finds out that Viv is my mate, she won't let her go."

"So they both have a mate mark. It would still say Mate Of in a language she could read, right?"

"I haven't claimed Viv," Mac admitted quietly. Gina looked at him sharply but didn't say anything.

Liam stood on two feet, completely bare-assed. "It's definitely a demoness. I swear I've scented her before. Remember the club a couple of weeks ago?" he asked Gina, who swore.

"We got called to a nightclub. It was more of a play club for nonhumans. A demoness showed up, seemed like she was okay to let in. They checked her ID, no issues, no warrants or arrests, no red flags from other clubs. They did their due diligence; she was just better at conning the system. They let her in, and she finds two people willing to play with her. They thought they were there to have a fun threesome. The club has video and audio in all the rooms to protect its regular members. The camera feed cuts out and they send security to check it out. By the time they get to the room, she had almost killed both of them. She cut them both, broke bones, raped them. The guy was small, he was a rabbit shifter. The girl about the same size, but she was a bobcat. Both of them fought back and even drew some blood, but they were no match for the woman when she took her demon form. They were in the hospital multiple days. We got a sketch from the victims and the video footage, but she managed to keep her face from a lot of the cameras. But the scent is the same as here. We never got far in the case. She's not registered in any of the criminal databases, human or other.

"I know it's not much, but there is physical evidence of her in the system now. I'll put in a breaking and entering report, as well as the missing persons. I'll contact both of their employers, so they won't have issues there once we find them. I'll plaster her description everywhere I can put wanted posters. If I hear anything, I'll let you know."

"Thanks. Lucifer is interrogating the Shadow to see if he can figure out where she might have gone. I'll let you know if we get any leads as well. We might need backup," Mac said.

Liam turned back into a German Shepherd and Gina opened the door.

"Thanks for coming out," D said. "Now what?" he asked when the door closed.

"See if you can focus on your bond. I need you to quiet everything else. Focus on Thomas, what he looks like, what he smells like, find your link to him and follow it. Let's see if we can't find them that way."

Mac watched as D focused. Mac closed his own eyes, bringing his mate to the forefront of his mind. They didn't have the mate bond, but he was hoping that his tracking skills would be helpful in some way. It led him to the couch, where there was a small puddle of her blood on the floor. Then nothing. Absolutely nothing.

"I can tell he's still alive, but I can't follow the bond. It's like something is blocking it," D said, frustration and desperation in his voice.

"Same here. She must have warded where she's keeping them."

"What do we do now?"

12

Viv woke slowly, her body sore. She must have slept really funky. Her head was pounding. She didn't even remember them drinking. She frowned, trying to remember what had happened last night. Oh. Shit. Demon lady. Where was Thomas? She sat up quickly, which caused a clanking sound. Her eyes flew all the way open, as she looked down and saw that she had an ankle cuff on. It was attached to a chain, which was connected to a metal hook in the wall. She pulled it, but it didn't budge. She was in a room, a cot thrown against the wall, a bucket in the corner. This was looking exactly like the movies that played at Halloween.

"Thomas?" she whispered. The room was so dark, she couldn't see much. There was a sliver of light coming in from a window, but it wasn't enough to see around the room. Putting her arms out in front of her, back of her hands out first like she saw in a movie once so you didn't break a finger feeling around, she slowly shuffled around the space. The chain made a horrible screeching sound as it scraped across the floor. Stupid, she scolded herself. She was trying to be quiet. She bent down to hold the chain off the ground with one hand. The floor was cold, and she realized that her socks and shoes were gone.

Chain held high, she resumed her shuffle around the room. She didn't want to break her toe on anything, so she went very slowly. She had just reached the other side of the room when the chain ran out of length. Lowering herself to the floor, she lay on her stomach, spreading her hands and non-chained leg out. She probably looked like she was making a weird snow angel. There was nothing. How could there be nothing? Where was Thomas, she thought, tears slowly escaping.

As the sun came up, she looked around the room, the growing light showing just how screwed she was. The flooring was ancient looking, cracked and worn, dirty. Everything was dirty. The window was a single pane, cracked and missing part of the upper left corner. The drapes were tattered and barely hanging on to the rod. The cot was the newest-looking thing there besides the bucket. Was the bucket for the bathroom? The room was otherwise empty. The door was missing the door handle, so even if she could reach it, she didn't think she could open it. The floral wallpaper was hideous and water stained. Large drooping flowers surrounded her. The ceiling was peeling, parts of the drywall missing to the point where she could see bare boards. There were a few dents or holes in the drywall scattered through the room. Maybe if she tried to look through the holes?

Grabbing the chain, she moved to the closest one. Viv slowly pushed her finger through the hole. She could barely touch the other side. Using her fist, she carefully opened the hole large enough to fit her hand. This was probably a stupid idea, she thought to herself. Who knew what was hiding in the walls. But she had to find Thomas. Taking a deep breath, she slid her hand through the hole. Once she reached the other side, she managed to scratch out a small opening on the other side, just enough to fit her finger. Crooking her finger, she tried pulling back toward herself. If the drywall she was destroying fell between the walls, the demoness might not notice that she was messing with the walls, she reasoned. She didn't get far, only about a quarter-sized hole, but she could see the hallway. There was some really gross-looking burnt orange carpet that had once been popular. She didn't see anyone in her limited view.

Moving to the wall with the cot, she had a few more options for holes. Viv tried to look through each one to see if there was a hole on the other side that she could use. Toward the back corner, it looked like there could be catty-corner holes, they were diagonal from each other, but she thought she could use them. It would be easier than trying to create a new hole with her finger again. Holding her breath, she slid her arm in the hole on her side, trying to angle her arm so that she would be lined up with the hole on the other side. She felt drywall, but not the hole. Viv huffed out a breath, feeling around cautiously. She winced as she felt cobwebs, hoping a spider wasn't now crawling on her. She scratched herself on a screw sticking out of the wood and in the back of her mind she wondered when she last had a tetanus shot. Her fingers finally felt a rougher surface, uneven and torn. She leaned hard against the wall, her feet pushing off the ground, trying to give her as much arm length as possible. She finally could just barely grip the edge of the other hole with her fingertips. Some of her fingers didn't want to bend and she was stuck using mostly her pointer finger and thumb. Pulling as hard as she could, she managed to tear a little piece off, but she lost the grip she had and fell backwards. The drywall scraped her arm, but she pushed herself back into position, adjusting so she had one leg pushing off the wall behind her to counterbalance when she pulled again. She found the hole quicker this time, getting a slightly better grip. She eventually managed to make a six-inch hole and could see a little bit into the room.

"Thomas?" she whispered. "Are you there?" She held her breath, her ears straining to hear anything. She heard a little whisper of movement. What was that? Was he waking up? "Thomas?"

Viv swallowed her scream as a mouse dropped onto her bed, scurrying across before falling to the ground and disappearing into a hole. Once the mouse disappeared, there were no more sounds from the other room. Collapsing on the bed, she looked around again, trying to see what she had missed. Her arm was now pulsing in pain, she must have scratched it worse than she thought. Looking at it, she saw a tear in her shirt, but it didn't really look that bad. Oh. She had forgotten about that somehow. Her hand had a hole in the middle of it from that bitch's shoe. She hadn't even noticed she was still bleeding. Gripping the arm sleeve that had a hole in it, she tried to rip her sleeve off. This was much easier in the movies, she thought, grunting as she pulled as hard as she could. This was going nowhere, she had managed to rip it maybe an inch. There was a jagged corner at the windowsill; maybe she could use that to tear it. Viv pulled her shirt off, placing the sleeve over the sharp wood, pulling it taunt. It took several minutes but she finally heard the fabric tearing. She stumbled as it abruptly separated from the rest of the shirt, catching herself on the wall. Viv pulled her shirt on before sitting back on the cot.

This was going to be awkward. She laid the strip of fabric over her leg, resting her hand on top. She really needed to wash it, but there was no sink or water nearby. This house probably didn't have running water anyway. She tried using the bottom of her shirt to brush as much dirt and grime away from the wound as possible.

"You're such a dumbass," she muttered to herself. "Didn't even remember you had a hole in your hand before you shoved it through the freaking walls."

It was too late to do anything about it now, other than wrap it up and hope for the best. She held one end against her palm with her thumb, wrapping it around her hand. She crossed the dangling ends, lifting her hand to her face so she could grab one end with her teeth, holding it so she could tie a rough knot. Her stomach growled, making her realize that she hadn't eaten since lunch yesterday besides the Fun Size Twix.

Viv had no idea how much time passed, other than the sun was fully up.

The door opened, the demoness standing there. "You're awake, I see. Lovely. Maybe you'll tell me which one of you is D's mate."

"No."

"Well, that just makes it more fun for me," she said with a grin. "Oh, by the way. Thomas was such a whiny little bitch that I finally gave in and brought him over to you. I only had one chain, so I had to break his leg so he couldn't get away. Have fun," she said cheerfully.

"What?" Viv asked, trying to follow the words spoken and not the cheerleader level of pep in her voice.

The demoness leaned over into the hallway, bending down to grab something.

"Thomas!" Viv rushed forward as the woman threw

him into the room. His leg was definitely broken, she thought, swallowing down the bile that threatened to erupt as she watched it flop. At least the bone wasn't sticking through the skin. Viv dragged the cot over to her friend, trying to figure out how to get him on it. It would be better for him to be off the floor. She wished there was another cot so she could break it apart and use the metal frame to splint his leg. She briefly thought about doing that to the cot now, but figured it was better for him to be off the cold ground. Thomas wasn't a big guy, but he was taller than her and as a dead weight, she quickly realized there was no way she was going to be able to pick him up enough to get him on the cot.

Gently laying him back on the ground, she looked him over. He had a large knot and cut on his forehead, from the coffee table she thought. There were a lot more bruises though. He had a black eye, red marks around his neck. Pulling his shirt up, his chest was a mass of bruises. She could see individual finger marks along his ribs. She must have been hitting him or dropping him a lot. She couldn't imagine how he got so many bruises otherwise. She didn't think the coffee table would explain this, especially the fingerprints. Viv laid his head in her lap, hoping he woke up soon.

"Thomas, I know you're not going to want to wake up, but I need you to. Just for a minute. There's a bed here, it's not much, but it's at least off the floor. I can't lift you up, I tried. Please. Please wake up for me."

13

Viv watched the door. The demoness had started coming in at all hours of the day. It didn't matter if the sun was up or the moon. Sometimes she just threw open the door and stood there. Sometimes she threw stuff at them. Sometimes she carried Thomas out and brought him back bloody. By the third day, Viv started feeling feverish. She had a feeling her hand was infected, but there wasn't much she could do about it. They got a bottle of water on day three, but she kept it all for drinking. She couldn't remember how long you could last without water, but she was sure it wasn't more than three days. There was only one bucket, and it had been filthy to start with, so collecting their own urine to drink wasn't an option. She wasn't sure when they would get water again, so her hand would need to wait. It wasn't like she had soap anyway.

She'd taken Thomas last night and hadn't brought him back yet and Viv was very afraid that her friend was dead. Hearing the board creak in the hallway made her feel hope. The demoness was coming back.

This time, she just dumped him in right by the door.

"He's a little sore right now," she laughed. "I'll be back later when he's aware. It's no fun to play with toys that aren't awake."

Viv waited until the woman left. The last time she tried to rush the door to grab him, she had gotten a kick to the ribs that sent her spinning across the room. Viv ran to the door, getting on her knees, reaching as far as she could to try to reach him. Her chain fell a couple of feet short of the door, but if she stretched enough, she could reach most of him. The cuff cut into her skin, and she could feel the scabs that had started to form reopen, but she ignored the pain.

"Thomas? What did she do?" Viv looked over his body frantically. He had burn marks on his chest. His left hand was swollen, several fingers clearly broken. Both eyes were now bruised, and when she checked his one eye, it was bloodshot, no white showing at all. While he was unconscious, she tried to ease his fingers back into place as best as she could. Ripping her other shirt sleeve off, she wrapped the fabric between each finger, before doing a loose wrap around his whole hand. It wouldn't keep them from bending, but it might help stabilize them a little bit.

She didn't want to move him until he woke up, in case something else was broken that she couldn't see. She waited by his side, holding the hand that wasn't broken until he started to stir.

"Shh. You're back in the room with me," she said quietly, trying to keep her voice soothing.

Thomas groaned. "It's cold."

"I didn't want to move you until you woke up and could tell me what hurt. I mean, I know most of you hurts, but more that I didn't want to move you and cause a broken bone to puncture something." She stayed next to him, trying to help him sit up as much as she could, letting him set the pace.

"I don't think any ribs are broken," he said. "This time she played around with matches and her fists." Thomas managed to get to one knee and hopped to standing using her shoulder to push off on. Viv stayed there, letting him get steadier, although he was swaying a bit. Viv jumped up, holding her arms out for him to grab. He hopped over to stand next to her.

"Do you think D will find us?" Viv asked, propping his arm around her shoulders, letting him use her as a crutch. It was the one hope that was keeping her going. She knew they had the mate bond and was hoping he could track them.

"I do. I think she has this place warded though, so he might not be able to as easily," he admitted. "But I do know he won't give up. He'll keep looking. I'm sure Mac is helping too."

"I'm sure. It's his best friend's mate that was taken. He should have some good resources to help." She didn't want to say too much in case the demoness was listening.

Thomas leaned his head on her shoulder. "You know he's got other motivation to help," he pointed out in a whisper.

Viv just shook her head. He didn't want her as a mate, so while he might feel bad that she got kidnapped and try to find her as part of his job, she truly didn't believe that he would be as devastated as D right now. Viv helped Thomas hobble over to the cot, his leg still very swollen and she worried about it healing right. She tried to help him raise his leg and lay it on the bed as gently as possible, but he still hissed in pain and paled. Viv sat on the floor next to the cot, laying her head on the edge, holding on to his hand. She hoped they came soon.

It was dark, barely any light filtering through the window. Viv wasn't sure what had woken her. The door creaked open, the demoness filling the doorway. This time she was in human form.

"It's adorable how you two snuggle together, as if that will make any bit of difference. I'm so happy you decided to wrap his hand. It just shows me which pathetic human is the one I'm after. It's been so much fun playing with both of you, but I really must insist that he and I have some one-on-one time right now." She transformed with a horrible smile, grabbing Thomas by his broken leg, waking him up screaming. She tossed him over her shoulder.

"No, please. Take me for a while, please. I could be a mate too. Let him go. I'll take his place," Viv pleaded. She didn't know how much more Thomas could take. They hadn't gotten any food since arriving, and other than the one water bottle, no water.

"No thank you. I'm good with the one I got." The demoness slammed the door shut behind her.

Viv sat in the dark waiting for her friend to be brought back. She stared at the door, willing it to open. It was another day before Thomas was dropped in the room. Viv had the bucket ready. She had dumped out their waste and was going to swing it at the demoness as soon as she brought Thomas in. She normally liked to gloat a little bit before she left, so it would give Viv a chance to beam her with the bucket. She didn't think it would do much, but maybe it would draw the attention to her instead of Thomas for a while. If she was really lucky, it would knock her out and Viv could search her for the key, although she knew that probably wouldn't happen.

The door finally opened, Thomas' body a bloody mess. He was missing his shirt and was covered in what looked like whip marks. Some were only red welts, some had clearly been hard enough to split his skin, some looked deep and were bleeding. Viv waited until she put Thomas on the ground. Reaching behind her to grab the bucket, she swung it with all her strength. The demoness was still bent over and Viv managed to nail her in the head.

"That wasn't wise," she said, storming over to grab Viv by the hair.

Viv struggled against the grip, kicking and digging in with her nails. The last thing she saw was the floor coming toward her face.

"Viv. Viv, wake up," a deep voice said that sounded familiar.

She opened her eyes, finding D leaning over her. "You're here," she said, full of disbelief.

"I am. Mac and I split up looking at different places, so it's just me right now. I can only take one of you at a time."

"Take Thomas. He needs help. She's broken his leg and fingers, I'm worried he has a concussion, he has burn and whip marks," she said.

D looked conflicted.

"Go," she urged. "Come back when he's safe."

"I will. I can't tell Mac where you are since it's warded. I'll be able to get back here though."

Viv sat on the cot, waiting for D to come back. She was so grateful that D had found them. Thomas was in bad shape and needed lots of medical attention.

"Where did my toy go?" the demoness demanded when she threw open the door only minutes later.

"He's safe. You can't hurt him anymore," Viv said with a smile.

"Hm. But I've still got you. This place is compromised, so I'll take you someplace else to play."

Viv fought, lashing out with her hands and arms, legs kicking, but it didn't matter. A blow to the head knocked her out.

14

Viv woke, her shoulders screaming in pain. A bucket of cold water was thrown in her face, some of it splashing up her nose. Coughing, gasping for breath, her ribs screamed in pain. She hoped they were just bruised. Opening her eyes, Viv realized she was in a different room. She was spread out, her arms supporting her weight until she stood up straight. Both feet and hands were chained to the floor and ceiling. She'd been stripped down to her underwear and it was freezing in here. Looking around, it appeared that she was in an abandoned building, the windows mostly broken out. The ceiling beams were in place, but there was no roof.

"I'm so glad you could wake up for me. It's no fun if I can't hear you scream and cry."

"What is it that you want? I'm not D's mate," Viv informed her now that Thomas was away safe.

"Oh, I know. But a little birdie also told me that you might be the mate of the Enforcer cunt that took my Shadow."

"I have no mate band," Viv stated, pointing out the obvious.

"Ah, you might not have a mate who claimed you, but you do in fact have a mate. He just doesn't want you. That's okay. I do. I want to have all kinds of fun with you. I'm going to play with you for a while before I use my tail on you. Have you taken a tail before? Unfortunately for you, I like to cover my tail in a barbed sheath. I like the pain and blood from my partners. My Shadow used to love to play. We'd find someone to share and play with. He'd fuck me while I raped them with my tail. It was so much fun watching what he could do to them, but he's gone now and I have no one to play with but you. Do you want to see it?" she asked, almost hopefully.

Viv debated on how to proceed, but figured she probably wasn't going to make it out of this unscathed or possibly even alive either way. "No, I don't. I don't want to play with you, I don't want to see your puny tail."

"That just makes it more fun," the demoness purred. She was tall but slender as a human and Viv wondered if she would have a fighting chance if she got free. The demoness shifted to her demon form, getting taller and bulking up. Her tail seemed normal until she pulled out a sheath that she clamped onto it. It was indeed covered in sharp-looking barbs. That would rip her up inside and Viv felt a moment of terror.

"I'm saving the fucking for later, but I'll introduce you to my tail now," the demoness whispered in her ear. Viv heard a whistling sound as pain exploded from her back. The demoness was using her tail as a whip and the barbs were cutting into her skin. She guessed she should be grateful that they weren't bigger; these wouldn't get far enough to hit bone. Viv bit her lip until she tasted blood, trying to keep her screams in.

"I'm not stopping until I hear a scream," the demoness told her. She jumped, spinning in the air, tail lashing across Viv's back, a leg flying out to kick the back of Viv's legs. She fell, her arms taking the brunt of her weight, the tail whipping around and getting the edge of her hairline near her forehead. With her own blood dripping into her eye, she had a harder time keeping track of the demoness.

"Did you know that as a mate to a demon you become immune to hellfire? Well, not you because your mate never claimed you. Are you curious to see what it feels like? I am. Let's see what you think."

Viv finally screamed as a line of fire traced down her back.

As far as Viv could tell, it was her third day in this building. The days got warm enough that she didn't freeze to death, but the nights were getting iffy. She could see her breath each night in the moonlight. With only underwear on, she didn't have a lot of protection from the weather. At least it hadn't rained or snowed, she thought, desperate to find one positive thing. The sun helped give the illusion of warmth, but Viv knew it was still cold. She felt like she had gotten sunburned, her skin felt tight and hot. Her time here was spent hanging, the demoness never taking her out of the restraints, waiting for the woman to show up. Each time it was with something new, little cuts, whipping, sometimes with the barbs, sometimes not. One time she burned the bottom of her feet, knowing she would have to stand on them. Sometimes it was just smacking or hitting. There was no bucket here, so Viv was also standing in a puddle of her own urine. She had tried to hold it as long as possible, but eventually had to go. She hadn't had any water since they had come here, so at least there wasn't a lot.

The demoness walked in, back in her demon form. She was so much bigger than Viv this way. "I brought some friends with me this time. They wanted to see what made humans so much fun to play with. Nonhumans heal much too quickly," she complained.

Viv's heart stuttered. She didn't think she could survive being raped. She really didn't. Please don't let that be what she meant. Five different nonhumans walked in, some shifted, some not. She could feel the tears falling down her face, but she bit her tongue to keep from making any noise.

"I thought it'd be bigger," the biggest guy said, disappointment in his voice.

"Some are. This one isn't," the demoness replied. "Now are you going to help me play or are you going to whine? Have fun, smack her, beat her, fondle. Just no penetration until after I have my fun. I get the holes first," she said, her teeth bared in what was supposed to be a smile.

The smallest one stepped forward. "I'd like to go first."

"No!" one of the men protested. "She'll be screaming and crying in minutes. I want to have some fun before you drive her mad."

"Yeah! Back the fuck up. You go last," another demanded.

A fight almost broke out, a large body slamming into

her, pulling her ankle painfully in the cuff. Her shoulder popped, and she had to bite her tongue to keep from screaming. That couldn't have been good.

"Don't break the toy before you play," the demoness scolded. "Play nice with each other or leave."

The big one stepped over, grabbing her face in his hands, squeezing her lips together. "Is this a hole?" he asked, cupping his crotch with his other hand.

"For now."

"Shame. I could break all her teeth out and gag her on my cock." He ran his hand down her body, squeezing her breasts painfully. He ripped her bra off, tearing her skin in the process. Viv didn't know if it was from his nails, the force of the fabric pulling against her skin, or the bra hooks. He ran a hand down her crease, pinching her lips shut. His other hand slid between her butt cheeks, his finger trying to thrust dry into her anus.

"Hole," the demoness shouted, smacking his hand away. "My tail is going to rip that shit up later. I'm making her bleed first. Not you. No holes until I'm done."

"This is boring then. I'm out," he said, backhanding Viv across the face, splitting her lip, before he left.

"More for me then," another one said, licking his lips, his eyes fixed on her bleeding lip. "Hm. Smells delicious." He blurred and she felt teeth tear into her skin, bites forming faster than she could register. He came close to her underwear but turned his head at the last minute, tearing into her inner thigh.

The other two circled, one taking his pants completely off, a scorpion-like tail emerging from his back. He walked behind her, the tail curving over her shoulder to caress her body. She shivered in disgust.

"I love the smell of blood in the air. Let's see if I can't make it last longer," he murmured, the tail just barely touching her. Viv waited for a bite, but instead the tail whipped back and flew at her, piercing her skin. The tip was as thin as a needle, but it burned as he injected her with something. She could feel it entering her body and spreading. Over and over, he stabbed her as the vampire bit, not seemingly concerned with the poison running through her body. She could feel herself getting weaker, the wounds showing no sign of closing or slowing down. The third one finally had enough and pushed the other two out of the way. He released a whip from his belt, staying in human form. Viv panted, trying to stay on her feet, but it was getting harder. Her world was colored by pain, black spots beginning to dance in her vision.

The first hit of the whip made her scream. He laid a strip right across the previous marks left by the demoness, across the bites and stings of today. She lost count at ten, her legs quickly losing strength. The fourth man finally approached.

"Fuck you all, she's going to be dead soon. Have your fun, but I'm taking my turn." He grabbed her face, forcing her to look into his eyes.

"Hello there, my pretty," he murmured. "I'm going to destroy you."

Viv's mind was awash in images of being raped, all of them taking a turn, all of them at once, ripping her to pieces, breaking her teeth out so they could force their dicks in without fear of being bit, of being whipped while someone else took their turn with her body. She screamed as she felt the vampire bite off her clitoris, holding it between his bloody teeth. The whip wielder cut through her breasts until they fell to the floor. She sobbed and screamed, all she felt was pain and anguish. She heard his voice chanting in her mind, horrible things coming from his mouth, how she was worthless, how no one wanted her, how no one would ever want her again if she lived.

Her screams filled the air. Her head hanging low, she was confused when she saw her body intact; she could still feel the pain of the assaults, but her body didn't show it. Looking up she saw the four men standing around her in a circle, their cocks out, some human-looking, some not. She twisted in the chains, trying to find a way out, but there was none. None of them touched her as they jerked off, spraying her body with their seed.

"It's my turn. Hold her," the demoness commanded. "I want her while she's still a warm body."

They all grabbed her, pulling her off the chains and holding her flat on the floor, spread eagle, no way to defend herself. Viv heard laughter behind her. She was so cold, her blood soaking into the floor from open wounds that wouldn't close. Maybe she would pass out before anything happened. The dark spots were getting larger, her mind trying too late to protect itself, but not before she felt them hold her ass cheeks open, claws digging into each side. She felt something big and sharp push at her entrance, pain blooming as it cut the sensitive skin near her butt cheeks and anus.

No, she wouldn't lie here, she thought. She might die, but she'd at least make it harder for them. She twisted, tightening her butt muscles, trying to close her cheeks. She fought with all the strength left in her body. Viv got one foot free, kicking backwards, twisting to get some momentum. She connected with flesh of some sort and heard a roar of anger.

"Hold her tighter!"

She tried kicking out again, but they grabbed her hair and slammed her head into the floor until she saw stars, blackness overtaking her vision. Something stabbed through her foot, holding her in place. The scorpion barb sticking through her foot was the last thing she saw.

15

Mac felt like he could finally breathe again. When D went back to get Viv, she was gone, fresh drops of blood on the floor. D had dropped Thomas off at the hospital and had ported back to get Viv within minutes, but she had already been taken someplace new. D had been blaming himself for leaving her there, but Mac knew Viv had been right that Thomas needed immediate medical attention. There was talk about surgery for his leg and they were worried about his one eye.

Mac had been working nonstop trying to find new locations and track down informants and leads. It took days but Liam had finally heard whispers among the degenerates of a small invite-only party. The party prize was a human. This had to be it. D was with Thomas who was still in the hospital recovering. They took him to a nonhuman hospital with extra security. It also meant that they had access to better medical care with witches and a shaman on staff. Liam and Gina were coming with him, along with several other Enforcers that Lucifer trusted. Some of them were Lucifer's own bodyguards.

They ported to the grounds. He took Liam while another Enforcer took Gina. They had also brought a witch healer just in case. There wasn't much around, only a partial building, and he could hear noises coming from that direction. He could also smell his mate's blood. A lot of it.

"We need to get to her," the witch urged in a whisper. "The amount of blood I smell is too much for a human. She'll die soon if we can't get her help."

Mac nodded. Using hand gestures Mac sent the team to surround the building. Gina waved her hand, creating a dome over the structure. She had the ability to create force fields and this one would keep anyone from teleporting out, making sure that they could capture anyone in there.

Mac crept closer, not hearing his mate's voice but he could hear her heartbeat. It was racing fast in fear. His team tapped their mics, letting him know they were all in position. Mac changed forms, knocking down the door.

"NO!" he roared. His demon took one look at the scene that would haunt him for the rest of his life and lost himself to rage. His mate on the ground, held in place by four nonhumans, one foot pierced to the ground by the scorpion shifter's barb. The demoness behind her, her tail encased in a barbed sheath, poised to force its way into her body.

Mac ported over before he could even form the thought, his claws out, slicing the throat of the demoness. Gripping her head, he twisted, ripping it from her body. His own tail reached out, firming to the hardness of steel, stabbing the scorpion shifter through the stomach. He grinned at him as he curled his tail and pulled it out, ripping out the man's intestines. His hand rose, stabbing the shifter through the ear with his claws. Pulling out his gun, he shot the one who was trying to run away. He was a mind fucker and Mac wanted to have a word with him before he killed him. Spinning to grab the one holding her left arm, Mac saw Liam had already ripped out his throat. Nodding at his friend, he turned his attention to the man trying to crab walk away from him. He kept slipping in the demoness' blood, so he didn't make it far. This one was a demon. How disappointing.

"Do you see this mark?" he asked, turning his wrist over.

"I'm sorry, sir. I didn't know we couldn't have this one."

"This one? This one's my mate." Mac watched as the demon's face drained of all color. "But regardless, this should never have happened." Punching his fist through his chest, he grabbed hold of the demon's heart. "Die. And when I see you next it will be in the deepest pits. Lucifer has a special place just for you," he told him. Mac let his fire come forth, burning the demon from the inside out. Most demons were immune to hellfire, but his was special, a gift known only to his family line. The body turned to ash in seconds, drifting away on the air.

Mac saw the witch working on Viv and he focused on the mind fucker. "You're going to die. How painful it is depends on you. I can draw it out for days. Or I can make it quick. You fucked with the wrong mate. Release her mind and any little traps you left, and you die quick. I want nothing of you or your magic remaining in her. We have ways of checking and if you lie, I'll let Lucifer himself have you."

"I'm just going to be in punishment anyway. It doesn't matter to me and it's amusing to watch her suffer."

"I don't think you understand. You touched what is mine. Look at me and see what I have planned for you. You won't die, but you'll crave it. I'll never let you go, and your pain will increase tenfold. Anything you love will die in front of you. There's no escape for you. I can crush your soul, or you can suffer eternal. I don't care which. There are ways around your trickery, it's just faster if you do it. Decide now or I'll decide for you."

Mac focused on all the depravity and awfulness he had seen in his many, many years working as an Enforcer. He thought of his teachings from his uncle who had seen much more than him. There were ways to skin a person alive, to keep them alive magically so they felt the painful pulse of nerve endings being exposed to the air. Ways to let the skin grow back only to start all over. He worked at keeping people safe, but he knew thousands of ways to make people suffer. To save his mate he would do whatever it took. Torture, killing. Nothing would stand in his way.

The mind fucker looked at him, trying to find a way to manipulate Mac's brain. "Not going to work, fucker. I'm immune. I'm just letting you see some of my ideas so you can make an informed decision."

The man paled. Mac knew he would cave then. They always did when they realized their tricks wouldn't work. The man looked at his mate, whispering words on the air. Mac grabbed his throat. "Nope. Loud enough we can all hear them. No bullshit."

The man spoke again, the witch listening intently. She had a mind gift as well, due to her mixed parentage. She placed a hand on Viv's head, focusing. When she gave a nod, Mac spoke to the man again. "You're going to see Lucifer. When we confirm her mind is clear of your bullshit, we'll destroy you. Until then, have fun." Mac stabbed him in the heart, twisting the knife. As soon as the life left him, Mac rushed over to Viv.

"How is she?" He wanted to touch her but wasn't sure where.

"Badly dehydrated and malnourished. They tried to rape her but didn't succeed. There's some bleeding at her anal entrance, but she wasn't penetrated. There are traces of scorpion poison in her system, keeping her wounds from healing. She's lost a lot of blood from bites. She's almost drained. Her hand is infected, and I'm worried it's gone into sepsis, but a lot of the symptoms are also associated with blood loss, so the hospital will have to run tests. I can't tell yet if her ankle is broken or badly sprained. She was also exposed to the elements, so hypothermia could be an issue. Some of her digits are showing signs of early frostbite. We need to get her to a nonhuman hospital. I need more healers if we want to save her. This is beyond my skills. I can keep her alive until we get there, but I'm not strong enough to heal all of this," she admitted.

Mac grabbed his phone. "Uncle, can you open a portal to the hospital? The witch needs to stay with Viv, and we need more healers when we get there. It's bad," he added, his voice breaking.

"It'll be done. She won't leave you," his uncle promised. Mac took solace in the words of his only remaining blood family member.

He heard a buzz and turned to see a large portal open, medical staff waiting on the other side.

"Can I pick her up?" he asked.

"Yes, but be careful of her ribs. There may be fractures," the witch advised, keeping a hand on Viv at all times. He could see the strain on her face, as her skin took a grayer tone. "We need to go now; I can't hold on much longer."

Mac lifted Viv as quickly as he could without moving her ribs and ran toward the portal, the witch keeping pace. As soon as they crossed over, he laid Viv on the stretcher and another witch placed a hand on her. The one that came with them collapsed, Mac catching her and laying her down, resting her head gently on the floor.

"Go, we've got her," a hospital member urged him.

Mac rushed after his mate, following them down hallways, only stopping when a large gargoyle stepped in his way in front of a set of large doors. "I'm sorry, sir. But that's the surgery. You can't go back there," he said, his voice apologetic. "There's a waiting room. Follow me."

Mac followed, receiving more than a few stares and people moving to give him space. They entered a waiting room. It looked like a standard hospital waiting room with bland walls, the smell of antiseptic and cleaner. A coffee and snack machine stood in the corner. The chairs here were a little differently shaped than human hospitals; the seats wider, some without backs to accommodate wings and tails. In another corner there was a glass-enclosed room with a heat lamp for the cold-blooded shifters. The opposite corner had a similar enclosure, but this was filled with snow and had blocks of ice to keep it cold. Those areas had their own seats inside of the enclosure, along with call buttons for the waiting room assistants.

It helped to have waiting room assistants; most of them had some sort of calming gift, helping to keep nonhumans as calm as possible and fights and rages to a minimum. They also ran to get food, drinks, anything the people waiting might need.

"Is there anyone we can call to wait with you?" the attendant asked.

Mac shook his head. Uncle would be helping deal with the ones he killed today. D was with Thomas, and he wasn't going to pull him from his injured mate's side. Liam was his next closest friend, but he and Gina were still at the site, cleaning up bodies and filing reports.

His phone chimed. It was his uncle.

Got them all. I created a new holding area just for them. I sent Belz to keep an eye on your mate. He'll make sure she's safe. Love you, Mac.

Mac found a small smile at that. His uncle didn't say it much, but Mac knew he loved him. He had helped raise him after his parents died. Belz was a demon, but he was trained in medicine and also had the ability to become invisible. Mac guessed he was in the surgery room. There were so many lights in those rooms, for a good reason, but it didn't leave any shadows for a demon to hide. Belz wouldn't have that problem.

He paced the room, wondering what was going on. His phone buzzed again but from a number he didn't recognize.

It's Belz. They have her on strong antibiotics. It went to sepsis. Hard to tell if in shock or just blood loss. Have blood transfusion and anti-venom started too. Had to wash her first to avoid additional contaminations. About to start surgery.

Thanks. What's the surgery for? Mac typed back.

Stitches for head, hand, foot, and some whip marks for sure. Shoulder will have to be reset. I'll let you know more later. They may find more. They're worried about ribs and possible skull fracture.

Thanks. Mac responded and closed his messages.

He took another lap around the room before grabbing a coffee. He hadn't slept in two days as they chased the last few leads that led to finding Viv.

How's Thomas? Has he woken up? Mac wrote to D. Last time they had spoken, Thomas had had surgery for his ribs, his leg set and casted, burns treated. They had him sedated to allow his lung to heal for a few days before allowing the sedation to wear off and let him wake up naturally.

He did briefly and was asking where Viv was, D replied.

We found her. We're here. She's in surgery now. They're all dead, Mac wrote back.

Do you need me to come down? D asked.

No. Stay with your mate. I'll keep you updated.

He stared at the white-ish beige walls and wondered why they didn't have pictures or something enjoyable to look at.

"Mac? Honey? Are you okay?"

He turned around and saw D's mom standing there. He wanted to give her a hug but his hands were coated in blood.

"I'm not hurt," he reassured her. "We found her. It's. It's bad. They were trying to..." he shook his head, unable to finish the sentence.

"It'll be a while, sir. There's a bathroom over there with a shower, if you would like to use it. I have a pair of scrubs that you can change into. I have slipper socks, but not shoes in your size," the room attendant said when she came over.

"Go," D's mom urged. "I'll wait out here in case there's news. You need a shower; you'll scare her looking like that. I sent Bill to grab a pair of D's shoes, you guys have always been the same size."

"Thanks, Ma," he said, giving her a wan smile.

The room assistant brought him over to the bathroom, the clothes already sitting on the bench. Mac looked at himself in the mirror. He was coated in blood, splatter everywhere. Yeah. He needed to get clean.

Mac sped through the shower, scalding himself but he made sure to get all the blood off his skin and under his nails. He quickly dried off and threw on the scrubs and socks. By the time he got out of the bathroom, D's mom was still sitting in the room, but she had a pair of boots for him. He asked the nurse for a plastic bag for his clothes. They needed to be burned. There was no saving them.

It took hours, but finally an exhausted-looking doctor came over. "Are you with the young woman that was brought in? Vivian?"

"Yes," Mac confirmed.

"Are you family?" the doctor asked.

"She's my mate and I'm an Enforcer," he replied, showing his markings.

"Let's go talk in a private room," the doctor said, leading them to a small conference room.

Ma sat with him, holding his hand.

"She had a lot of injuries, but I can at least say she wasn't raped. They tried and there's some cuts around her anus, but a few stitches took care of those. Some of the whip marks needed stitches, her shoulder was dislocated and we have that set. We have it immobilized for now to let it heal. She had signs of a concussion, but we did a CAT scan and didn't see anything too alarming in terms of brain swelling. She had a skull fracture. We had to administer antivenom before we could perform surgery or she would have bled out. It was close enough as it was. We repaired the nerves in her foot that were severed. She had a hairline fracture in her ankle. She also had several bruised ribs and a large burn down her back and on her feet. She's on antibiotics and pain meds for everything. We're keeping her lightly sedated so she doesn't thrash around and cause more injuries. She was dehydrated and malnourished on top of the blood loss and hypothermia."

"Can't you use a healing potion? Cost is no problem, whatever she needs," Mac offered.

"The Lucifer already took care of it. It's more that her body can't handle too much more strain. She's human and not used to rapid healing. We gave her a few small doses to heal the concussion and skull fracture so we could put her under sedation and used healing salves to heal the burns and most of the whip marks on her back. Some were deep enough to scar though, even with the cream. We're hesitant to use any more on her right now until we see how her body reacts. We had to do the same thing with her friend that was brought in earlier. Treating humans is a little trickier if they haven't been exposed to our healing before. If she does well, we'll try additional potions in a few days. She's going to be kept sedated until then to reduce the risk of further injury.

"Her ankle is in an air cast at the moment to keep it stabilized. She can use a walking boot once she's awake and feeling up to being mobile. The biggest issue was her hand. The puncture wound went all the way through, severing a nerve. It was also septic. We repaired the nerve as best we could, but the combination of the infection and the severity of the wound might cause long-term issues. We'll have to wait to see. We applied a few drops of healing potion to help get the infection under control, to boost the antibiotics. The foot was pretty straightforward. I don't anticipate any long-term problems from that. As a normal human, she may develop aches in the bone as she ages, but nothing from the nerve issue."

Mac sat back, stunned at how much her small body had endured.

"Is that it, doctor?" Ma asked, gripping his hand tightly.

"You're mates?" he asked again, hesitantly.

Mac nodded.

"We did a swab and a quick pregnancy test to make sure that none of the ejaculate made its way into her body. She was lucky, nothing entered, and the scan was clean.

She won't become pregnant from them ejaculating on her."

Mac felt lightheaded. He hadn't even thought of that as a possibility since they said she wasn't penetrated. Holy crap.

"Head between your knees," the doctor said, shoving his head down. "I don't need to stitch you up too if you hit your head passing out."

Mac took several deep breaths, calming himself before sitting up.

"When can we see her?"

"Give us a half hour or so. Someone will come get you."

16

They were finally all home. Thomas had been released a few days ago and D had been frantically cleaning the apartment getting it ready for him to come home while his mom sat with Thomas. The broken coffee table and chair were thrown out, the dents in the wall repaired and painted over, the broken phones replaced. All the blood had been scrubbed away, although they had to throw out some of the pillows and the rug.

They had been able to take Viv off sedation and used a little more healing potion for her hand. Unfortunately, she started having a reaction to it and they had to stop the dosage. The doctors thought it was best for the rest to heal on its own. At least the infection was gone, the antibiotics and healing potion having worked. After she came off of the sedation during her last couple of days in the hospital, Viv had started having nightmares. Nothing seemed to help; Mac finally had slipped her a knife, one spelled to always return to her, thinking it would help her feel safe. He had been hoping she would rest better when she came home, but if anything, the nightmares seemed worse.

He was starting to get worried that any progress on her health would regress and finally brought it up to his friend the second full day she was home.

"She's not sleeping," Mac said quietly to D. "She stares at the door like she's expecting someone to bust through it again. She's not going to heal much past what they did in the hospital if she's not eating or sleeping. She can't go on like this for long."

"I have an idea but let me run it by Thomas first. He knows her best. He's been losing his mind over how to help her."

Mac sat with Viv as she stared at the apartment door. She was on the couch, her new phone in her injured hand, the knife clenched in the other.

"Viv. She's gone. She can't get you again," Mac said gently. Viv shook her head.

"I'm here. I won't let anyone get you, okay. You're my mate. I was stupid before. There are fuckups in every race and I'm hoping you don't hold her against all demons. I realize now that's what I did. I was too scared of being hurt again to trust. Can you forgive me? I don't want to lose you. I must be pretty stupid, because it took almost losing you to make my walls come down. I know I don't deserve it, but I'm willing to work at getting a second chance. Do you think maybe you could trust me enough to keep you safe? I'd been doing okay at it until that day. I should have left D behind. I didn't think it was a distraction to get us away from you," Mac admitted.

"What do you mean, until then?" Viv asked, her voice still rough from screaming and disuse. She hadn't spoken other than a few sentences in the hospital.

"Right. So. This is going to sound stalkery, but I didn't mean it that way. I knew you were my mate, and while I didn't want a mate, I didn't want anyone to hurt you. So, I kind of followed you on your dates, hung out at the library. Your second date was a doozy, I had lots of fun causing the drinks to spill all over him. I followed him home and realized what a scumbag he was and left a little tip for the cops."

"You were my shadows?" she asked. "I always felt safe when my shadows were there."

He nodded. "I wanted to keep you safe." He had to school his face, keeping the shock from it when she crawled into his lap. He held her tight enough that she wouldn't fall out, but not so tight as to feel bound or restricted. Her head tucked into his shoulder, and he could hear her breathe in deeply. She must like his scent because her shoulders dropped and he thought she actually fell asleep.

D stood in the doorway. "Asleep?" he mouthed.

Mac nodded. D held up his phone. Mac tilted his head to where his sat on the table. D walked silently over to hand it to Mac. After making sure the phone was on silent, he texted D.

I think she's finally asleep. I confessed I was hiding in the shadows watching her before. She said her shadows made her feel safe, climbed in my lap and fell asleep.

D nodded as he read, typing out a response. *I bought that house and had contractors in fixing it up. I just got the all clear that it was ready to move into while they were in the hospital. My thought was we move in right away. Get new living room furniture so it doesn't remind them of the apartment. Move what we can today, maybe have movers get the rest. I think a new area would help them both. Thomas agreed and said Viv was awake for more of the attack in the apartment. He was groggy from getting thrown into the coffee table right at the start.*

Mac nodded. It made sense. They could set up a camera security system so they would all have access to look around at all times. He'd ask his uncle to help set up wards over the house. If she knew no one could simply come through their door, he thought it would help her sleep. *Let's do it,* he typed back. *How quickly do you think we can get it done?*

I bet my parents will help transport furniture into the house. If I can get living room furniture delivered today, we can get them in by tonight. I'd like for it to be daylight if possible so it's not as potentially scary looking, D replied.

Let me get ahold of Uncle and see if he can send someone to ward the house. We can add our own, but at least it will be ready when we get there, Mac wrote.

Sounds good. I'll call my parents and see if they can help, D added, walking out of the room. Mac assumed to call his parents and not wake up Viv.

Uncle. Can I ask a favor? Can you send someone to D's new house to set a ward? We want to move in today. I think it will help Viv sleep. D's getting his parents to help move the bedroom furniture, but we're going to buy new stuff for the living room so there's no association with it, Mac typed.

Consider it done. I'll send living room furniture too. Think of it as a mating gift.

Mac smiled. *Thank you. But she hasn't accepted me yet. I have a lot of groveling to do. I rejected her and made her feel awful. I should have acted like a mate.*

You did. And you do. But you can also explain why. Not that it excuses your behavior, I raised you better than that, but maybe she'll be more open to you, his uncle replied. *Love you, nephew. Good luck. Don't worry about the house.*

Thank you, Mac replied.

He wasn't sure if D was still on the phone with his

parents or sitting with Thomas, so he sent him an update via text. *Uncle is sending over living room furniture and someone to ward the house.*

Mac sat on the couch, holding his mate, his best friend in the other room, his uncle more than willing to help him. He had a pretty darn good life, he just needed to get his brain to follow what his heart wanted. Viv wasn't anything like his first mate; she helped protect those she loved. Even when she didn't know D very well, she still kept the secret of nonhumans. He needed to figure out how to be there for her, how to show her he was sorry and for her to trust him with her heart. He wasn't sure how, but he figured he might have a chance since she climbed into his lap and felt safe enough to sleep.

Viv woke up as she felt her body move, gasping and her heart racing.

"Shh. I've got you. We're just moving rooms," Mac said gently.

"Where are we going?" she asked, laying her head back on Mac's shoulder.

"D found us a new house and has it ready for us to move in. His parents helped move the furniture we would want, and we'll pack up the kitchen stuff later," Thomas said, hobbling over in his walking cast. With his broken fingers it was too hard to use crutches and they had sped up the recovery of his leg using magic enough for him to be able to use a walking cast. They didn't want to push his body any further than that and were leaving it up to his natural healing to do the rest.

"Not the couch," she said.

"Nope. We're getting all-new living room furniture," Thomas said firmly. "I saw pictures of the house and it looks amazing. D found a ranch that spreads out; it has a living room and kitchen in the middle of the house, with wings on either side that he converted into our own living spaces. It's great for me right now since I don't have to manage stairs. We can still live together but will have our own spaces. There's a nice back porch with a big yard. Maybe we can get a dog now," Thomas suggested.

"I'd like that," Viv said. She loved dogs and had always wanted one. She thought it would help her not feel scared of being alone in the house.

"Are you ready to go?" Mac asked.

She had forgotten he was still there; he had been so silent. Which was kind of ridiculous since he was holding her. "I need to pack some clothes," she said.

"We already ported your entire dresser over," Mac replied. "D's mom got the things in your closet and bath-room. Once we get you home, you can send me to get anything you're missing," he offered.

"Okay. I can't wait to see it," she said, trying to come up with the enthusiasm she knew she should have. She had been excited when D had first brought it up before the demon lady. She was hoping that being in a new place would help her sleep. She felt much better after taking a nap, but she couldn't sleep on Mac all the time. She vaguely remembered him saying he was sorry for before and that he had been watching over her. It would explain why she felt safe with the shadows. But she had a hard time believing that he suddenly changed his mind about wanting a human for a mate. She thought he was feeling guilty over her being taken and hurt, and that wasn't a good reason to accept his mate claim. He needed to want her, to want to love her, not do it out of a feeling of responsibility or guilt. She had come to terms with her mate not wanting her. Kind of. But she didn't want a pity mating either.

Thomas gave her a hug, which ended up including Mac. D came over and picked him up, opening a portal and stepping through.

"Ready?" Mac asked.

She nodded, breathing in his scent to help calm her. She hadn't been awake for two of the portal journeys. The last one brought her home from the hospital and she had been in pain, nervous about seeing the apartment, and dealing with emotions that had caught up to her after the last week. Viv watched as a portal opened in front of them, Mac holding her tightly as he stepped through. As it closed behind them, she looked around the new living room. It was bright and cheery, the walls a pale gray with darker gray and blue curtains. White wood slat blinds hung on all the windows. She liked that they would be able to close the wood blinds if it was glaring but still have light come in and close the fabric curtains when it got dark out. There was something creepy about people being able to see into your house at night. She never understood the people who left their windows uncovered at night. You could see right in when the lights were on.

The two couches were a Chesterfield style in a deep midnight blue, placed in an L shape facing a fireplace. A large screen TV sat on the mantle. A matching leather recliner sat at the open end, a light gray throw blanket over the arm. The rug between the couches had grays and blues in an abstract swirling pattern. She saw a few throw pillows on the couch. It looked like it had an open floor plan, with the kitchen behind the living room, separated by a half-wall. The kitchen walls were also a light gray color, letting the two rooms flow together. The wood cabinets were in a dark midnight blue with silver handles. The appliances looked like stainless steel from here. There was a double oven, which she was thrilled to see. She had always wanted one and it would make Thanksgiving dinner so much easier to cook. Last year it had just been the two of them, as Thomas' parents had gone to visit extended family, and he didn't have that much time off of work. His school had the Wednesday, Thursday, and Friday off, but to drive out there would have taken maybe two days each way so it hadn't been worth the trip. Now Christmas was a good break for him with two weeks off. The library was closed on Thanksgiving, Christmas Eve and Day, and New Year's Eve and Day. Viv normally saved her vacation time for summer when she and Thomas would go on a vacation together. It wasn't fun traveling alone.

"Do you want to see your side of the house?" Mac asked.

Viv nodded, eager to see her space. She was sure Thomas had given D an idea of where her furniture should go. Mac walked over, pulling open the door.

"Each wing has a door so you can close it off if you want to, especially if either of you had guests over. You can't see it from where we were, but there's a bathroom over by the kitchen for guests and a door that leads out into the garage. D is talking about expanding the garage. It's a three car right now. He has a garage door opener for your car on the kitchen table. I can bring your car over for you today so you have it. I don't want you to feel trapped here if I have to leave," he offered.

Viv hummed in response. She wasn't sure what the best

answer for that was. It seemed like he may be planning on staying here, but she certainly wasn't going to offer to share a bed. She looked around, seeing some of the pictures and artwork from her room at the apartment had been hung in the hallway. Mac stopped by the first door.

"This is the second bedroom. I thought I'd stay here if that's okay with you? I can move over to D's side, but I wanted to be close in case you needed something. Thomas will have D there to help."

Viv hated to admit it, but it made sense. She was still feeling pretty weak, and though she knew she was going to try to do it all herself, it would make her feel better knowing someone else was close by. "That's fine," she said.

Mac continued down the hallway. "This is the second bathroom. It's a full bath and has a fun clawfoot tub. It has a shower curtain around it so you can take a shower as well. The door across the hall here is a closet. I guess for linens or something, Thomas said. There's a big coat closet by the front door and living room."

He stopped in front of the last door. "This is your room. It has an attached bathroom and a walk-in closet." He adjusted his grip on her so he could open the door and she gasped in surprise. The walls were a pale grayish blue, her bed placed in the middle of the room, looking toward the door. Her dresser lined the right-side wall. On either side of her bed were built-in shelves, the ones closest to the bed had built-in chargers, both the normal three-prong wall outlets and USB outlets. There were also small lamps on either side. Some of her book collection and collectible trinkets were placed on the shelves. Although she would probably move a few things around, it was nice to have them already unpacked. Her nightstand was set up just the way she liked it. The room was bigger than her apartment room and there was an oversized chair in the corner, perfect for curling up and reading.

"How did you get this done so fast?" she asked. She hadn't taken that long of a nap, maybe an hour or two.

"D and his parents worked on the bedrooms. Thomas sat with us at the apartment. My uncle sent someone to ward the property and he sent over the living room furniture. We'll have to set up the kitchen later and bring all of that over, but it's good enough for today. I figured we'd get a grocery order for delivery and order in some dinner. Whatever sounds good to you."

"Thanks," Viv replied.

"There's one more room to see," Mac said. He thought she would like this one the best. "This is your closet," he said pointing to the door next to the dresser. "This is the bathroom," he said, crossing the room. He shifted her in his arms so he could open the door. The bathroom had a shower, a toilet, double sinks. It was a decent size, but not too large. The shower could fit two people though. D's mom had moved over her toiletries.

"This is the living space for this wing," he said, opening the last door. It wasn't a big space, but it had built-in bookshelves, a TV, a small desk for working and her laptop, a loveseat and two chairs.

"Oh, this is perfect!" she said. It really was. It would be nice to have her own space to read or watch her shows. Thomas and D were just down the hallway and they could still get together in the common space, but when they were busy or she needed alone time, she now had someplace that wasn't her bedroom to hang out in.

"D's mom helped decorate and hang your stuff, but she didn't know what to do in this room, so she left it pretty plain, just a couple of blankets and pillows."

"Where did the furniture come from? I didn't have anything like this."

Mac cleared his throat and she watched as he turned red. "I, uh. I picked it out. I wanted you to have someplace to relax when you moved in. If you don't like it, I can have something else delivered." He had ordered it from a Netherworld shop so D could port it into the house for him.

"I do like it, thank you," she said softly. She wasn't sure how to feel about him buying her furniture. She loved the room, but he wasn't her boyfriend, just a potential mate.

"I'm going to let you get used to your room, without me hovering. Where would you like to be set up? There are phone chargers in both rooms. Oh! D had emergency alerts installed in each room. In your bedroom, it's the button on the wall by your pillow. In here, it's on the underside of this side table."

"I think I'd like to sit in here, please," Viv replied.

Mac set her gently on the loveseat, helping her get comfortable. He laid a blanket over her, handing her the phone cord. "I'll leave the doors open so you can call out and reach any of us," he said, giving her one last look before walking out.

17

Viv sat in her new sitting room, in their new house, taking in everything around her. She still felt a little disassociated with her body, like her mind wasn't fully there or it was floating. It had been that way since she had woken up in the hospital. She really wanted to talk to someone, but there was no way she could open up to Mac and she didn't want to disturb Thomas.

As if he sensed her thinking about him, her phone dinged with a message.

The guys are putting in a grocery order. And a dinner delivery. Does Chinese sound good to you? Or burgers? Thomas asked. She was glad he hadn't asked about pizza.

Either is good. General Tsao or a milkshake and fries. Both sound good. They actually did sound good. She hadn't had much of an appetite since she had woken up in the hospital but being here made her feel hungry again.

Awesome. I'll let him know. Can I come see your room? Thomas asked.

Of course! She typed back. *I'm in the sitting room.*

"Hey lady. How do you like your rooms? D did good,

didn't he? I don't know what I expected when he said he bought a house, but it wasn't this." Thomas slowly hobbled his way in a couple of minutes later.

Viv stared at her best friend. She was glad he was alive. He was looking better; he still had bruises, but they were quite faded. His eye had been okay once they used the healing potion on it. As a precaution, he had needed to wear a patch for a couple of days, but it was now off. His leg had been set, along with his fingers. He had told her that they had an amazing burn cream at the hospital, and he wouldn't have many scars. They had used both healing potions and cream on him, so his whip marks and burns were taken care of, along with some of the deeper cuts. His leg and fingers had had their healing sped up, but he still had time to spend in the casts. His body had taken to the healing potions better than hers had.

Thomas sat in one of the chairs, his casted leg stretched out on the ottoman. She was terrified of what to say to him. It was her fault that the woman had found out Thomas was D's mate. Viv hadn't been thinking when she ripped the other sleeve off her shirt to brace his broken fingers. With both of her arms exposed, it had been clear that she didn't have any mate bonds. Thomas had been whipped after that and she knew some of them had cut deep enough to scar.

"I didn't mean to let her know you were D's mate," she said softly, willing her tears not to fall. This wasn't about her. She wanted to apologize to her friend for allowing him to get hurt.

"Honey. Is that what you've been upset about?" Thomas cried, grabbing her hand. "No. No, no, no. This wasn't your fault at all. She was playing with us. She got a phone call the first day she had us. She was in the room with me and I overheard; they were telling her that D was gay. She knew from the first day that I was his mate, she just wanted to play games. Why do you think she focused more on me until D got me out?"

"Really? Don't lie to me on this, Thomas. I'll know. I can't handle it if you lie to save my feelings," Viv said sternly.

"Honest, Viv. She was just a crazy bitch who liked to cause pain. There was nothing you could have done differently. You gave up the one bed to keep me off the ground, you helped treat my injuries. You did everything you could. I owe you because you told D to get me out first, leaving you there with her."

"You were hurt and needed to get to the hospital," she stated. There had been no other choice in her mind.

"Except then you were hurt too," Thomas pointed out.

"I..." Viv didn't know what to say. She didn't really want to talk about it, and she definitely didn't want to make her friend feel bad about what happened to her.

"Can you tell me, please? I think it would make you feel better. You know pretty much everything she did to me, and I want to be able to help you too."

Viv took a minute, wrapping herself up in a blanket that faintly smelled like Mac. "She came back after D left and was angry you were gone. I tried to fight her, but she hit me in the head and knocked me out. I woke up in an empty warehouse or something. It was a big room, windows, a door that I could see, brick. But clearly old and abandoned. There wasn't a roof. I was chained up, my arms to the old ceiling beams, my feet to the floor, in an X shape. It was cold and I only had my underwear on. I was soaking wet too since she threw a bucket of water on me to wake me up.

"The first two days, it was just her. The third day was when Mac and his team found me. That day, she had brought five guys with her. One left almost right away when she wouldn't let him penetrate me. She said they could all have a turn when she was done, but they could do whatever else they wanted until then. The vampire drank. A lot. I started to feel lightheaded, but he didn't stop. They all took turns hitting or punching me. The one was a scorpion shifter and he let his tail out and kept stinging me, all over. Nipples, breasts, neck, I think he even got near my clit. It burned so bad. There was one guy who didn't touch much, but he had some kind of mental power. I could hear him in my head, filling it with all kinds of images of them raping me, cutting my—cutting pieces of me off. I could feel the pain too, it wasn't just in my head. He kept telling me how I was just a human, how no one would want me, how when they were done with me that no one would ever want me again. I asked at the hospital to make sure, but they didn't rape me. She tried, but it seems like Mac got there before she could penetrate all the way." Viv pulled her legs up, her sore ribs protesting, but she laid her head on her knees, not wanting to look at Thomas.

"How did she..."

"Tail," Viv answered.

"Oh, honey. I'm coming over to give you a hug, scoot over," Thomas said. "Now listen to me. Even if you weren't raped, it was close and you have the mental stuff to deal with from that. I am here whenever you need to talk, or we can find you someone to talk to as well. When you decide to get physical again, I want you to remember that you are loved. You are sexy. You are an amazing person. And tails are fun when used the right way," he added.

Viv's head came up. Thomas' cheeks were red, but he nodded when she looked at him. "D has used his before and it's...um...it's a lot of fun. Big fun. Orgasmic fun. I'm not saying you should be jumping into bed with anyone, I just don't want you to think tails are bad either. Especially if Mac—"

"Nope. Not going there. He rejected me, remember? I don't care if he was stalking me and keeping me safe in the shadows. He still said he didn't want me as a mate."

"Wait. What?" Thomas looked confused.

"Oh. Right. So. Um. I had a feeling the shadows were watching me. For a while, a little after we saw Mac the first time at the apartment. But they seemed like nice shadows? I felt safe when they were there. Apparently, it was Mac. Watching me at work and on dates."

"Like a creeper," Thomas responded. "And you never told us?"

Viv shook her head.

"We'll talk about that later. But I do want to say something about Mac. He's a douchebag. I'm not saying he's not. He acted like an ass. I get he was hurt in the past, but if he got to know you at all, he would have seen how amazing you are. I am not saying you have to give him another chance. I will keep my 'No Mac Allowed' rule if you say the word. We can kick him out of the house for good and if you need to, you can stay in the extra bedroom on our side of the house.

"Now. I will say he was gutted when he realized you were missing. I heard stories from D. I also saw him in my hospital room when he realized you had been taken to another location. He was terrified. After you were brought in and were stabilized, he stopped by to give an update in person. He clearly hadn't been sleeping. When D brought up the house, he jumped at it and asked his uncle for help. He likes to be self-reliant and not ask for help from anyone, from what I understand. But he asked this time. As much as

I don't want to like him because of how he treated you, I do think he finally got his head out of his ass and realized what a great gift he had been given. If you decided to give him a chance and he treats you like you deserve, I'm all for it. If you decide no or he's a jerk, I'll block him from this house. I already had this talk with D. He can hang out at either of their houses in Netherworld or go to a movie or dinner, or whatever to see him, but not here."

"I don't know what to do," she admitted. "I'm attracted to him. His scent calms me. Even after everything, I'm still drawn to him. But he hurt me; he was mean and pushed me away with his words and actions."

Thomas held her for a minute, thinking. "Do you want my opinion?" he asked.

Viv nodded.

"You're mine, my best friend, my family. I will support whatever you decide. I never thought fate was real, had no idea mates were even a thing outside of those romance novels we read. I will say I have never been happier. He completes me, as corny as that is. He bolsters what was there, encourages me, loves me for me. Even if I have a few extra scars now. Even if I always have a limp, which they don't think will happen, but if it did, I have no doubt he would still want me. There may have been times where mates didn't work out, but I think ninety-plus percent of them do. All that to say that it might be worth giving him a cautious second chance. Take it slow. Make him work for it. Make him grovel. But maybe see if you can grab hold of some happiness. See if you can come together and be a couple," Thomas said. "Only if you want to."

"Thomas, he didn't want me when I was perfect before. Well, not perfect, but not all marked up and almost gang-banged. Why would he want me now?"

18

Mac made himself leave Viv's room, giving her time to herself to adjust. He really wished he could have called it their room, but he knew he had to give her time. He walked back to the common area, already filling out a grocery delivery order.

"What do you want for dinner?" D asked as Mac came into the room.

"I'm good with whatever. I want Thomas and Viv to pick, if it's something that sounds good to them, then they'll probably eat it."

"I'm getting better," Thomas said, hobbling back into the room. "The heavy-duty pain meds made me sleepy and I think I just didn't feel hungry anymore. I bet Viv's the same way, but she's lost weight."

They both had, Mac thought but kept it to himself. "I've got a grocery delivery order started, so let me know if there's anything you want. I have just the basics right now."

Thomas nodded. "Can I send you a list? I know what Viv usually gets. I'll see what she wants for dinner." He set his phone on the counter, typing a message with his good hand.

"That would be great. Do you guys mind if I sit out here? I wanted to give her some space," Mac said.

"I'll go sit with her, have some bestie time," Thomas said, giving D a kiss on the cheek.

D watched his mate walked down the hallway.

"How's it going with Viv?" he asked quietly.

Mac shrugged. "She seemed okay with me staying in the guest room on her side and she really liked her living space. I don't know what to do to show her I need her, that I was stupid at pushing her away."

"Ma probably has some good wooing ideas," D suggested.

They placed the grocery and dinner orders and sat in the living room brainstorming until there was a knock on the door. D checked the camera. "It's dinner."

Mac waited until D shut the door to go tell Viv and Thomas that dinner was ready. As he entered the room, he heard her confess that she didn't think he would want her anymore and it hurt his heart.

"Because you are beautiful and strong. You survived and you fought for your friend. You are loyal and loving and see the best in people. You want to help others and share your love of books and learning and reading with everyone. Because you were willing to move out of the apartment that had been your home to give your friend and his partner their own space. Because even on your bad days, you don't take that out on anyone else. You're smart. Those are just a few of the reasons I want you. It doesn't matter if you feel sad, or feel broken, or angry. It doesn't matter if you want to take it slow or tell me I'm just a friend. It doesn't matter if the marks some assholes put on you leave scars. You're still all the things I just said."

Mac moved to crouch in front of her, making sure she could see his face and hopefully see that he meant what he said.

"I let my past haunt me and blind me to the gift I was given. My first mate tried to kill me, saying I was an abomination, evil, filth. You have never made another person or being feel that way in your life. It's not in you to treat anyone like that. Believe me when I say my rejecting you had everything to do with me, not you. I was stupid. And if you let me, I will treat you like you deserve and show you how much I want you as my mate."

Viv's eyes met his and the disbelief and wariness in there killed him. She hadn't looked at him like that until he so harshly said he wasn't interested. At the time he had told himself that it was better for both of them; for him it removed any hope of her being interested in him and tempting him to give her a chance later, for her it meant forgetting about him and being able to find someone else she could love and settle down with. Mac should have realized even back then he was being stupid. Any free time he had had been spent watching over her. He paid more attention to conversations when her name was mentioned. He had been an idiot and hurt the one person he was supposed to protect above all others. D had tried to tell him, but his muleheadedness meant that it took her getting abducted to break through his walls.

Her eyes searched his for a minute until she looked over at Thomas, who gave her a slight shrug and head tilt in response. He wished he knew what that meant. Thomas would be the one person who might sway her opinion in his favor, but he could understand if he didn't give his approval either.

"I will accept that you're sorry. I will be open to spending more time with you and seeing where it goes. I'm not agreeing to anything beyond friendship right now. You were unnecessarily cruel the last time we spoke and while you may think you feel differently now, you might change your mind again once the shock of the situation wears off," Viv said hesitantly.

Mac nodded, accepting her terms. He knew he wouldn't change his mind, but only his actions and time would prove that to her. "I will agree to those terms. I know the only thing that will prove it will be actions." He stood up, thinking he really needed to talk to D's mom; even though she would probably yell at him, she would have some ideas from a female perspective.

"Dinner arrived. We got Chinese. When the groceries come, we also got the things to make milkshakes or sundaes for dessert."

Mac helped Thomas off the couch; with a broken leg and a broken hand, it was hard for him to push himself out of the couch. He waited until Thomas was stable to help Viv up. She wasn't as wobbly, but her ankle was still weak and in a walking boot. He let them go ahead of him, but stayed close enough to grab them if they lost their balance. Reaching the eat-in kitchen, he pulled out a chair for Viv.

"Thank you," she said.

Mac grabbed her cup, filling it with her favorite coffee and creamer. "What do you like to eat?" he asked. "We got a lot of different things."

"General Tsao and fried rice, if we have it, please."

"We do. Thomas said it was your favorite. I can make you a plate," he offered.

"That would be wonderful, thanks," Viv replied with a small smile. Maybe he could do this, he thought. Little things would show her he cared.

The food was wonderful, and he thought this would be a new favorite restaurant. It wasn't far from the house either, maybe a ten- or fifteen-minute drive. Viv and Thomas both ate an entire plate, which made Mac feel like celebrating. He was happy to see her appetite coming back. He and D had started clearing the table, when the doorbell rang. Viv's whole body tightened, stress pouring from her, her face pale and her eyes darting to the door and back down to her bedroom.

Mac rushed over to her. "It's the groceries. See, D is checking the cameras first." He grabbed her phone and showed her the alert on her phone. "You can check all the cameras too; Thomas helped us put the app on your phone. The wards won't let anyone who means harm in. You're safe."

He stood, standing between the door and the kitchen table as D opened the front door.

"Thanks," he heard D say. Mac walked closer as the person turned around and left. Between the two of them, it didn't take long to put the food away. They created a pile of things that went to the separate bedrooms, like shampoo. Viv started getting color back in her cheeks. He hated that she associated something like the doorbell with the attack; it made sense, but it was something that could happen every day.

"How about milkshakes or sundaes?" he asked. "We have chocolate and vanilla ice cream, chocolate and caramel syrup, cherries, nuts, malt powder."

"Sundae?" D asked Thomas, who nodded.

"Do we have peanut butter? Can I have a peanut butter chocolate milkshake?" she asked.

"Yup. I love peanut butter too. There's this place that makes an amazing peanut butter pie. I'll have to bring some to you soon. It's the best I've ever had."

"That sounds good. Do they use creamy or crunchy peanut butter?" she asked.

"They have both, but I always go for creamy. I'm not much of a crunchy peanut butter fan," he admitted. If she was, he'd just get a slice of each.

"Me neither," she replied.

Mac smiled back before turning to grab the blender. They forgot to bring the one from the apartment, but they just added it to the grocery list. It wasn't as nice as the other one, but it would do for now. Neither he nor D had wanted to leave the house tonight. Washing it out quickly, he added the ingredients for the shake, pouring it into a tall glass, finishing it with whipped cream and a cherry. He added a straw and handed it over. He made himself one as well but added the malt powder. He loved malts. He hummed happily as he took a sip. He set his glass off to the side, filling the blender with water and a squirt of soap, running it to help make cleanup easier.

He sat back down at the table, enjoying the evening. He could have had this the whole time if he hadn't been so stupid and stubborn.

19

Viv sat at her desk in her sitting area. Mac had been following her everywhere in the house. Not like all up in her business, but he didn't leave the house if she was there. He checked in with his work through phone calls and video calls, but he stayed there. She could tell he was trying; he had flowers and chocolates delivered. He even had a book that she had been looking at sent to her. The doorbell continued to freak her out, but she had been talking to an online therapist and she was working through some of it. She had been lucky enough that this one was a nonhuman. Thomas was also going to her.

The nightmares were still a problem. Not every night, but they happened at least several times a week. Mac assured her that the mind bender had been destroyed and so had any trace of his magic, but she could still hear his words. She could only imagine how much worse it would be if his magic was still influencing her. She knew they had double-checked at the hospital as well. This was just her own brain not letting go of the negativity. Her mate had rejected her before this, so her subconscious was thinking that maybe there was something to what the mind bender had said. Her therapist said it was complete bullshit. They were working on it.

Today she had a follow-up appointment with her doctor from the hospital. He wanted to check on her hand. The stabbing from the shoe had been seriously infected by the time they had found her and it had gotten into her bloodstream. They had been able to treat it and stitch her up, but it was time to see if the stitches could be removed and test the range of motion in her hand. They had been worried about nerve damage. She was also due to see her ob/gyn to make sure the damage from the attempted rape had healed correctly. It felt like it had healed, but she also couldn't see it herself with it being at her ass. She wanted to talk to her doctor about any potential problems too. One day she wanted to have kids and she wanted to make sure the poison from the scorpion hadn't caused any long-lasting damage. The hospital staff had thought that it had only prevented her blood from clotting and her body from healing, which was treated by the anti-venom. But she wanted to ask and was grateful that her long-time ob/gyn had turned out to be a nonhuman mate herself. D had asked around for her, trying to find out if it was safe to talk to her about what had really happened, and she had been relieved that she didn't have to hide anything from her or find a new doctor. She was trying to find a way to tell Mac to stay at home for these appointments, at least the ob.

"Are you ready to go to your appointment?" he asked, knocking on her door.

"I am, but for my second appointment, I was thinking I could drive myself," she said.

"Is your ankle up for that?" he asked. He loved being

able to port her around and between her hand which she wasn't supposed to move until today and her ankle, which was still wrapped, he thought driving might be a challenge.

"Oh, I forgot about that. Um. Could you stay outside during the appointment, then?"

"Sure. Anything you need," Mac replied. Thomas had already warned him which doctor the second appointment was at. He could understand why she wouldn't want him there.

"Thanks," she said.

Mac helped her put on her winter coat. It was cold out and while they might miss that with the portal, he knew some medical offices ran cooler. Taking hold of her hand, he opened the portal and stepped through to the doctor's. It helped that it was at the nonhuman hospital and porting was normal. Viv let go of his hand and went to check in at the front desk. He was hoping they had good news for her. She wanted to get back to work, even if he wasn't convinced that she was ready. She wanted the routine and to feel normal again. Which he did understand.

"Vivian?" a voice called out at the other end of the room. Turning, Mac saw a nurse standing there with a clipboard.

"Hi," Viv replied as she walked up to the nurse.

"Let's get your weight and temperature real quick and then we'll get you in a room," the nurse said.

Mac was happy to see she had gained a few pounds back from when she had left the hospital.

"If you'll wait here, the doctor will be right in. If the stitches are removed, they'll also test your grip strength," the nurse added before closing the door after herself.

Mac gently guided Viv to sit in the chair furthest from the door. He wanted to be between her and the entrance.

She still had reactions to doors opening. It was getting better, but she was already on edge with seeing the doctors today. And it made sense; for a week or so, anytime a door opened it would bring pain.

"What if I have lasting damage?" she asked quietly. She was afraid of what that would mean for her job, driving, etcetera. Her therapist said they would tackle that issue if or when it happened and worrying about it now was causing unnecessary stress.

"We deal with it then," Mac said calmly. "You drive mostly right-handed now, you're right-hand dominant, so it shouldn't affect things too much. Cutting things up to eat, maybe, or putting a ponytail in, but there's ways around that too. I think you could still do your job just as well. You may have to henpeck with one hand if it's bad, but you could still do it. I am positive that you can do things you still love if that's the case, but I'm hoping it won't be."

Viv nodded, taking a deep breath. He was right. She could still drive using mostly her right hand, she could push books aside with her left if it was feeling weak and use her right hand to pick up books to reshelve. It would be okay, she told herself. Mac turned toward her, reaching across her lap and held her uninjured hand, his thumb lightly rubbing across her skin. It helped soothe and settle her.

There was a knock on the door with a few seconds of delay before the door opened.

"Good morning. Let's see if we can't get these stitches out," the doctor said cheerfully. He reminded Mac of a smaller Santa Clause. Of course, he was a gnome, so that was probably why. Rounded belly, white hair and beard, jovial. He helped put Viv at ease.

He rolled a small table over before setting out a clean

cover, tools to remove the stiches, a cream, and bandages. "Let's see what we're working with," he said, holding out his hand for Viv's.

She placed her hand in his. The doctor examined it, looking closely at both sides. "I think we can take the stiches out. It looks like that part is healing well. Then we'll see about your range of motion."

Mac laid his hand on her leg, letting her feel he was still there, but not getting in the way of the doctor as he laid Viv's hand on the tray. "You might feel some tugging or small discomfort. If it's too bad, let me know so we can make sure something isn't wrong. The internal stitches are dissolvable, so this will just be the surface ones on either side of your hand," the doctor reminded her.

It took maybe five minutes to remove the stitches, Viv wincing a few times. The doctor wiped off the small drops of blood from the stitches and placed a bandage over the areas. "Okay. Your hand is going to be stiff, but I'm going to have you try to make a fist. Stretching and mild pain is okay. If it's sharp, tearing, or very painful, stop and we'll see what's going on."

Viv nodded, slowly making a fist. Mac could tell when it started getting painful, about halfway closed. The doctor spoke up before he could. "Stop there. Try to close each finger one at a time." He gently grasped her hand between his fingers, allowing him to feel the muscles and tendons move.

Her thumb, pinky, and pointer fingers seemed to do fine. It was the middle and ring fingers causing problems, which made sense since that was where the damage had been done. The doctor had her try a few more movements as he gently poked and prodded.

"There may be some lasting damage, or it may still be

healing. Your body has gone through a lot, and it may just take time. You have enough range to be able to do most things, especially with your pointer finger and thumb having full range of motion. I'm going to send you some exercises to do to try to help loosen any tightness. Do not push yourself. Follow the directions and if it aches, that's okay. If it hurts, stop. If it gets worse, call the office and come in. The exercises should help, so make sure to do them each day. Ice afterward."

Viv nodded, taking the handouts he handed her. He gave her what looked like a stress ball and small metal balls to work on her grip and motion, as well as a brace to wear on days it bothered her.

"Call if you need anything," he said as he stood up.

Mac took hold of her newly stitch-free hand. He gently pressed a kiss to the bandage, trying to let her know that none of that mattered to him. "It sounds pretty good," he said, keeping his voice light.

"I guess. I was hoping it would be completely healed, at least back to normal motion," Viv admitted, her voice a little more downcast than before.

"It will get there. And if it doesn't, we can work around it, remember? It's not enough to affect your daily life and work. If it aches, we'll find ways to help ease it. Maybe massage. Maybe something else. We'll find ways to make it feel better," Mac promised.

"Okay," Viv said, giving him a small smile.

"Do you want to grab a coffee before your next appointment? Do we have time?" Mac asked.

Viv looked down at her watch. "I think so. There's a coffee shop across the street from the building, if you want to go there."

"Are they nonhuman friendly?" Mac asked. He had

driven by last night to make sure he knew where to port to, but hadn't noticed the coffee shop.

"I'm not sure," she admitted. "I still can't tell nonhumans apart when they're in human form, and it's been a while since I've been there."

"I'll port behind the medical office then and we can walk across. I'll be able to tell when we get there. I just don't want to port if it's humans and scare someone," Mac said.

"I didn't think of that," she replied. "Can you get there, or do we need to get my car?"

"I drove by yesterday so I could get us there," Mac said.

Viv nodded, touched that he took the time to make today easier on her. She led the way to the check-out desk to pay her co-pay. She hated to see what her bills would end up being as she hadn't even checked to see if this hospital was in-network or not. She was a little surprised when the receptionist said they would bill her later, after they billed insurance. She was used to having to pay a co-pay or a deposit of some sort. Maybe it was a nonhuman thing?

Mac held out his hand, opening a portal. Viv took his hand, feeling more comfortable doing so. They stepped through, landing in a...shed?

"This was added by a nonhuman doctor who works here for those of us who teleport," Mac said. "Let's get your coffee so you have time to drink it. I'd like to walk you to the office and make sure you get there safely, if that's okay? I'll stay out in the waiting room or hallway, whichever makes you feel better," he assured her.

Viv took a minute to think it over as they crossed the street. "Waiting room is fine," she said. She felt safer the closer he was. Maybe her subconscious knew he wouldn't let anything happen to her.

Mac took her hand as they crossed the street, holding the door open for her at the coffee shop. There were some medical personnel from the nearby offices, a few moms, and business professionals, but there were still plenty of open seats.

"Hi," she said, as she walked up to the cashier. "Could I get a small mocha, please?"

"I'll have a medium black coffee, and could we get two of the sugar cookies as well?" Mac ordered.

Mac pulled out his wallet to pay before Viv got hers out of her purse. "I asked you to coffee," he said.

"Thank you," Viv replied, her heart jumping a bit. Stupid girl hormones, she chided herself. The point of this was to start slow and get to know him, see if she even wanted to give him another romantic chance.

"Have a seat and we'll bring it out when it's ready," the cashier said.

Mac led them over to a corner booth, letting her slide in first before taking his seat. "I thought I'd make dinner tonight. Does spaghetti and meatballs sound good? Garlic bread too? With or without cheese, your choice."

"I'd like that, it sounds good. I like garlic bread either way, so whatever way you like it sounds great."

"I'll make it half and half then. D likes his plain and I'm not sure what Thomas likes."

"He eats it any way too. He's a bit of a bread whore," Viv confided. Not that she was much better. She loved anything bread.

Their coffees came and she looked at the leaf design they had created on top. "I love it when they make designs in the coffee," she said.

"I've never really gotten one, I drink plain old boring black coffee," Mac said. "It is pretty fun." He wondered if he could figure out how to make them at home. It couldn't be that hard, could it? He would watch some YouTube videos and practice when she was asleep or at work. It would be fun to surprise her.

Viv ate her entire cookie and her coffee. He wondered when he would stop cataloguing what she ate, maybe when she was back to her normal weight. He took the cups and plate back to the counter. He held her coat out for her to put on, glad he had grabbed it before they left. Even the short distance they had to cross over to the office building was a cold walk.

Mac sat in the waiting room while she checked in. He noticed she was favoring her ankle and he hoped she would be willing to go home afterward to rest it.

"I'll be back soon," she said when they called her name.

Mac nodded, pulling out his phone to check his email and text with D's mom to get a few more wooing ideas. He had a book and games on his phone if it went long.

Viv followed the nurse back, changing into the dreaded paper gowns. She hated these things. She always felt like she was going to moon someone in the hallway when the door opened. She sat sideways on the table, not wanting to put her back to the door.

"Hey, Viv," her doctor said as she knocked and entered. "I see you've been through a bit of an ordeal. The hospital sent over your records," she added, holding her file.

"Yeah. I. Is everything in there?" Viv asked. She really hoped so. If she didn't have to tell the story again, she would be happy. Her therapist kept telling her that talking about it would help her heal, but talking to someone outside of Thomas, her therapist, or maybe Mac seemed like a lot to her right now.

"Yes, they sent the reports with your statement and someone named Mac's statement as well. What brought you in today?"

"I wanted to make sure everything was healing. I don't feel any pain there anymore, but I also can't see it. And I wanted to make sure the poison wouldn't affect anything when I wanted to have kids or the babies themselves."

"Scoot on down and put your feet in the stirrups and I'll take a look," her doctor instructed. She kept her gaze lowered as she asked the next question, as if knowing it would make it easier for Viv to answer. "The report says they didn't penetrate, is that correct?"

Viv nodded, then realized she would need to use her words. "As far as I know. They held me open and she tried to, but I got loose, I think. I passed out before she tried again, but Mac says he stopped her and they did an exam at the hospital when I was unconscious. It doesn't feel like it was an internal pain," Viv said.

Her doctor nodded, leaning down to look. "I'm going to do my own exam, just to make sure, if that's alright?"

"Okay." Viv tried to relax and not tense up, breathing deep. She normally didn't have both entrances examined at the gynecologist, so it was a weird experience.

"Easy, almost done," her doctor said, her voice soothing.

It took a minute but she sat back up. "I didn't find any internal tears or scarring, so I believe the hospital report is correct. Everything looks like it healed nicely. There are a couple of scars where they must have pierced the skin while holding you. Next part is completely up to you. I can do a vaginal exam, even use a small scope to try to see if there is any scarring or damage from the poison. It sounds like he used his to affect your healing and blood clotting, so I don't believe it was directed to your organs, but I can check if it would make you feel better."

"Yes, please. I think it would make me feel better to know for sure," Viv replied.

"Okay." Her doctor leaned back down, pulling out a speculum. "Little bit of cold and pressure," she said.

Viv concentrated on breathing deeply, staring at the ceiling. She had never been more grateful that her doctor put funny comics and memes on the ceiling tiles.

"Everything looks good so far. I'm going to use the scope to get a closer look, but you shouldn't feel anything," her doctor said.

It took another couple of minutes before she sat up. "Everything looks healthy. I can't see into the ovaries from here to examine the eggs, but I don't see scarring or unhealthy tissue. We'll keep a close eye on you if you decide to become pregnant, just to be on the safe side, but I don't think you'll have any issues. Give me a call when you decide to try to become pregnant and I'll call in a prenatal vitamin to take. Once you have a positive test, give us a call back and we'll set up a plan. Any questions?"

Viv shook her head, sitting up.

"I'm glad you're healing and you're alright, Viv." Her doctor squeezed her shoulder on the way out the door.

She got dressed and checked out at the counter. She could see Mac from here, he was sitting in a chair, looking at his phone. As if he could sense her, his head popped up and he smiled at her.

"Already to go?" he asked when she walked into the waiting room.

"I am. Do you mind if we go home? My ankle is getting sore. I haven't been on it this much at the house."

"Nope, I think it's a great idea to give it a rest." Mac found an empty corner in the hallway and opened a portal to the house. It would mean less walking for her this way.

20

Viv was going back to work. She needed to feel normal again, do normal things, have a routine. Her boss had been very sympathetic and understanding when it came to the whole situation. She hated lying to him, but she couldn't say a demoness attacked them. They had modified the story, saying the apartment had been broken into and they had kidnapped them to try to get more money through ransom as there wasn't much in the apartment. Viv thought it was a sketchy explanation, but Liam had talked to both their employers in his police uniform and people were more likely to believe someone in uniform.

Thomas wasn't going back for another week, waiting until all his bruises and cuts were fully healed. He didn't want to scare the kids and a walking cast was a familiar enough sight that they wouldn't question it too much. He was hoping that his fingers would be healed enough that he could get that cast off before he went back.

Mac was driving in with her. He wanted to teleport, but decided on driving in case he got a work call and had to leave. He had put some wards around the library yesterday to help keep her safe. D had done the same thing at Thomas' school. He didn't think anyone else would be coming after them, but they did work in punishments so there was a rare possibility it could happen again. Mac was bringing his laptop so he could finish writing some reports and get some research done on a few open cases.

Viv had her brace in case her hand acted up, but she was going to try to use her right hand for the majority of typing. It might be a little slower, but she had already talked to her boss about her new limitations. He had been very under-standing. Luckily, it wasn't her dominant hand, and her job didn't require paragraphs of typing so she didn't think it would make a huge difference. If she was still in the running to take over the library when her boss retired, she could always invest in a voice-to-text software if needed. Mac had pointed out all her options last night when she was stressing out about not being able to do her job anymore. Her hand had gone numb, and it had taken a while for feeling to come back to the middle and ring fingers. She had been in tears thinking she wouldn't be able to do the job she loved. He had patiently held her hand, massaging it, and then laid out all her options. He was right, there were ways she could make it work.

Viv walked into the kitchen, Mac at the stove, Thomas sitting at the table.

"Morning! Are you sure you're ready to go back?" Thomas asked, concerned.

"I need to. I need to feel normal again, get back into my routine," Viv said.

"Alright. I packed you a lunch. And some pain meds in case you need them," Thomas said, giving her a hug.

"Thank you for the lunch." She grinned.

"Anytime."

Mac handed her a plate with eggs and buttered toast. "I'll get your coffee as soon as it's done brewing. Eat, please."

Viv sat, looking at her scrambled eggs. She was surprised that he had made her breakfast.

"Thomas, here's a plate for you too," Mac said, bringing another one over.

Thomas looked at her, waggling his eyebrows. She stuck her tongue out at him. Yes, a man who could cook was sexy. He gave a tiny nod in Mac's direction, quirking an eyebrow. She shook her head. No, she was not ready to give him a romantic chance just yet. She was taking this time to get to know him and to make sure he wouldn't run scared again.

Although cooking for her and her bestie definitely got him bonus points.

Viv let Mac drive, worried her hand would flare up again, even though she usually used her right hand the most. It could have been so much worse; she was just grateful that she had grabbed her phone that night with her left hand. She was extremely right-hand dominate and it would have been horrible to lose mobility in it. At least this way she could compensate a lot easier. Mac parked in the front, turning to her as soon as the car stopped.

"I know employee parking is in the back, but there's better lights and public visibility out here and if we can get you to a closer spot, then it's less of a walk for you."

Viv nodded. It made sense. The employee lot required them to walk to a side entrance or the front entrance, there wasn't a separate door that led to the back lot. There were lights, but not quite as many as the front, and the front entrance faced the main streets.

Mac smiled. "Thank you. I'll be working on my computer, but if something comes up and I have to go, I'll let you know before I leave," he promised, handing her the car keys.

He followed her in, already blending into the background. Her boss was waiting for her at the desk.

"Viv! I'm so glad you're okay. Now, if I know you, you don't want to talk about it and want to get back to your routine, but if you want to talk, I'm here. Okay?" he said, giving her a hug.

Viv smiled, hugging him back. He knew her well. Of course, she had been working here since college and they had had many conversations over the years.

"I added a stool so you can sit but still reach the computer easily," he said, pointing out the barstool. "I'm only here for opening but call my cell phone if you need anything. And welcome back," he said handing her a small bag.

"Thank you, Ted," she said, opening it to find a cannoli from the bakery down the street and a new coffee tumbler that had an image of three towering and leaning stacks of books with the words 'I like big stacks, I cannot lie.' "I love it, thank you," she said, smiling at her boss.

"I just made a new pot of coffee, if you want to get some before you start and eat the cannoli."

"I will, thanks."

Viv led Mac to a table where he could see her at the main desk and the employee door leading to the break room and the stacks. "I'm going to wash this and get a cup. Did you want some coffee? We have extra cups," she offered.

"I'm good for now, thank you though," Mac replied.

Viv washed her new mug, filling it with coffee and her

favorite creamer. She had brought a new bottle from home, thinking the other one had probably gone bad by now. She stuck her lunch in the fridge and grabbed a bottle of water for Mac. She sat next to him at the table, handing him the water. She took a bite of the cannoli, giving a tiny moan of happiness. These were so good and she hadn't had one in a long time. Mac looked at her out of the corner of his eye.

"You want a bite?" she offered. She could share.

Mac leaned over, opening his mouth. Viv fed him the cannoli, watching as his lips closed around it. He took a small bite, licking his lips when he was done.

"That's delicious," he said.

"It's my favorite bakery," she replied. "Which is bad since they're down the street. It's too tempting to stop in at lunch every day." She finished the last few bites, wiping her face and her hands before grabbing her coffee cup. "I better get to work," she said.

Mac nodded, watching her go. Viv headed to the desk, letting her boss clock out and leave for the day. She let the sounds and rhythm of the library flow around her, soothing her. She honestly loved her job, and it was one of her happy places. Not that they didn't get the occasional jerk, but in general people at the library were pleasant. She loved being surrounded by books. A couple hours into her shift, she was grateful her boss had put a stool there. She rested her butt on it, keeping her left foot on the ground, but allowing her right foot to hang and get the pressure off. It looked like he had also upgraded the mouse to a weird vertical-looking one that was supposed to be more ergonomic. She didn't have issues with her right hand, but if she was going to be using it more often, it made sense to try to lessen the strain, she supposed. She really did have the best boss.

Her first day back was going better than she even

expected. She had a few regulars come in saying they missed seeing her and they hoped she was feeling better. Her boss had told everyone she had been in an accident and had been hurt. It was nice not to have intrusive questions about being abducted.

By the time her scheduled lunch break arrived and the assistant came over to relieve her, Viv was ready to sit down and take a break. Her foot was aching even with the chair and her fingers had tingled as she tried to grab a piece of paper on the other side of the desk.

"I'm going on my break," she said quietly to Mac. She didn't want him to look up and not see her.

"Thanks for letting me know." He smiled at her. He really was handsome when he smiled.

Viv made it to the break room, fixing herself another coffee and grabbing a water. As she opened her lunch, a plethora of food stared back at her. There was a small note on top, reading *'Ask your mate to lunch. ;) Love ya. Thomas.'* Viv shook her head but smiled at the nod of approval from Thomas. Mac must be winning him over for him to pack him a lunch and encourage her to take a step forward. She closed her lunch up, keeping it cold, and walked out to the main area. Mac was seated at a table near the employee only door. He must have moved to be closer.

Viv cleared her throat. "Would you like to come back and eat lunch with me? Thomas packed a lot of food," she said.

"I'd love to," Mac said, shutting his computer and standing up.

Mac sat in the library watching his mate work. She really shone at her job; you could tell she loved it. He stuck to the shadows or worked on any paper or computer work he had. He was actually surprised that she had let him come with her for so long. He had been coming in with her every day this week. He thought that maybe she looked forward to the car ride conversations too, or maybe she simply felt safer when he was there. His phone chimed, using the tone he had assigned for work. He sighed, pulling it out of his pocket.

Sorry to interrupt, but I need you for an assignment. I don't think it will take long, maybe a day or so. If you're worried, add a ward to cover the parking lot and her car so she'll be safe when you're not there. I hate to give this one to you, but it falls under your specialty. "Dammit," Mac muttered. It was bound to happen sooner or later, but he was hoping for later. He pulled up the app for his job, logging on to see what the new assignment was. There was an angel going rogue, trying to set up their own religion. He had gotten quite the cult following already and there were signs it was going to take a deadly turn as he was now asking his followers for proof of their devotion.

Mac packed up, heading over to the help desk. "Viv, I have to go. Work just called me in. I'll be gone a few days at most, I hope. I'll let you know if it's going to be longer. If something seems weird, you call D. I'll try to answer too, but if I'm in the middle of an arrest or a chase, I may not be able to. I'm going to ward the parking lots and your car before I leave. I don't know why I didn't think about it sooner, but my boss mentioned it. You'll be safe."

"Be careful," she said, grabbing his hand and giving it a squeeze.

"I will. You too. Make sure you take your Tylenol and ice if you need it."

Viv nodded. She decided to risk it and leaned over the desk to press a quick kiss to his cheek. "Text me and let me know you're safe?" she asked.

Mac nodded. His phone dinged again and he gave her a wave as he walked out the door.

21

It had been a week since Mac left. The case was taking more time than anticipated. He was trying to get to the angel, but he had surrounded himself with humans. That wasn't the problem. The problem was that he apparently had multiple locations and kept porting to different ones. Mac was also left trying to disarm the multitude of booby traps that the guy had set at all his camps. He had installed bombs or kill-switches of some kind that were able to be remotely activated. Mac was trying to be as covert as possible to avoid triggering anything, but it was taking a lot of time.

Both God and Lucifer were pushing for a quick close, which he would love to provide so he could go home and get back to wooing his mate. He had had phone service most of the places he was at, so they were texting and calling each other at night. At least they were getting to know each other even though he was gone. He had learned Viv's favorite color was blue, she preferred dark chocolate, and loved watching meteor showers and eclipses. He only discovered that last one because when he had called, she had been sitting in the backyard waiting for a meteor shower. It didn't matter that it was freezing out, she was bundled in blankets on the outdoor couch, waiting for the show to start. She had switched to video call and shown him the sky. It had been nice sharing it with her. He wondered if she would be willing to visit the Netherworld with him if they mated. They had some pretty spectacular eclipses with their two suns. One glowed red, one blue. Their moon was a deep green color. He had no idea why they were such odd colors, but it certainly made it pretty.

Tonight, he was meeting up with another Enforcer, an angel by the name of Bert. He had worked with him before and was hoping the guy would have some insights into their perp.

"Hey, Mac," a deep voice said behind him. Turning, he saw Bert. Bert wouldn't fit anyone's stereotypical image of an angel. Short, shaved head, goatee, tattoos, worn jeans with holes in the knees, black biker boots, black t-shirt showing off his abs and biceps, carrying a leather jacket. All that was missing was his motorcycle, but Mac assumed he had just ported in.

"Hey, Bert," he responded. "Anything new on your end?"

He shook his head. "I've cleared two other locations, but he keeps jumping. Between the two of us, we should have come across him by now. I don't know if he's getting tipped off or if he's just that lucky."

"I wish people would stop listening to him. He's gaining followers every day and they don't even realize that he's using them for his own goal, whatever that is. For gods' sake, he has self-destruct mechanisms at every location I've been to."

"Same here. The bastard's always been charismatic. We

grew up together and even went to training together for a short period. We weren't friends, just grew up in the same area and went to the same schools. He was always looking to be the center of attention and he loved shortcuts of any kind. He never made it past the first year of Enforcer training. He tried shortcuts there too and almost got his team killed. I don't know how he managed to stay off the radar for this long. You would think someone would have picked up on his behavior before it reached this level."

"You think he has help?" Mac asked.

"It's the only explanation I can think of. I've been letting Base know which direction I'm heading just in case there's problems. If there's a leak, it would explain why he's already gone. What I haven't figured out yet is why he has all these booby traps but hasn't set them off yet."

Mac hummed, letting Bert know he heard him but was thinking. "Killing an Enforcer would bring a lot more heat on him, for sure. Instead of one or two of us, he'd have everyone gunning for him. That could be a reason. Or worst-case scenario, he could be planning on detonating them all at once. I don't know what he would gain out of that. Unless it's as clichéd as he had them all put him in their wills and he's going to collect the money when he kills them."

"That wouldn't surprise me actually. It's a type of shortcut to get rich fast. We live a long time and human money is needed if we're going to live for any amount of time on Earth and not Netherworld or Arlysium. If he can get the attention he wants here, then he's going to need to find a way to sustain himself while he's here. Although he could also be mooching off his followers for things. But he's getting these properties somehow and it's not triggering anything in our system. I don't know if he's using an alias or if his followers are giving him the properties. I'm thinking there is someone covering for him somewhere in our system. There are too many things that should have thrown a red flag before now."

"Got anyone in mind?" Mac asked.

"He's got a couple of friends and family that work for Arlysium. Want to help tackle breaking into their computers? If we can figure out which one is tipping him off, we can take them in for questioning and hopefully get an idea of where this guy's going to be next. I want to get him before he causes any destruction," Bert replied.

"Are we hitting their work computers or their home computers?" Mac asked.

"Let's start at the office. It would make sense if they tried it there, they would have more access to the database. For the level most of them are at, their at-home access would be limited."

"Makes sense. You lead, I'll follow," Mac replied. He figured Bert already knew which offices and desks to hit.

Before he ported out, he sent a text to Viv.

Off to follow some leads with Bert. I'll try to call tonight if it's not too late, Mac typed out.

He got a reply almost immediately. *Who's Bert?*

Another Enforcer. He's on the Arlysium side.

There's an angel named Bert?! Viv replied. *Be safe, please.*

I will. Have a great night. You should be getting something delivered tonight, he sent with a smiley face emoji. He had arranged a delivery from her favorite bakery to drop off some cannoli for dessert. He hated being away from her this long, especially since she seemed to be opening up to him more. Of course, maybe that was because it was over the phone and that made it easier. Whatever the reason, he was just grateful that she was giving him another chance.

He had hopes that it would lead to a second chance to be her mate, but he'd take it one day at a time and be grateful she was even talking to him after how he acted.

Mac put his phone away, opening a portal to Arlysium's base office. Stepping through, he saw a cubicle-filled space. It didn't look much different than any other office setting, including the Netherworld's home office. He didn't do well in cubicle land. When they were in Enforcer training, they had been stuck in the office to learn the other side of the process; how reports came in, how to file their reports, all that good stuff. Back then it was all handwritten, computers and even typewriters hadn't been invented yet. But the general layout of desks after desks, no wall between him and noisy chewer Jimmy, drove him insane. He did much better out in the field. He technically had a desk at the Netherworld office, but he was rarely there. He checked in maybe once a week but didn't stay long.

Bert was already at a computer, logging in and running a scanning program that all the Enforcers had. It picked up a lot of things, but they would probably need to do a deep search themselves as well.

"Hey. I've got four computers to look at in this office. Can you get started on one? I put a pink sticky note on top of the cubicle wall to show which ones we need to inspect."

Mac nodded and walked down the rows looking for pink. Finding one, he sat at the desk, pulling out his USB drive with the scanning software on it. As it opened, it overrode the login screen, letting him type in his own password to gain access. Hitting the run command, he took a look around the desk. There were family pictures, one of them including the angel they were looking for. He looked so normal. There was a pad of paper, the top sheet had been messily torn off. Mac borrowed a pencil and lightly rubbed it over the paper, trying to find what the last thing that had been written was. It looked like a grocery list. Boring.

The program beeped as it finished. Mac typed in the angel's name, Angel's Love Church, the last known locations, and a few other keywords. He dug around in the desk drawers, looking for any other clues or indications that they had been in contact with the guy. There were pieces of scrap paper with all kinds of notes, nothing that made much sense, but if it was an address or phone number, he took note. He'd cross-reference them later.

Bert had moved on to his second desk, a scowl on his face. Mac would bet that the first scan hadn't turned anything up. He looked at the screen as it beeped again. Nothing suspicious. He took over and did a manual search, but it also was a dud. Disconnecting the flash drive, he made sure to close the computer and leave everything as he had found it. He moved to the last desk, starting the whole process over. This person was a little more organized, but there weren't a lot of personal items around.

"You get anything?" Bert asked, disgruntled.

Mac shook his head. "I have a few random phone numbers and addresses that were on scrap paper thrown in a drawer, but I have a feeling that they won't lead anywhere. You?"

"Nothing. I have one more desk to search, but I need your help with this one."

"What is it?" Mac asked.

"His brother is a supervisor here. I never heard bad things about him, he was always in John's shadow. He's the youngest one and used to follow John everywhere. I have a hunch he's part of this somehow, but he has cameras in his office. Which in and of itself is weird. I don't have the ability to cloak myself in shadows like you do and would be seen for sure. Can you slip into his office and log on?"

"Sure. But how am I getting into the office? If I open the door, it will trigger the cameras. I'm assuming he'd have alerts if there was a portal that opened in his office too."

"He might. I didn't think of that. He would have access to the files at his home, since he's higher up. We can port to his house and try a computer there, or I can open the door to his office and pretend to leave a note or something. You slip in behind me and run the program. Do you think that will work?"

Mac shrugged. "Might as well give it a try. I'd rather do it here than risk going to his house and having civilians involved. If his brother has kill-switches at all his properties, I don't want to risk that he might have the same setup."

"Makes sense. Alright. Let me get all official looking," Bert said.

Mac laughed as he simply smoothed his beard and grabbed a padfolio from someone's desk.

"That's your official look?" he teased.

"Yup. Have a padfolio or a clipboard and people think you're in charge. I don't know why, but it works. Okay, his office is one floor up. Let's port there, since that's what I would normally do, especially since there's no one here right now to let me in the building. Let's meet back here to talk about what we find," Bert said.

Mac nodded and shadowed himself before porting after him. This floor was all the supervisors and their assistants. He followed Bert to an office. It looked like any other office, but when he looked closer, he saw there were small cameras pointing in all directions. They were small enough that most people wouldn't even notice them.

Bert politely knocked on the door before trying the doorknob. It was unlocked, which struck Mac as strange. Of course, with all the cameras, maybe the guy felt safe. It wasn't like the public could really access the building either. Mac stuck close to Bert as he entered the room. Bert leaned over, blocking the computer screen and keyboard from view. Mac crouched on the floor, throwing the USB into the drive. Mac held in a laugh as Bert placed his padfolio on top of the screen to write, and in the process knocked the mouse, making it look like the screen turned on because of him. It also blocked the view of the screen. It was an awkward position to try to reach up and around Bert to type, but Mac made it work. He quickly ran the scan, using the same keywords as last time. He had hits within seconds, and he downloaded it to the drive. He could examine them later. The important thing was that they got the proof. The scan and download finished, Mac popped out the drive and tapped Bert's leg to indicate he was done.

Bert left the note folded on the keyboard. He had left the door wide open when he had entered the office, so Mac exited first, walking around the corner to open a portal to the floor below. Seconds later Bert appeared.

"What'd we get?" he asked hopefully.

"I think we got good stuff. I didn't get a chance to look at it much, but from what I saw we definitely have enough to talk to him. Do you want to grab him first, or head to one of our offices to go over the data?" Mac asked.

"Let's go to my office since we're here and we can get a better idea of how involved he is," Bert suggested.

Mac nodded, following Bert to the Enforcer's floor. Bert's desk was just as bare as his was. Locked drawers, a few pens, a notepad. There was a stack of notes and mail in his corner box.

Bert quickly scanned through the papers, dumping most of them in the garbage. "I'm not here much," he said.

"I'm the same. I'd rather work from home or in the field. I don't do well in an office setting," Mac agreed.

Bert unlocked his drawer, pulling out a laptop. Mac handed over the drive, grabbing a chair from another desk.

They scanned through all the documents. "We're going to get him," Bert said gleefully. "His brother is definitely in on it. At the very least, he's helping cover John's tracks and suppressing the property information. I wonder how much he knows. Feel like talking to him tonight?"

"Let's do it. I want to get this case finished and be able to get home," Mac said.

"See you there," Bert replied, porting out.

Mac shook his head and followed.

22

Viv stared at her phone. She hoped Mac was alright. She hadn't heard from him since yesterday afternoon. He was chasing a lead, so maybe he was busy with that and didn't have time to update her. He hadn't called last night; she had stayed up until she finally fell asleep holding her phone. There were no missed calls this morning. She had missed their nightly chat. It was easier to talk to him without seeing him. In person, she still heard his words about not wanting a human mate. Over the phone, her brain didn't shove that little tidbit at her for some reason.

She had learned that he absolutely hated Brussels sprouts but loved broccoli. His favorite color was red, he loved board games, and played Gardenscapes at night to relax. He enjoyed detective novels and she had set a few aside for him to look at the next time he came in. He had a dry and sometimes dark sense of humor, which given what he did for a job, a darker sense of humor seemed to fit. In the days he had been gone, she had received daily little things that showed he was thinking of her. Some were notes that he had written and left with D to give her. There was a flower delivery a couple of days ago, the cannoli delivery last night, and a cookie bouquet mixed in there as well. There were little touches that showed he was listening to her, like the flowers were wildflowers and sunflowers, with a few roses mixed in. Sunflowers were her favorite.

Viv checked her phone again, noticing it was time to start urging people to leave and close up for the night. She grabbed the intercom, making the announcement that there were ten minutes before the library closed and to check out now. As soon as she finished, she felt a shift in the air, the shadows once again watching her. She could tell it was Mac.

"Welcome home," she said. "I'm glad you're back. You'll have to tell me all about it at home."

Her phone dinged, showing a text message with a thumbs-up emoji.

She walked the library, shooing out the stragglers, cleaning up as she went. Her shadowy bodyguard following. As soon as the door was shut and locked, she turned around looking for Mac.

"Where'd you go?" she called out. She thought for sure he would be right behind her.

"Tables," he said, his voice low. He sounded exhausted.

Walking toward the tables near the desk, where he normally sat, she saw him slouching in the chair. He glanced up, his face drawn and a little gray.

"What happened?" she cried as she ran over to him. His poor face was scraped up on one side, stitches splitting his eyebrow. His wrist was in an air cast, the fingers looking a little swollen and bruised. His clothes were dirty, dusty and ripped in places, wet and darker looking in others. As she got closer, she realized that was blood.

"We found him, but he detonated one of the booby traps," Mac replied, his voice slow. "We found out his brother had been hiding his trail and we got his location out of him. We called in reinforcements since the asshole keeps evading us. As soon as we arrived, we had another Enforcer with us throw a containment spell so he couldn't port out again. He had a bunch of humans at the property, but Bert and I got them out first. When we went to grab him, he detonated the explosives he had throughout the building. The blast knocked out the Enforcer who cast the containment spell, so he couldn't revoke it which meant that none of us could port out. I got buried under some rubble. Bert was knocked back, but luckily the blast shoved him behind a pillar that stayed upright so it protected him. Once he was conscious, he dug me out. We had to climb our way out of the house to get far enough away that we could port out. There were Enforcers who had been stationed outside, surrounding the building in case he tried to run and they helped. They found the guy's body. He was dead from the explosion. I had to stop at the hospital, or I would have been here sooner," Mac said.

"You asshole!" Another voice rang out in the library. Viv grabbed her knife, the one that Mac had spelled to always stay with her and stood guard over her mate. "I can't believe you left the hospital against orders!"

Mac touched her lower back. "It's okay. It's Bert."

A short but muscular bald man came limping toward them.

"Ah. You must be Viv," he said, holding out a hand. "I'm Bert. Did this idiot tell you what happened?"

"He said there was an explosion and you got him out. That was about as far as he got," Viv replied, shaking his hand after she put the knife away. This was not what she pictured an angel looking like. There were no white robes, no halo. Just a bruised, tatted-up, biker-looking dude. He seemed nice though and she felt safe being near him.

"He had a piece of shrapnel lodged in his leg, his skull was showing through that eyebrow, his hand and wrist were literally crushed from a huge piece of the building, like they were bone powd—"

"That's enough, Bert! I'm fine. They gave me some healing potions, set the broken things, and stitched the rest. I just wanted to go home. I'll heal better there than in a hospital anyway. You know we don't deal well with those kinds of places. Home has a comfy bed and lots of wards," Mac pointed out.

Viv looked at him carefully. He really did look horrible.

"Does he need to go back?" she asked Bert. "Nope, you shush," she scolded Mac when he opened his mouth to protest.

"Probably not, but I didn't save his stupid life just for him to be dumb."

"I'll keep an eye on him," she promised. Bert didn't look all that much better. "Would you like to come back to our house? You can get a shower and we'll find you some clothes. Thomas' might fit well enough. We can get some dinner and you can always stay in the spare room or the pull-out couch," she offered. Bert came here instead of going somewhere else, so he might not have a family to go to. Plus, he had saved her Mac. She could at least make sure he had a good meal and could relax and feel safe for a bit.

Bert looked at Mac, who nodded. "I would like that. Thank you."

Viv grabbed her phone and sent a message to Thomas.

Mac home. Hurt. Bringing home an angel for dinner. Can you set up the extra bed?

What?! An angel? Seriously? Who is it? D wants to know, Thomas replied.

Bert. He's an Enforcer who was working with Mac.

There was a pause as she was sure Thomas was passing it on. *D says he's good people. I'll order in Chinese and some pizzas. See you soon.*

I'm driving home, so it'll be a few, Viv responded.

"Okay. Dinner is being ordered, Chinese and pizza. Will those work?" she asked Bert.

"I like them both," he replied.

"Let's head to the car. Mac looks like he's going to pass out," she said worriedly. She wasn't sure what would happen if he passed out trying to open and go through a portal. Viv leaned down, putting her shoulder under Mac's arm. She made sure to use the one that hadn't been dislocated. The last thing they needed was her to reinjure herself or drop Mac.

The three of them slowly walked to the front, two of them limping. She locked the door behind them, helping Mac into the front seat. They must have been lucky because traffic was light and they caught all green lights. As she pulled into the driveway, D came out.

"Hey, D," Bert greeted as he climbed out of the back seat.

"It looks like you guys had quite the night," D said dryly.

"You could say that," Bert snorted.

D opened Mac's door. "You ready to go inside?"

"Maybe in a minute," he said, his eyes closed.

D shook his head, bending down to pick him up. He ported them inside.

"Come on in, Bert. You look like you need to sit down," she said worriedly.

She dropped her purse and coat by the front door, making sure Bert made it to a chair before rushing to look for Mac. D had him in his room, helping him lie down.

"Is he okay?" she asked.

"He will be. He should have stayed in the hospital longer," D said.

"Wanted to be home," Mac slurred.

Viv startled as a tiny package dropped onto the nightstand. There was a note laying on top of the small box.

Tell my idiot nephew that one healing potion is not enough to heal an entire building falling on you. Here's another two for him, as well as one for Bert. If you need more, tell Mac to call me. Opening the box, she found three small bottles. D helped Mac raise his head, Viv opening the bottles and helping Mac drink them.

"Can you stay with him? I'll bring Bert his," she asked D.

Thomas was now in the living room, giving Bert a bottle of water. He must have been in the other guest room making up the bed. As soon as Bert swallowed his potion, she ran back to check on Mac. He was already looking better, the scrapes on his face healed.

"Dinner should be here in ten minutes," Thomas said, coming into the room. "Bert is in the shower. I gave him a pair of sweatpants and one of my looser t-shirts. I hope they fit him, he's a bit bulkier than I am."

"We can always give him one of mine," D said. "Come on, Mac. I'll help you get in the shower. Those potions are working but you're going to be a bit wobbly still."

Viv watched as Mac leaned on D, letting him take some of the weight off his leg as he worked his way down the hallway to the bathroom. The clawfoot tub was cool, but it would probably be hard for him to climb into on his own.

"That is not how I pictured angels," Thomas murmured with a grin.

"I know! A tattooed biker who looks like he could bench press me was not what I pictured either. He seems nice though and from what Mac told me, he saved Mac's life."

"What in the world happened?" Thomas asked as they headed toward the living room.

"I'm sure there's more to it, but the short story I got was they found the guy, threw a containment spell over the building so he couldn't portal out, got the humans out. When they went to arrest him, he detonated the building. The containment spell was still active, so they couldn't port out either. The building collapsed on Mac, Bert had been thrown back and was saved by a piece of the building that didn't fall. Bert dug Mac out and got him outside so they could port to the hospital. Other Enforcers were there too. The guy died in the explosion. That's about all I know," Viv told him.

The doorbell rang, startling both of them. They were getting better about noises at the door, but sometimes it still took them off-guard. They checked the cameras, making sure it was the delivery person. Even if they opened the door and it wasn't, the wards wouldn't let anyone in the house that they didn't allow or who were evil torturing bitches. Thomas opened the door, Viv standing off to the side. It was the pizza delivery guy and they could see the Chinese food driver pulling up. Viv took the pizzas and ran them to the kitchen counter. She made it back to the door as the next delivery person was walking up.

"It smells so good," she said, helping Thomas set the table.

"Do you need any help?" Bert asked as he came back into the living room. He was looking much better.

"No, sit. What would you like to drink?" Thomas asked.

"Just water, please."

Viv grabbed waters for everyone. Thomas was lining the counter with all the different food so people could grab what they wanted. It was quite the spread, but she figured with three big guys, her and Thomas, plus the fact that two of them were healing, they would probably eat most if not all of it.

Mac came out, still moving a little slowly, D hovering behind him. "Stop hovering like a mother hen! I'm fine. Thirty more minutes or so and I'll be all normal," Mac snapped.

"Don't be mean to D. He's worried about you," Viv scolded.

Mac frowned. "Sorry," he muttered.

"Sit down. What do you want to eat?" she asked him.

"Little bit of everything, please," Mac answered.

"Bert?"

"Uh, same, please. Thank you.

It was quiet once the food was at the table, everyone digging in. Mac and Bert were clearly tired, almost falling asleep at the table toward the end. D helped Bert to his room first, coming back to get Mac.

Viv helped clean up, putting the few leftovers in the fridge. She thought she could sleep all the night through tonight. Her family was all here.

23

Viv woke on a scream. Stupid freaking dreams. She should have known better than to expect to sleep the night through. She just hoped that she caught the scream before anyone heard her. She turned over, looking at the clock. Two o'clock. Great.

Mac came bursting into the room, knocking the door into the wall.

"What's wrong?" he demanded, looking around the room frantically.

"Nothing, go back to sleep. It was just a dream." Or a nightmare. Maybe it was seeing Mac and Bert injured and bloody that brought it on this time. She had dreamed she was back in the building, strung up. This time though, her toes were turning black from the cold, frostbite setting in. She had woken up right when they were about to rape her. Even though it hadn't happened in reality, her brain liked to show her the what-ifs. Asshole brain. Her hand cramped, the nerve that had been damaged making itself known. It had been getting better, but sometimes when she was stressed it seemed to aggravate it. Maybe it was all mental.

"Scoot over," Mac said, climbing on top of her bed. He stayed above the covers, but lay next to her, taking her hand between his and massaging it.

Viv watched him for a few minutes. "I'm glad you're here," she said.

"Me too," he said simply.

The heat radiating from his body and the relief he was bringing to her hand drew her toward sleep again.

"Sleep. I'll keep you safe," he said quietly.

Viv gave in and slept.

She was so warm and safe. She didn't want to get out of bed. She couldn't get out of bed. Viv's eyes popped open to stare at the arm wrapped around her waist. Mac. Mac had come into her room last night, soothing her from the nightmare. She lay still, trying not to wake him. He needed his sleep to finish healing, even with the healing potions.

"How'd you sleep?" a gruff voice asked.

"Good. You?"

"Better than I have in a long time. I gotta go check in with my boss today, but I'm only a phone call away, okay? I'm going to grab a shower," he said.

She felt a kiss to the back of her shoulder before the bed dipped as he sat up and climbed out, shutting the door behind him. Viv rolled over, hugging his pillow, noticing it now smelled like Mac. She made herself get out of bed, running through her morning routine of brushing her teeth, showering, and then getting dressed. She was off today, so she kept it comfortable in jeans, a t-shirt, and a hoodie.

Walking into the kitchen, she noticed Thomas already up and making a pot of coffee. She could smell bacon in the oven too.

"So... I went to check on you when I heard you scream, and lo and behold, I see a sexy man walking into your room," Thomas teased.

"Nothing happened," she protested. "He heard the nightmare and came to check on me."

"Mhm," Thomas uttered, disbelief coloring his tone. "Oh, honey. Is your hand bad today?" he asked, looking down at her hand.

"It flared last night. It seems okay this morning, I put the brace on just to give it a little more support today."

Viv waited for further interrogation from Thomas, but he was quiet on that front. Mac came in, grabbing a piece of bacon and a travel mug of coffee before giving her a kiss on the forehead and porting out. Bert wandered in a few minutes later.

"Mac leave already?"

"You just missed him," Viv said.

"Alright. I'll give him a call later. I need to go to the office to finish some paperwork. Thank you for dinner and letting me stay last night. It was nice to meet you," he told Viv.

He disappeared, leaving Thomas and Viv alone in the kitchen. She had a feeling D was hiding on their side of the house, giving them some room to talk.

"What's really going on with Mac?" Thomas asked.

Viv groaned. She'd known it was coming, but at the same time she had hoped he would drop it. "I don't know. I really don't."

"Walk me through it. Let's see if I can help," Thomas suggested.

"You know how he avoided me. You know his past. You know what he said to me. He did it to be mean on purpose to push me away. I get all that, but he still said it, you know? My brain has those words in the back of my head, as well as the words from the mind bender, which play off each other.

"He's been sending me little things. Not every day, but pretty close. Flowers, coffee delivery, a surprise lunch at work. Sometimes he sits at the library and does his own work remotely. Sometimes he's hiding in the shadows, but I know he's there." Viv paused, trying to figure out how to express what she was feeling.

"He's trying to show you he values you and is thinking of you, but you're worried that it's still leftover fear from the kidnapping, or that he feels bad that his work affected you."

"Close enough," Viv admitted.

"I'm not going to lie. I do think the kidnapping played a role in his change of heart, *but* I think it was simply the catalyst that sent a wrecking ball through his walls. You're a pretty awesome person; I think he would have come around at some point anyway. This just sped it up. He hasn't run scared since, not from the nightmares you still have, not from the doctors' appointments, not from the times your hand goes numb and you drop things."

"Yeah," Viv said, still not convinced.

"Did you miss talking to him when he was working and couldn't call? Did you look forward to hearing from him or getting his texts? Do you still have butterflies in your stomach when you hear his voice?" Thomas asked, waiting for her to nod. "Then you still want him. He is meant to be your mate, and I refuse to believe the same fate or design or whatever that brought me D would screw you over and give you a mate you couldn't have.

"Plus, where did Mac go when he was hurt?"

"The hospital," she said, admittedly a little densely, trying not to think of the implications for his choices.

Thomas lightly flicked her in the arm. "Don't be dumb. He left before he was fully healed so he could come 'home.' To you. That doesn't seem like a man who's running anymore, to me."

Viv leaned her head on Thomas' shoulder. She took a deep breath, slowly letting it out. "What if we're having sexy times and his tail comes out and all I can think of is the bitch?"

"If that's what happens, you pause and snuggle and let him slowly introduce you to his demon form. Nothing is insurmountable. She didn't try that with me, but the first time I saw D in his demon form after, I freaked out. He was porting in from work and I saw him out of the corner of my eye. Total meltdown. It was so stupid, because I know his form, I've seen it a lot of times. Something about him porting in off to the side where it was a little darker triggered something in my brain. It took a bit of time, making him port in different locations and times for me to get used to it again. If that happens and you have flashbacks, you let him introduce that side of him slowly and not during sexy times," Thomas said, wrapping his arms around her.

Viv nodded.

"I don't see you jumping into bed for sex right away anyway. Maybe ask him if you can see that side of him so you can get used to it."

Viv leaned against her best friend, thinking over what he said. Mac had dragged his feet and ran away the first time. This time she was the one dragging her feet. Not that she didn't feel like she had some good reasons, but if they were ever going to move forward, she needed to accept he had been an idiot and forgive that. She needed to take a step forward or they would be stuck here, because she had a feeling Mac wouldn't make any other moves to push her forward other than leaving her little gifts.

Maybe she could plan an easy date, take a tiny step forward.

24

Mac ported to his uncle's, eager to catch up and see what had happened since the last time he saw him.

"Uncle?" Mac shouted out as he ported into the front entryway.

"In the kitchen," came a faint reply.

Mac walked through the house, entering a door to a back area that was kept for family. The walls went from plain and boring, to more colorful with family pictures hanging on the wall. There were pictures of Mac's parents with his uncle, pictures of Mac and his uncle, pictures of Mac playing with the Hellhound puppies that always seemed to be around. He had a good life growing up.

Walking into the kitchen, he saw his uncle on the floor, three hellhound puppies crawling over him. It was a side of him not many saw.

"Who had puppies this time?" Mac asked, squatting down to let them sniff his hand.

"Clarice. Braedon's the father."

"That's a good pairing. These will be good protectors then," Mac said. He was familiar with all of his uncle's dogs.

"I think so. They're weaned now and I'm just starting to get them housebroken. I had a thought I wanted to run by you," he said.

Mac nodded, letting his uncle know he was listening, but he was really playing with the little balls of fur. Not that they would stay little for long. Hellhounds grew to be about Great Dane-sized in height but were built more muscular. If you combined the strength and cunning from a Doberman Pincher, a Rottweiler, and a Pit Bull, with the training of a German Shepherd, that was a close enough description of the Hellhounds. They were Netherworld in nature, so they too could transform their shapes, often with flaming fur and the lights of hellfire in their eyes. They could be terrifying and once they latched on to their person, they would destroy the world for them. His uncle knew which dogs paired best with each other to create the next generation and he was always careful to train them himself. While some other demons did get their own Hellhounds, most still belonged to his uncle. They often accompanied him or the Enforcers for work.

"Once I get these trained, I would like to give one to your mate. I know you worry about her when you're not there, even with the wards in place. I can make a Service Animal accreditation for him, so she can bring him to work. What do you think?" his uncle asked, looking at him.

"She's been wanting a dog," Mac said slowly. "I think she would accept one. Which one were you thinking?"

His uncle pulled out one of the squirming puppies, placing him in Mac's hands. "This one."

Mac studied the dog, noticing it met his eyes square on,

a little growl forming. "That's enough," he said firmly. "Are you going to protect my mate?" he asked the pup.

The whip-like tail went crazy, wagging like mad, a little woof giving him the answer. "That's a good pup," Mac said, holding the pup up to his face, letting him scent him.

"I think it's a good choice," Mac said, grinning as a little tongue licked his nose.

"Great. I'll work on training him so he's ready. Would you like to visit the punishment levels today?"

Mac knew this was his uncle's way of asking if he wanted to go mete out punishment to the ones who hurt his mate. It was very tempting, especially with the scream of last night's nightmare still fresh in his mind. But he didn't want to go back home with that energy on him.

"Not today. I know you're punishing them for me." He sighed. "She had another nightmare last night. She doesn't talk to me about them, but I think she does to Thomas and the therapist she sees online."

"You need to give her time. No one should have to endure what she did, or Thomas did. I thought I had made it very clear years ago that anyone who tries to hurt my boys will be dealt with by me," his uncle said, his voice hard. "Apparently they need a reminder."

Mac grinned, knowing his uncle had unofficially adopted D when they were younger. It was always fun getting both families together during the holidays. D's parents were probably the only other ones who got to see his uncle in his family life. Everyone else only got to see the work version.

"Thank you," he said. "Got any more ideas on wooing my mate?"

"You tried flowers? Chocolates? What about love notes?"

"I don't know that love notes are really my thing," Mac replied. "Where are you getting these ideas?"

His uncle blushed. "Magazines. What?" he asked indignantly when Mac started laughing. "It's not like I have a mate," he protested. "I've been single for longer than you've been alive. No one wants to date me, thinking I'm just my job. And I haven't come across my mate yet," he pouted.

Mac squeezed his uncle's shoulder. It would be wonderful if his uncle found his mate. He needed someone to come home to, someone to relax with.

"I tried the flowers and chocolates. I sent over coffee and cannoli, one time I sent her lunch. She's been talking to me, but I don't know that I'm making much progress otherwise."

"You are. By being there consistently and showing up, you're showing her that you've changed. It might take some time. You were an idiot."

"Thanks, Uncle."

"Well, you were. She's dealing with you and your change of mind, plus all the trauma and residual scars of being abducted. You need to have patience. Being there for her is what she needs from you."

Mac nodded, knowing he was right. It was fun getting to know her. She was funny and he loved hearing some of the stories that came from working in the library. Like the other day when she found an older couple getting frisky in the back corner, thinking no one could see them. Or the little girl who finally finished a book on her own and couldn't wait to tell Viv about it. He had been there for that one and it had been adorable. Viv was so good with the kids, well with everyone really. He couldn't believe he was dumb enough to not have seen it and had lumped her in with his first mate simply because she was human.

His phone vibrated in his pocket, causing Viv's pup to nose at it. "I'm getting it," he said, laughing, gently pushing his nose away. He read the message, not quite sure if he was reading it right. He read it again, a grin spreading over his face.

"You look creepy," his uncle pointed out. "What's going on?"

"Viv asked me on a date."

Viv was nervous. She had hit the send button before she could second-guess herself.

"Good job," Thomas praised her, his teacher voice coming out. "Now what? What are you going to do?"

"The park has an outdoor movie tonight. Maybe pick up some food and have a picnic and watch the movie?"

"What kind of movie is it?" Thomas asked. A horror movie or even a murder mystery probably wouldn't be the right kind of movie for a first date.

"It's a rom-com. It's an old one I've seen before. It's a little cheesy, but it should be fine."

Her phone chimed. "He said yes and wants to know when."

"Tell him tonight. You can drive together and either pick food up on the way or have it delivered right before you leave," Thomas suggested.

Viv nodded, typing out the details and sending it. She pulled up the food app, thinking that having the food delivered would be easier than driving someplace and waiting for it and trying to make it back in time for the movie. She decided on barbeque. There was a place close by that did really nice green beans with diced onions and bacon. The pulled pork was always good and she loved their cornbread. It was moist, which was hard to find. She found most places had dry cornbread, but she loved this one. She added two different sauces, not sure if Mac liked a sweeter or spicier BBQ sauce. She added another side of mac and cheese and coleslaw since she knew how much he could eat, and a couple of drinks.

"Can you ask D if we grabbed the picnic basket from the apartment and where it might be?" Viv asked. The first few days of the move were a blur.

"I think I know where it is. There's a storage closet in our hallway. Let me go look," Thomas said. Viv followed him to his side of the house. She hadn't been over there much, other than the first tour he gave her. They tended to leave each other's rooms alone and stuck to the common spaces. The closet was packed. It looked like everything that they didn't know where to put or if they should keep it, ended up in here. Thomas dug in, searching through piles and towers of stuff. "Found it!" Thomas slowly started pulling it out, trying not to send the tower of stuff tumbling.

Viv helped get it out and then ran to the shower. She wanted to look nice for tonight, even though she knew nothing was going to happen. This was their first date, despite knowing each other and texting and talking on the phone. She was nervous, which seemed ridiculous, but if this went well it had the potential to change her life. She would have a mate and would live a long time. And if it didn't...well, her heart would be broken again.

25

Mac ported home, having taken a shower and changed at his Netherworld house. He still had clothes there that he thought would work for a first date.

"Don't be an idiot again," his uncle said as he was leaving the house. "You're going to need to be a little vulnerable with her. She needs to see all of you, see what a good guy you are. Don't fuck this up."

He was pretty sure he had rolled his eyes, but it was decent advice. He wanted to apologize to her. Again. And explain his history a little more. There were things that not even D knew about, but he thought it would help her understand him. He had dressed in a pair of black boots, his dark wash jeans that hugged his ass and thighs, and a black button-down shirt with a black t-shirt underneath. He grabbed a coat, even though he generally didn't get cold. But with Viv being human, she might get chilly as the night went on.

Stepping through the portal, he saw Thomas standing there, arms folded. "Hi," Mac said, uncertainly.

"She's taking a step. Don't fuck this up."

"Why is everyone saying that to me?" Mac asked, throwing his hands in the air.

"Probably because you already messed up," D pointed out very helpfully.

They all got quiet as they heard her bedroom door open. Thomas pointed at his own eyes and then back at Mac in the universal 'looking at you' sign. Mac shook his head, but he was glad his mate had such a good friend.

Viv came out, dark jeans encased her legs, a soft comfy-looking sweater hugging her torso, her hair down, the waves falling loose against her shoulders. Her naturally pink lips were glossy, inviting him to press a kiss. He'd wait, but he really wanted to find out if her lips were as soft as they looked, what they tasted like. She looked gorgeous.

D gave him a pointed look.

"You look gorgeous," Mac said, loving how her cheeks turned pink at his words.

"Thank you. You look very handsome. I have the picnic basket all ready to go when you are," Viv replied.

Mac nodded. He had smelled the wonderful food when he came home. He grabbed the basket and opened the door for her. He had brought his truck over when he had moved in. He opened the passenger door, helping her climb up before placing the picnic basket in the back seat. He wanted to drive tonight, for a couple of reasons, one of which was the heated seats. If the temperatures dropped a lot, it would help her stay warm. He also didn't know if this was a park and watch kind of movie, like a drive-in, or if this was a park in a parking lot and sit on the grass kind of event. He had thrown a few extra blankets in the back of the truck just in case.

"Thank you for setting this up," he said as he pulled out

of the driveway. "I haven't been to a movie in a long time, much less one in a park."

"It's something the city sets up. Thomas and I used to go a lot in college, but I haven't been in a while either. I thought it was something different. How did the meeting with your boss go?" she asked, plugging in her phone to provide directions.

"Good. It ended up being less about work and more about catching up. I did get to see the new batch of puppies, which was fun."

"Puppies?"

"Mhm. Hellhound puppies. They're tiny now, but they'll end up being about as tall as a Great Dane."

"Do they have three heads like Cerberus, or just one?" Viv asked, curious. She wondered how many things were wrong in religions and myths, since angels and demons were nothing like she had expected.

"Just the one," Mac replied with a smile.

"Did you get any new cases, or do you get a bit of a break since you just finished one?"

"It depends on what comes in. Right now, I don't have anything, just finishing paperwork. If something comes up that I'm better suited for, then I'll get called in. Luckily, there's enough Enforcers and most nonhumans don't behave badly enough for us to be overwhelmed. I know it probably doesn't seem like it since I've had several cases since we met, but there can be a lot of down time," Mac replied.

"What do you normally do in your off time?" Viv asked. They had talked about a lot of things, but not so much about his job and home life.

"I'm kind of boring. I hang out with my uncle or D, sometimes a few other work friends. I'll read, mostly detective, suspense, or true crime type of books. TV sometimes. D and I go to the range. Oh! I like making bread too. Smacking the dough around is relaxing and helps get rid of any work frustrations."

"Huh. I did not see you as the baking sort," Viv admitted. She loved the smell of baking bread and loved eating warm bread with melty butter even more.

"Just bread. I tend to burn cookies and whenever I try to make a cake, it turns out dry. It got to the point where my uncle very nicely asked if I baked his birthday cake or not before he took a bite."

"Oh, no! He wouldn't eat it if you made it?"

"No, he was a good sport, and he ate it. He just made sure he had plenty of coffee or milk to go with it." Mac grinned. "A really, really tall glass of milk."

"Oh, that's nice of him," Viv laughed. She had a picture in her head of the scene, but she wondered if one day she would get to see it in person.

"I promise to buy your birthday cakes," Mac said. "I won't subject you to my horribly dry cakes."

"It's the thought that counts," Viv said, a little touched he was planning on celebrating her birthday with her. It was still a while off. "I love making Christmas cookies. Thomas and I spend the whole day baking and decorating. Maybe you and D can help this year," she offered.

"I'd like that," Mac replied, quickly looking over to smile at her. He pulled into the parking lot, noticing it was pretty full already.

"I'm surprised they still have the movies when it's this cold out," he admitted.

"This is the last one for the season, I think," Viv said.

Mac climbed out, grabbing the picnic basket and a

bunch of blankets from the back of the truck. "I brought some extra blankets in case we get cold."

"That was a good call. I have one packed in the picnic basket too," Viv said. "I have a base layer on, which should help."

They walked over to the movie area, a large screen set up, with several couples and a few families already sitting around. Mac could smell hot chocolate and saw a drink vendor, as well as a popcorn machine and a roasted nut truck sitting off to the side. That was smart. Mac laid down a few blankets, thinking it would help stop the chill from seeping into them from the ground. He kept one out to wrap around Viv if she got cold.

The food was wonderful, the movie cheesy with a bit of a predictable storyline. He enjoyed having Viv snuggle up next to him, his arm wrapping its way around her back. Mac draped a blanket over their laps as the temperature got a little cooler. They had finished their dinner, leaving their cookies and mini brownies for dessert and the second half of the movie. There was a brief intermission, where people got more snacks or took bathroom breaks. He jumped up and grabbed them two hot chocolates.

As he sat back down, Mac thought he could use this time to explain things to Viv. The darkness made it feel easier to talk about these things; probably like Viv had felt when they talked over the phone. He waited until she had her hot chocolate and was situated under the blanket again, their legs touching.

"So. Um. You know I had a mate a while ago. And that she tried to kill me. There's a bit more I haven't told you, some of it even D doesn't know."

"You don't have to tell me, if you don't want to," Viv responded, laying her head on his shoulder.

"I want to," Mac said. "It doesn't excuse my behavior, but it might explain it a bit."

He took a deep breath, trying to gather his thoughts in a coherent line.

"My parents were awesome. They were mates and had met each other a little later in life. My paternal grandparents were gone by then as well, but my uncle raised me when they died, my dad's brother. My mom's parents didn't approve of their mating and stopped talking to her long before I was born. I was an only child, which isn't all that uncommon in the nonhuman world. We tend to only have one to three, spaced widely apart. They were on a vacation one year. I was staying with my uncle while they were gone. All of a sudden, he jumped up and had a guard come watch me and he left. It all happened in seconds. He came back, covered in blood. It was the only time I've seen him cry. My parents had been killed. Someone saw my father perform some magic and even more so back then, humans were a fearful superstitious bunch. A group of them surrounded my parents and killed them. My uncle brought their bodies back to bury and I lived with him from then on."

Viv made a sound and hugged him tighter but let him carry on his story.

"I avoided humans for a long time; I was scared I would end up like my parents. Uncle taught me how to blend in with humans and how to interact with them. There were a couple of Enforcers that had human mates and they helped as well. Time passed and I slowly got more comfortable being on Earth. One of these times, I was near a small village and scented the most amazing smell. I followed it and found my first mate. She was beautiful. She seemed to get along well with everyone in the village. She had many beaus courting her. Her father was a rich landowner and men came from all around trying to tie their houses together. I pretended to also be a rich landowner; I had land and some riches, most of it was in Netherworld. I courted her for months, bringing gifts for her and her family. Her father accepted my proposal and I was the happiest I had ever been.

"I took her on a carriage ride and brought her to a local pond. It was still public enough to conform to societal restrictions, but private enough that I could quickly show her my other side. She was taken aback but seemed to accept that side of me, telling me that she would accept me in either form. Looking back, I should have paid more attention to her body language and actions than her words. She didn't touch me after that, climbing up into the carriage on her own, rushing out after giving me an air kiss whereas before she had been kissing my cheek.

"About a week later, I received a message saying she would like me to come to her father's house for a luncheon. When I arrived, it seemed quieter than normal, more subdued. I was escorted into the waiting room, nothing out of the ordinary, but there were men there I didn't recognize, including a priest. I wasn't sure what was going on, but didn't think anything bad. She came in, dressed in black, which seemed odd. I asked if she was in mourning, what had happened. She came close to me, hands held out like she wanted to hold my hands. I held mine out as well, but a pair of cuffs were slapped on instead. A noose thrown around my neck. The men had surrounded me while I was distracted by her. The priest tried to perform an exorcism, which doesn't work. I had salt and holy water thrown at me. When that didn't work, a couple of the men shot me, but it takes a lot to kill one of us. As they held me down, I watched as my mate walked toward me. She stood there, staring at me with hatred and disgust in her voice saying she would never love me, she loved another. She would have gone through with the marriage to get the riches for her family, but there was not a chance she would associate with such filth. She stabbed me, I believe going for my heart, but she missed by an inch or less. I would have died otherwise. I managed to open a portal and got to the nonhuman hospital.

"I was despondent for weeks afterward. I had been so hopeful that it had been someone overhearing or seeing my change that had set the whole thing up. I knew when she stabbed me that she had been actively involved in it. Uncle sent an investigator and they found out that she had married another, days after trying to kill me. I didn't want any part of me tied to her, even if she would die much sooner than I would. I didn't want to risk having my soul tied to hers in the future. It's rare, but you can break the mate bond; have it dissolved so that your souls will never be tied together again, no matter how many times they may be reincarnated. It became my mission to have that done. It's not easy to do and the higher-ups have to do some pretty intrusive and dicey things to break it. The bonds aren't meant to be broken and they only try in severe cases. Uncle petitioned on my behalf, pushing them to accept my bid to have it broken. I don't know what made them do it, but I was so relieved when it was done. I was unconscious for part of it, delirious with pain and fever for the other part. D doesn't know how bad it got; I never told him. I had to be in the hospital while they tried to break the bond due to the risks associated with it. It took about a week, and I almost died twice. I did flatline for a couple of seconds before Uncle forced my soul back into my body. I had to stay in the hospital for another week for all my vitals to stabilize," Mac said, pausing as he tried to figure out what to say next.

"You weren't tempted to break our bond?" Viv asked.

"You aren't a bad person; I just couldn't bring myself to trust in a mate bond or a human again. Your soul is beautiful and something in me didn't want to even think about breaking the bond. I was drawn to you over and over again, even following you on dates to make sure they were good enough for you. I wanted you to be happy, even if I couldn't see it with me."

"And now you think you can?"

"I do. You care about others, you're loving and giving. I was just stuck in my fears and not willing to let myself be hurt again. When you were taken, it was the most fear I have ever felt in my life. Even more than when Uncle ran out of the house when my parents were taken from us, more than when I thought I would die trying to break the first mate bond. I realized just how stupid I had been. I would love to be able to show you that I can be the mate you deserve, not the one that I was when we first met. I want to show you me; not the version that was determined to push you away and was cruel on purpose even though my demon raged at me the entire time. I'm normally not that big of an asshole, I swear."

"Okay," Viv said simply.

"Okay?" Mac repeated, not sure if she was acknowledging his words, agreeing with his last statement, or agreeing to give him a chance.

"I don't agree with what you did, but I understand why you felt like it was too big a risk to take me on as a mate. I'm not saying we are going to finalize the bond tonight, but I am willing to be your mate. We just need to keep getting to know each other better; I think that's best for both of us."

"I agree. And thank you for giving me another chance," Mac said, pressing a kiss to the top of her head. He wrapped an arm around her and drew her back in to snuggle. The movie started moments later, letting them relax again after their heavy conversation. Mac felt lighter than he had in a long time.

26

It was Thanksgiving. So much had happened since Halloween. The whole kidnapping and torture thing, Mac changing his mind and trying to woo her. Moving. She really needed to talk to Thomas today to see what all they were telling his parents. When his parents had heard about the kidnapping, they had been understandably upset. When they moved out of the apartment, she thought they sounded relieved thinking it would be safer for them. They had offered to help them move, Thomas had told her, but he told them they were getting movers. His parents were older, and they wouldn't have had them lift things anyway.

Thomas had asked them for some time before they came over, which they mostly managed at least until Viv went back to work. While they had stopped over a couple of times, both at work and at home, they had kept it brief. Viv was grateful they knew her so well; she hadn't been ready to talk about anything then. They had cancelled their vacation plans so they could have Thanksgiving with them.

They were bringing the fruit salad and mac and cheese, things Thomas' mom was known for. Yum.

Throwing her hair into a ponytail, Viv started walking to the kitchen. She needed to get the turkey started.

"Morning," she said, as Mac stepped out of his room.

"Hey. Is there anything you need help with?" Mac asked. "I can help chop or other things that don't require much skill before I get out of your hair?"

Viv looked over at him. "What?"

"I thought I could help before I went to Uncle's," Mac replied.

"Oh. I didn't know you had other plans," she said softly. She had thought he would eat Thanksgiving with them.

Mac was quiet for a moment before speaking. "I think maybe we missed something," he said slowly. "I was going to Uncle's so you guys could have your Thanksgiving with Thomas' parents."

"Do you celebrate Thanksgiving in the Netherworld?" Viv asked.

Mac shook his head. "It's just another day," he replied. He was really confused now.

Viv bit her lip. "Do you not like Thanksgiving or not want to be around Thomas' parents?" she asked. She knew Mac was trying to get over his hatred of humans, besides just her and Thomas, but it was a work in progress. Humans hadn't shown him the best experiences after all.

"It's fine. I think they seemed like nice people at the engagement party."

Viv was confused. "Then why would you not stay?"

Mac stared. His mouth opened and shut. "I didn't know I was supposed to?" he said, the tail end of it raised like in a question.

"This is your home too. We're dating. I think I made

assumptions and maybe didn't express them clearly to you. I thought you would have Thanksgiving with us, especially since you didn't mention anything with your uncle. I'm sorry I didn't make that clear," she apologized, grabbing one of his hands.

"And I'm sorry I didn't ask. I just assumed you wouldn't want me there, and instead of asking I pouted. It was all in my room, so you didn't see it, but I definitely pouted," Mac replied.

"I'd love it if you stayed," Viv said.

Mac nodded, raising their hands and kissing the back of hers. "Uncle didn't know I was going to pop in anyway. He would have told me to work on my communication skills and talk to you first, so I was just going to drop in," he added sheepishly.

Viv shook her head at him, smiling. Dork. They both needed to work on their communication, she thought.

"What about your parents? Are they coming too?" Mac asked. He hadn't heard much about them.

"No. They do their own thing at the holidays. My parents like to take vacations for holidays, but it didn't always line up with school breaks. Thomas' parents actually hosted me for the holidays a lot while we were growing up. I'm an only child, so it worked out pretty well. They're in Florida right now, I think."

Mac had to pause to think of how to phrase his next question. He had seen Thomas' parents in the house when they popped in to check on him, or he had seen them when they dropped by the library to drop something off for Viv. Heck, he had even heard them on phone calls and video calls. What he hadn't heard or seen much of was Viv's parents. "Do they know about you being abducted?"

"Yeah. I called and let them know. Not everything, just the same version we gave to work," she reassured him.

That wasn't reassuring at all. Even that version included Viv and Thomas being injured and tortured in some way. And her parents hadn't even come to visit once?

"And they still didn't want to come for Thanksgiving?" Mac finally asked.

"That's not who they are," Viv responded softly, shaking her head. "They had me because it was expected of them to have kids. I don't think they ever really wanted any. They're not mean, just a little reserved and standoffish. I'm sure they're relieved I'm better now, but since it had already happened and I was fine, they wouldn't see the need to rush over to check on me. They offered to send money if I needed help with the bills since I missed so much work, but that's about all I expected from them. Thomas' parents were really where I got the parental support growing up. They're amazing, always treated me like one of their own. If they had known about the kidnapping earlier, which I know why they couldn't because they wouldn't stand a chance against nonhumans, they would have been out there searching as well."

Mac drew her in for a hug. He didn't know what to say to that, so he kept his mouth shut. He would show her love and he knew his uncle was waiting impatiently to meet her. His work kept him in Netherworld, so it would need to wait until they were mated, and he could safely bring her down there. "I look forward to officially meeting them. What do you need me to do?"

"Can you roughly chop some onions, celery, and carrots? I'm going to use them with the turkey. Leave some celery and carrots for the salad though," she added.

Mac pulled out the larger knife and cutting board,

getting to work on the vegetables. Viv had pulled out the turkey, removing the giblets and neck from the cavity. Mac watched out of the corner of his eye. He didn't think he had ever made a turkey. She placed butter and seasonings under the skin, added more on top of the skin before wrapping bacon over the top. What deliciousness was this?

"Bacon?" he asked.

"It helps keep the turkey moist as it cooks. I'll still baste it, but it turns out well. Plus, then there's bacon to eat, and who doesn't like bacon?" she laughed.

A few minutes later, Thomas and D stumbled out of their hallway. "You got started already? Did you eat breakfast?"

"Not yet," Viv replied.

"I'll go get some donuts or something," D said, opening a portal.

"I'll get the coffee started. What all needs to be done?" Thomas asked.

"Mac's cutting vegetables and then I think the salad," she said, looking over to Mac for confirmation. He nodded. Salad should be easy enough for him to do. "I think we decided on mashed potatoes, stuffing, rolls, and green bean casserole? Or was it Brussels sprouts?" Viv asked. She knew they had bought things for both but couldn't remember what they had picked.

"Let's do both," Thomas suggested. "It's not like it won't all get eaten," he joked.

Mac grinned. He and D could eat a lot. In fact, sometimes they had to run to the grocery store twice a week to keep them in enough food. He finished with the vegetables for the turkey, setting them off to the side. He went to the pantry and grabbed a larger glass storage bowl and the rest of the salad ingredients from the fridge. The salad he knew how to do. He'd seen Viv make one often enough. He focused on his task, letting Viv and Thomas carry on a conversation in the background. He was still finding his way in the whole group dynamic. He thought it was easier with D there to act as a sort of buffer. He knew Viv had accepted his apology, but he thought at times Thomas was still withholding judgment. Although he had encouraged Viv to give Mac another chance, so maybe it was all in his head.

"How are we handling your parents?" he heard Viv ask. He tuned in a little more, not wanting to stick his foot in it when they were here.

"I think keep it as simple as possible. They already know the public version, kidnapped for ransom type of thing, and that the one kidnapper was rough in the process resulting in our injuries. I don't think they're going to ask too many more questions on that front other than how we're feeling. They don't know anything about which hospital we went to or your attempted assault. Mac was here when they visited and we said he was a friend of D's. I don't think we mentioned him living here, but we can double-check when D gets home."

"Mac, are you alright with being introduced as my boyfriend?" Viv asked.

"I'd be honored to," Mac replied, smiling. He loved that she was claiming him and putting a human label on them. That more than anything made him secure in the knowledge that she was really giving him a second chance.

"Donuts!" D shouted as he stepped through the portal. "I managed to get the good ones," he said proudly.

Viv finished setting the turkey up, placing it in the roasting pan and scattering the vegetables around it. A few onions, carrots, celery, and some butter got stuffed into the cavity, broth poured into the bottom of the pan. After tenting it with foil, she moved to the oven. Mac ran over to grab the oven door, letting her slide it right in. Thomas was peeling the potatoes. Mac had always bought pre-mashed potatoes. It made him realize just how little he cooked for himself. He knew how, his uncle had made sure of that. But it was always easier to just throw a burger or something on the grill and heat up a bag of vegetables. If he didn't have those, he would cook something easy like boiling broccoli or cauliflower. He never spent a lot of time making food for himself. It seemed like a waste of time to do extravagant things for one person. When he and his uncle ate together, it was usually at his uncle's house.

"Set timer for two hours," she said to her phone. When she saw Mac looking at her, she explained, "After that I'll start basting it and take the foil off."

They washed up, grabbing coffee and sat down to eat. Mac loved mornings like this when they were all here.

27

Mac was surprised to find himself enjoying dinner with Thomas' parents. They seemed very nice and had welcomed him to the family when Viv introduced him as her boyfriend. He hadn't been able to stop the grin on his face when she said that.

"How did you two meet?" Beth, Thomas' mom, asked.

"Through D," Viv answered. "Mac came over to see him at the apartment one day and we met there. We were just friends at first, but then decided to see how we did at dating."

Mac was both surprised and grateful at her answer. He had no idea what to say and hers was almost the truth. With a few bits and pieces of him being a stubborn ass left out.

"Oh, that's nice. I think being friends with your partner is the best thing to keep a relationship healthy. It means you can hang out and do things together besides just nookie. I mean one day you'll be old, or even just have a cold and not feel like it, and you still need to be able to relate to each other. I'm so glad both my kids have found someone they can both be friends with and have a sexual relationship with," his mom replied.

"Mom!" Thomas shouted, his face red.

Mac didn't dare look at D or he had a feeling they would both lose it and start laughing. Viv's face was just as red as Thomas'.

"That's a good point, dear," Thomas' dad said.

Mac bit his lip hard when he heard a snort escape D.

"I'll be right back, gotta run to the bathroom," D said, his voice strangled.

"Traitor," Thomas whispered low.

"Would you like more to drink?" Viv asked, trying to change the subject. She loved his parents, she really did, but sometimes they didn't have much of a filter. Of course, it all came from a place of love, so she would deal with the occasional embarrassment gladly. It was much better than her own parents' standoffishness.

Mac jumped up to help her grab the wine bottles and refill the water pitcher. "Are they always this much fun?" he leaned down and whispered to her.

Viv nodded. "Yup. All the time. Hearing the stories that came out of parent-teacher conferences was always the best part of the school year. My favorite was when his mom asked why they weren't teaching safe anal sex. They were teaching safe sex for hetero couples, and she thought it only fair that they taught both types. Afterall, not only gay men enjoyed anal. The teacher couldn't look Thomas in the eye for at least a week! They did add it to the curriculum though. Thomas wasn't the only non-straight kid there. There were other gay and bi kids. They even added safe sex practices for female couples. There were one or two parents who caused an upset but I heard they shut up pretty quickly after his mom spoke up at a parent night. I have no idea what she said, but I would have loved to have been there."

"They sound amazing," Mac admitted. He was glad he had this chance to know them. He was a little sad to realize that they would be gone one day. Granted they could have another thirty years or so left, but one day they wouldn't be here. He resolved to get to know them better; they were like Viv's other set of parents after all.

"They really are. They're great parents," Viv replied.

They carried the bottles back to the table, sitting down. D came back, seemingly composed now. Mac couldn't blame him, he had almost burst out laughing as well. The rest of dinner went pretty smoothly. Mac tried his best to eat his weight in mac and cheese. It was delicious, big curly type of noodles, lots of gooey cheese, a sprinkle of bread-crumbs made crunchy in the oven. He needed to see if Viv knew how to make this. He would gladly eat this every day. It was that delightful.

D made another pot of coffee, pulling out the pumpkin pie and whipped cream for dessert. Mac helped clean up the table and put the few leftovers away. They ended up sitting in the living room for dessert. Thomas' parents sat on one couch, Thomas sat in D's lap in the recliner, and he and Viv sat on the other couch. He thought they needed one more chair to even out the seating. That way no one had to sit on each other's lap, although D and Thomas didn't seem to mind. Mac grabbed his phone to send a quick text to his uncle to see where he had gotten the chair. He wanted them to match.

As he ate the pumpkin pie, he wondered why it was only served at Thanksgiving time. It was a nice pie and the whipped cream on top made it even better. Was it because fall was when the pumpkins were harvested? But there was canned pumpkin available at the store all year long. Maybe it was one of those 'it's tradition' mysteries.

They hung out after dessert, playing a few board games. Thomas' parents shared a few stories of Viv and Thomas when they were younger. Mac enjoyed himself thoroughly. He really should have given humans another chance before this, he thought to himself.

"Thank you for inviting me," he told Viv as he helped load the dishwasher after the parents had left. "I had fun."

"I'm glad. It's hard not to have fun near them," she said.

"I'm off to bed," Thomas said, coming over to give Viv a kiss on the cheek. "It was delicious as always. Thanks, honey. D is taking out the garbage and then we're done for the night," he said with a wink.

Uh huh. She knew that meant to stay away from their side of the house. "Sleep tight," she teased as D came back in and he and Thomas said goodnight and walked down to their room.

"I somehow don't think they're going to sleep," Mac said dryly.

"No, I don't think so either," Viv responded.

Mac wasn't sure how to ask her to stay up with him a bit longer. It had been a long day and he didn't want her to miss out on her sleep, but he did want to spend some alone time with her. "Would you want to turn on the fireplace and relax on the couch with me?" he asked. They had a gas fireplace, so it would be easy enough to turn off when they wanted to go to bed, no waiting for the embers to burn down.

"Let me run and get changed. I want in comfy clothes. I'll be right back," Viv said.

Mac took the opportunity to run to his room to change into sweatpants. He had eaten enough to be almost uncomfortably full. He was bending down to turn on the fireplace when he felt a light smack to his butt. He spun around, seeing Viv laughing at him.

"I mean...you stuck it out there," she said, laughing.

"Uh huh," Mac said, shaking his head at her in mock disappointment.

Viv climbed onto the couch, sitting cross-legged. Mac turned the fire on, adjusting the flames a bit before sitting down on the couch. He placed one of the decorative pillows against his side and grabbed a blanket. "Come here," he said, patting the pillow. Viv moved to lie down, resting her head on the pillow. As soon as she was settled, he threw the blanket over her. "Comfy enough?" he asked, not wanting her to be in a painful position.

"I am. This is nice," Viv said, burrowing her head into the pillow.

Mac let his hand brush over her hair, running his hands through it, gently massaging her scalp. Viv made a low moaning sound, causing his dick to twitch. "That feels good," she said.

"I'm glad," he replied. Watching the flames helped distract him from the occasional moans and sounds of pleasure coming from his lap region.

"Did you have a good first Thanksgiving?" Viv asked, hoping he at least had some fun.

"I did. We'll have to see if they want to come again next year. I was thinking we should get another chair, or even a loveseat, for in here. Then if we have three couples, there's room for everyone to sit. Not that Thomas or D seemed to mind sharing a seat," he said.

Viv flipped on her back, looking up into his face. "I'm glad. I think the extra seating is a good idea. Do you think your uncle would ever come to visit?" she asked.

"Maybe? Work keeps him in Netherworld quite a bit. I can't even remember the last time he left. Could be why he hasn't found his mate yet," he said, trying to remember the last time his uncle left their home world. It might have been when he had collected his parents' bodies. Maybe he was having some issues to work through with humans as well. It's not like he ever saw the best of them in his line of work. His uncle saw even more of the depravity and evil that existed than he did.

"Will I be able to meet him when we are mated? I can go there safely if we're mated, right? I think that's what D said when he took Thomas," Viv said.

"Yup. Once we're fully mated, you'll be safe to go. You'll have an immunity of sorts to the things that could drive a human mad if they had just wandered in. Not that you can really wander in, but you know what I mean. I would love to show you around. My house isn't much, but it's nice enough for when we go visit. It's close to my uncle's as well."

"What do demons do when they mate? Not the sex part," she hurried to add, "but do you have a ceremony like a wedding or anything?" She hadn't heard Thomas talk much about it, although they were engaged.

"Not so much. There's a vow you exchange during sex to accept each other as mates, but it's a private thing. Some demons who are mated to other nonhumans or humans, usually do whatever is common for their mate's culture. I would love to marry you," he said softly.

"How would that work? Do you even have a birth certificate, or anything like that?" Viv asked.

"Magic or really good hackers," Mac pointed out. "If you wanted to get married, I would make it happen."

"I think I would like that," she said quietly. "It could be

small, just us and Thomas and D. Maybe your uncle and Thomas' parents."

"That sounds nice," Mac replied. He wondered if Thomas and D would be interested in a double ceremony. He couldn't imagine why they were waiting to get married. Maybe it was a human custom he didn't understand?

Viv sat up, looking him in the eyes. "I'm not ready for more yet, but how do you feel about kissing for a while? A make-out session."

Mac's breath caught. He didn't think she would have made a move tonight, but he was more than willing to see how soft her lips were. "I'd love to," he said, his voice raspy with sudden need.

Viv stood, moving to straddle his body and sat on his lap, a leg on either side of his. She leaned in, his head moving to meet her. His tongue darted out, licking his lips before they covered hers. He kept the pressure gentle, letting her set the pace. Her hands came up, cupping his face, pulling him in closer. Viv parted her lips, letting his tongue slide into her mouth. His tongue swirled around hers, his body heat almost burning. She squirmed slightly in his lap, adjusting her position and letting her body relax into his. Oh boy, she thought as she ran into evidence of his pleasure. He was hard, she could feel the heat of his erection through his sweatpants. His length felt long and thick and she moaned a little as she rubbed against him. She had thought her dry-humping days were behind her, but making out on the couch made her feel like a teenager again. Viv forced her hips to stop, not wanting to give Mac the wrong idea. Kissing was all she was ready for tonight. Mac's hand grabbed her ass, pulling her in closer, his shaft resting against her mons. She couldn't wait for the day she would feel that inside her, she thought. Her hands found their way into his hair, those dark strands silky smooth. She clenched his head, keeping his face against hers, her teeth biting into his lips. She felt pin pricks on her cheeks and realized his hands had shifted into their demon form. She pulled her head back a bit.

Mac's eyes opened, the dark vastness lit by small flames, his demon side poking out. He drew a deep breath. "I can smell you," he rumbled. His voice was so rough and deep like this, her pussy clenched in anticipation. "I think we need to stop for tonight," he said, regret in his voice. Viv nodded, giving him one last tame kiss before climbing off. God, she could feel how wet her underwear was just from kissing him.

"Night," she said before she hurried to her room, her body horny and aching. She dove for her bed and her side drawer, pulling out her trusty dildo. It wasn't too long, about five inches, but it had these lovely nubs where the balls would be, and they felt amazing against her clit. She ripped off her pants, sliding a hand down to her lips, finding them puffy and wet, she moaned lightly as she glanced over her clit. She slid the dildo between her folds, teasing herself, letting the nubs rub against her clit, no penetration yet, she gasped as she rubbed a little harder, feeling a gush of liquid between her legs.

A groan sounded from the doorway, the door she had forgotten to shut.

"Don't stop, love. I'll stay here. Let me see what you like. Gods, you're beautiful, you smell so good," Mac rasped. His cock straining against his pants, his hand pressed against it.

"I want to see too," she said, licking her lips. She felt daring as she spread her legs, placing her feet on the bed, letting Mac see her vagina, how she shaved herself smooth, her lips were engorged, her arousal dripping from her.

She whimpered as he drew out his cock. It was uncut, which she would have expected with how old he was. Although she didn't know much about demon anatomy either. His balls hung heavy beneath his shaft. His penis though, that was what drew her eyes. It was thick, it looked like she might not be able to close her hand around him, he was long, about eight or nine inches, the tip dark red, dripping with precum. He had a Prince Albert piercing, she realized in shock.

"Fuck yourself, love. Let me see," he ordered.

Viv kept her eyes on him as she slid the cockhead over her clit, rubbing it in circles, ramping her arousal up. "Mac," she gasped as pleasure shot through her.

"Yes, love. Like that," Mac groaned, his hand wrapping around his dick, slowly stroking it up and down. "Slide it in and match me," he said, his voice dropping another octave, his demon coming out a little more, his dick gaining another inch in length and girth. Oh gods, how would he fit in this form, she wondered. His skin darkened, making him look tan, the flames growing in his eyes, his hands sporting wicked-looking sharp black claws where his nails were. She could see his tail lashing behind him like a cat.

"Eyes on my dick, love," he reminded her.

She slid the dildo into her channel, wishing it was the kind that heated. She could imagine it was his dick then. Her other hand found her clit, her middle finger pressing against it, rubbing in circles. As his hand slowly sped up, she tried to match his pace. She felt the cock slide against her walls, rubbing in all the right ways, the veins providing extra stimulation. She pulled it almost all the way out, letting just the tip rest in her entrance, keeping her spread as she rubbed the nubs over her clit, causing a riot of sensations to rush through her body.

"That's it. Beautiful. You look amazing taking your pleasure. One day, I'm going to be between those thighs. I'm going to feast on you, keep you begging for hours until I finally slide my dick into your cunt. Do you think you can take me? I bet you can," he grunted as he sped up again, his hand twisting around the head of his shaft.

She looked closer as the foreskin drew away, watching as the silver barbell popped through his fingers. She wondered what that would feel like inside her. She tilted her hips, crying out as the dildo found her spot.

"Faster, love. Almost there," Mac said, his voice strained.

Viv tore her eyes back to his face, seeing the tension there, his forehead glistening with his efforts. She followed a bead of sweat down his neck, down his chest, down the six-pack until it disappeared into the wiry curls at his pelvis. The veins were more prominent in his shaft now, the precum leaking steadily. She watched his hand, mesmerized by the flashes of the silver, her finger pressing hard on her clit and she gave one last hard thrust of her dildo.

"Mac!" she cried out as her orgasm rushed through her. She watched as cum shot through his fingers, his orgasm seconds behind hers.

Mac leaned against the doorframe, panting softly. "Thank you, love. You were beautiful," he said before pulling up his pants. "Sleep tight," he said, closing the door behind him.

Viv pulled the dildo out of her body. Did that really just happen?

28

Viv thought it would be awkward the next morning knowing they had masturbated together. But instead, it was a nonissue. Not quite like it didn't happen, but Mac had only come over and given her a light kiss and a "Good morning, beautiful," the word he had called her last night. He hadn't called her that before. Maybe he was waiting for her to say something, or he didn't want to embarrass her.

She kept watching as she got ready to run a few errands. It was a huge shopping day, but she was able to buy a few things online this morning. There were a few in-store-only sales that she wanted to check out.

"I'm going to go shopping this morning, if you wanted to come," she offered, looking at Mac.

"Shopping?"

Viv nodded. "It's Black Friday. The day after Thanksgiving is a big sale and shopping day in the United States. It's geared toward Christmas presents, but it's a good time to stock up on things you might need anyway. There are only a few things I was going to look for that I couldn't get online. I know shopping's not very exciting," she said.

"Do you guys celebrate?" Mac asked.

"We do. Sometimes it's just Thomas and me, sometimes it's with his parents. It depends on if they found a great deal on a vacation now that they're retired. We always celebrate with them, sometimes it's just a little before or after Christmas. This year they found a great cruise to go on, so we'll be celebrating with them on New Year's."

"Should I look for gifts for D and Thomas then?"

"If you want to," Viv replied. She didn't want to push him into something he didn't want to do.

"That sounds fun. I'd love to go. I think it would be hilarious to get my uncle a Christmas present. What do we do for Christmas?" he asked, bending down to put his boots on.

"If his parents aren't here, we keep it pretty relaxed. Pajamas or other comfy clothes, sit around watching movies and playing games. Sometimes we order in fancier food, sometimes pizza, sometimes Chinese or burgers, just depends on what we're in the mood for."

"That sounds like a good day," Mac said. He was looking forward to a day of hanging out with his mate and his friends. He wondered what he could get Viv for Christmas. It was a month away, but he needed to think of something good. Maybe he could ask Thomas or maybe she would look at something today. He'd have to pay attention, he decided. He grabbed their coats from the closet. "Where are we going first?"

"Target and Costco. They're close to each other, so we can park at one and walk over to the other if we manage to snag a parking spot. There's a new air fryer combo thing

Thomas has been wanting. I already told D I was getting it," she said with a grin.

He would guess that D had been lost for ideas and she had snagged that one first. There was a lot of triumph and gloating in that grin. "I've never been in a Costco," he admitted.

"Really? Oh, you're going to love it. Well, maybe not today. Today is going to be crazy busy. I'll have to bring you back when it's calmer, maybe right at opening during a weekday. It's like a little treasure hunt; they change stock so often that there's almost always new things to see. They have everything from socks and shoes to refrigerators and washing machines, rotisserie chicken to laundry detergent. Probably not today, but they offer samples a lot of the time. They also have cheap hot dogs and pizza at the food court. The Costcos are different too; Texas can carry something different than Maine, Canada and other international ones have some different food court options as well."

"Let's go; you can show me. I'm excited to spend the day with you," Mac said. It didn't matter if they sat on the couch or shopped, he wanted to spend time with Viv.

As they climbed into the car, he finally broached the subject. "Are you okay with last night? I didn't want to push you too far," he said. He watched as a faint blush stole across her cheeks.

"It was perfect, not too far," she said, her cheeks turning even redder.

"Good," he said simply. "Now what should I get for Thomas and D?" he asked.

"You could always give them a joint gift, something for both of them. Maybe something for their wedding if they pick a date by then, or tickets to something. Like a play or an event, or something to do. I don't know if we'll get enough snow, but Thomas likes going snow tubing. Or a class together. One year we gave his parents a pottery class together. I'm not entirely sure what class they could agree on though, so that might be a bad one."

"That's not a bad idea. Maybe I could pay for a vacation, like a weekend getaway?" he wondered aloud.

"Sure," Viv said. She didn't know Mac had that much money that he could pay for a vacation for a friend. "Do you know what you might want to get your uncle?"

"No. I'm hoping something jumps out at me. I have time at least to find something," Mac replied.

Viv nodded, focusing on maneuvering through the parking lot. It was extremely crowded, but she finally found a parking spot on the fringes of the lot. She grabbed one of the carts from the parking lot, thinking it would be easier to get one out here. The corrals were pretty full, the employees in the process of bringing some in.

"Stay close," she said. "I get a guest in with my membership card. If you want to buy anything, just put it in the cart and we'll use my card."

Mac nodded, amazed that all these people were holiday shopping. It seemed like madness; oversized carts and people buzzing about. The noise level was deafening. You could feel the tension, stress, and anxiety in the air. Viv found the air fryer and he reached high to grab it.

"Let's get in line to check out. I'll bring you back and show you the fun of Costco another day when it isn't a madhouse," Viv said, after looking at his face. She began working her way to the cash registers. There were lines stretching far back, both for the cashier lines and self-check-out lines. She wanted to ditch the cart since they only had one item but knew from experience it acted a little like a blocker or shield around them. She really did want to show Mac the joys of Costco, but today was not going to be that day. Taking someone who didn't really go shopping and throwing them in the deep end of Black Friday madness was probably a bit mean. She should have thought it out more but had been eager to spend more time with him.

They finally made it to the front of the line and checked out within minutes. They walked to the car. Viv turned to look at Mac as she put the air fryer in the trunk.

"You don't have to come in for the next one, I know it can be overwhelming. I try to do as much online shopping as possible to avoid stores on Black Friday."

"You must be crazy if you think I'm going to let you go into that madness without me!" Mac exclaimed, his eyes wide in disbelief. Was she out of her mind? The humans here were overcome with stress, greed, desperation, and a sense of urgency. Nothing good ever came from that cocktail mix of emotions. He needed to be there to protect her.

Viv laughed. "It's not that bad. This is Target, I shop here all the time. Just be glad I'm not dragging you to Walmart."

"Why Walmart?" Mac asked. How could it be worse?

"I'm not going in, but it's right over there," Viv pointed out. "Feel free to port in, no one will notice today. Just shadow first so you don't get caught on a security camera. Stay in a corner and watch for a minute. I'm not in a hurry."

Mac looked at her suspiciously but ported into the store. He looked around in disbelief. People were shoving each other, grabbing things out of each other's hands. Children were crying, adults were shouting. Oh, this was much worse. How did the poor employees deal with this? That woman just stole a toy out of someone else's cart! He stayed in the shadows, cloaking himself, and moved the toy back to the original cart. He walked around the store, viewing the insanity. He took video to show to his uncle. Recreating this would be a great addition to some of the lighter punishment levels. Mac ported back to Viv's car.

"I would be eternally grateful if we never experienced this shopping day there. Ever. I feel so bad for the employees there. People were quite rude. I did get some inspiration though. I think I can recreate a punishment level that is perpetually a Walmart Black Friday sale and the souls in punishment have to work there as employees," Mac told her.

He smiled when Viv burst out laughing. "Oh my god. It would be a great punishment! You should Google videos of it later for more ideas. There are some doozies. It's made the news several times.

"I only have a couple of things to get at our next stop, and if the line's not long we can get a coffee while we're here. They have a Starbucks in-store."

"I could use a coffee," Mac said. A large coffee with a shot of whiskey maybe. Or three. He was glad they didn't have anything like this in Netherworld. As bad it was here, adding in hellfire and magic would make it deadly.

Mac looked down as his phone rang.

"Uncle? Is everything okay?"

"Mac! Are you in danger? Do I need to come?" his uncle asked, his voice stressed and worried.

"What? No. Why?"

"You sent a video."

"Oh! I'm out shopping with Viv for Black Friday and she told me how bad this store was. I went to see for myself. That was the video. I'm safe. I was thinking we could recreate it for a punishment level."

"I can see the potential there," his uncle mused. "Okay

then. Have fun. Stay safe. You know how crazy people can get."

"I will. Bye." Mac clicked off.

"Uncle was worried when he saw the video," he explained when Viv looked over at him in question.

Viv shook her head. These guys. "Come on. I'll keep you safe," she teased.

Mac followed her to the store, noting that compared to the other, this wasn't so bad after all.

29

Viv was helping a patron at the desk. They were trying to research how different obscure poisons worked. It would have alarmed her, but they had explained that they were an author and showed her their books as proof. Viv knew the library carried some of them, and sure enough the photo on the book matched with her customer. She wrote dark suspense romance, more along the lines of murder mystery where the detectives find a love interest. She wondered if she could talk the author into having a talk or a signing at the library. It would be great to promote a local author.

She felt a shadow of a brush against her left arm, a signal that Mac needed to talk to her.

"Let me run and see if I can find this for you in the stacks. I also want to talk to you later about maybe doing an event here at the library, if you would be willing. I'll be right back," Viv said, locking her screen and heading toward the stacks. It was usually empty and there were plenty of shadows for Mac to hide in there.

Walking into the stacks, she headed toward where the

book would be located, knowing Mac would be porting in soon. She felt warm arms wrap around her from behind, Mac's scent surrounding her.

"Hm, this is nice," she said, leaning her head back on his shoulder.

"I've got to go to work. I should be back tonight. I was thinking we could go out to dinner tonight? Maybe to this steak place I know? They have cheesecake and chocolate cake on their dessert menu."

"Mm, bribing me with desserts," Viv teased. "I'd like that. Do we need to make reservations?"

"I already did. For eight o'clock. I know it's late, but at least I should be home in time," Mac said, turning her gently around for a kiss.

Viv parted her lips, eager to taste him. His tongue swirled around hers, tangling together. One hand holding her waist, the other cupping the back of her head, he held her close. He pulled back after a minute.

"I've got to go. Be safe. I'll let you know if I'm going to be too late to make dinner. If that happens, I'll reschedule for tomorrow. Your author might like *Grim Sights*, it's more of a Victorian type of book but has arsenic, vitriol, and strychnine poisonings in it. It's not as well known, so she might get a kick out of that." Mac looked at the bookshelf, pulled a book out and handed it to her. Leaning down, he gave her one last kiss and ported out.

Viv looked at the two books, thumbing through the one Mac handed her. It was perfect. She hadn't even known they had this; she didn't think she had ever seen it before. Viv headed back to the front desk.

"Sorry for the wait. There was another book down there that I think will help you as well," Viv said, handing over both books.

"These look perfect, thank you." The woman took the books and sat at a nearby table, using her phone and paper to take notes since they were reference books and couldn't be checked out.

The rest of the day passed pretty smoothly. She had a story time in the children's room, a knitter's group that reserved the meeting room once a week, and a few study groups came in after school let out. It was a good day and she felt content when she locked the doors behind her. Looking at her watch, she had plenty of time to grab a shower and get dressed up a bit for their date.

Things had been going well with Mac. He was making an effort to spend time with her doing all kinds of things, even if it was as simple as helping wash the dishes or cut up vegetables for dinner. They had gone on a couple of dates since the movie picnic and she was getting more comfortable with the idea of becoming his mate. He was sincere in his efforts to prove he was letting go of his bias toward humans.

Pulling into the driveway, she saw the lights on inside. Thomas must have beaten her home today. Opening the garage door, she smelled lasagna.

"Honey, I'm home!" she called out teasingly. She didn't want to walk into another couch scene if she could help it.

"Hey! I thought you had a date tonight? Mac was asking D for advice," Thomas explained.

"We do, but it's later. He needed to go into work, so the reservation's at eight. I'm going to grab a quick snack and then get a shower. It smells amazing in here," she said.

"Yeah? Good. I wanted to do our own little dinner date." Thomas grinned.

"Just make sure you're not getting frisky in the living room when we come home," Viv teased.

"One time! One time in all the years we've known each other. Are you ever going to let that go?" Thomas complained, but he was grinning so it didn't hold much weight.

"Nope," she said, popping the 'P.' She walked back to her room laughing, eating an apple she grabbed off the counter.

She stopped in front of her closet, trying to decide what to wear. There was a cute black handkerchief dress. It was about knee-length at its longest tip, so it would work for dinner. She could dress it up with some silver thread earrings and a pendant. She moved to her dresser next. She wasn't planning on seeing Mac naked again tonight, but she wanted to look nice if she did. Last time she had been wearing pajamas. This time, she wanted to make sure her bra and underwear at least matched. She pulled out a pale pink thong. It had a metal square that connected the two sides that sat right above the swell of her cheeks. It was plain from the front but looked amazing from behind. She had a matching bra, a pale pink with a fine lace overlay. It was lower cut, so it wouldn't show with the dress.

As she waited for the water to heat up in the shower, she debated on washing her hair, knowing it wouldn't dry in time. Taking a sniff, she wrinkled her nose. It smelled like the gyro she had for lunch, which was great for food but not so much for her hair. She would just throw it up and let it be wet, she decided. Viv took time to shower everything, shaving her legs again. When she got out, she dried off and applied lotion. Brushing out her hair, she pulled it up into a bun. She was never very fussy when it came to dressing up. She actually hated makeup, so the most she ever put on was a tinted lip gloss. She threaded the wire through her ears, making sure it hung evenly. The pendant had a bright blue stone, bringing some color to her outfit. She grabbed her lower heels, not wanting to wear tall ones tonight.

Finishing the last few touches, making sure she hadn't missed any strands of hair when she was twisting it up, she looked at her phone. No messages yet, she thought. Yay, the date was still on. She had about a half hour or so until Mac should be home, so she sat in her reading room and pulled out a new book. These were a lower-angst series with paranormals finding love with their fated mates. She liked how the series went through each couple but still kept the previous characters involved in the story.

Getting lost in the words, she startled when there was a knock on her door. Getting up and smoothing the bottom of her dress into place, she answered, finding Mac on the other side. Oh my deliciousness, she thought. He had changed into an all-black suit, black dress shirt, a deep red tie that looked almost black from far away. The suit clung to his shoulders, emphasizing his strong build and slim waist. He looked amazing.

"You look gorgeous," he said, holding out a rose. Its petals matched his tie, the red so deep and dark it was almost black.

"Thank you, so do you. Handsome, I mean. Well, you're gorgeous too," she said, face-palming her forehead. "Ignore me. I don't know why I'm rambling. Thank you for the flower, it's beautiful."

"I'm glad you like it, it's a special one from the Netherworld. I have it spelled so it won't die either," he said.

"It's perfect," she replied, bending to smell it. It didn't smell like a normal rose. It was floral but with slight hints of sweetness like a dark chocolate, and a very slight undercurrent of smokiness. "Oh wow, that's different. I love it." She took another sniff. It was so different than other flowers she had smelled. "Let me put this in a vase and we can go," she said. "Does it need water?"

"No, it will stay like this without water. I grabbed a vase on my way here; D gave me a heads-up that they were having their own date in the kitchen, and I didn't want to disturb them," Mac replied, pulling out a bud vase from behind his back.

Viv placed the rose on her dresser where she could see it easily every day. "How are we going to sneak past them to the front door?"

"The owner of the restaurant is a nonhuman, so there's a portal safe room in the back. I thought we could port there and then we don't have to risk seeing anything we don't want to," Mac said.

Viv laughed. "I already had a talk with Thomas. I guess you heard about the time I accidently walked in on them? I can do without that again," she agreed, taking his outstretched hand.

"Got everything?" Mac asked.

Viv reached over and grabbed her purse and phone off the dresser and nodded. She walked through the portal with Mac and ended up in a seating room of sorts. You could hear the bustle of the restaurant and kitchen, but it was nicely decorated with a loveseat and a couple of uphol-stered chairs to sit in.

Mac placed his hand on a sensor and the door popped open. Stepping out into the hallway, she heard sounds of the kitchen to the left. As they turned to the right and began walking down the hallway, she looked at the different doors. To the left was a large dining room, barely visible through the heavy velvet curtains. They were open just enough to walk through. It was a gorgeous room with leather and dark woods. The booths were high backs, giving the feel of privacy. She imagined they may also help keep the sound down. The tables had plenty of space between them, the dark red leather chairs looking plush and comfortable. There were a variety of sizes, anywhere from a cozy two-seater to a large table that looked like it could fit twenty people. There were a few rounded corner booths as well, probably fitting six to eight. The space had a variety of chandeliers, all clear glass, all different sizes and types. Some looked like octopuses with long dangling crystal strands, others were shaped like a mushroom or a UFO, while others were more traditional. They were bright enough to light the space, but not so bright as to take away from the intimate feel. Continuing down the hallway, they passed the manager's office on the right, another separate dining room on the left, and then the bathrooms on the right. Turning to the left, they entered the waiting and hostess area.

Mac led her to the hostess stand. The woman smiled and Viv thought she saw a brief glance of fangs, but when she blinked and looked closer, they were gone.

"Reservation for Mac," he said, keeping a hand on Viv's lower back.

"Right this way," the hostess replied, leading them back to the room closest to the rear of the restaurant. Viv wondered why they separated the two dining rooms; maybe to keep the noise level down?

They were led to a smaller booth, although it could still fit four people. There was even a sliding door to separate it off from the rest of the room if they desired. The menus were laid on the table.

"Your server will be right with you," the hostess said, this time definitely showing fang.

"Thank you," Mac said. Once she was gone, he leaned

forward, resting his hand palm up on the table, inviting Viv to take it. "So, a few things about this restaurant," he started to explain in a low voice. "Because it's owned by a nonhuman, there are two different clienteles they cater to. It's a five-star restaurant in the human world, and they are served in the first dining room. If you are a nonhuman, you can request to be sat in the back. This is only for nonhumans; if you are a mate or come with a nonhuman, you are allowed in. The food back here can be different than the front, as it caters to a much wider palate. For example, there might be warm blood brought for vampires. Some dishes have foods found only in the different planes like Arlysium and Netherworld.

"I wanted to introduce you to some of my childhood foods, but we can order regular steaks from the other menu as well. We also don't have to be careful what we say here, unless it's about work, so you could ask me any questions that you have or might come up," Mac said, looking a bit nervous.

"She really did have fangs?" Viv asked.

Mac nodded.

Viv leaned back in her seat. She knew Mac would protect her and the restaurant had such amazing reviews, although they were probably all from the human side. She didn't know what to think on this. It was exciting, but at the same time she also had bad experiences with strangers in the nonhuman world.

"Do you want to sit on the other side? We can totally move," Mac asked. Maybe this hadn't been such a great idea, he thought.

Viv took a deep breath. She was doing the same thing she accused Mac of; judging a group by a select few and that wasn't who she wanted to be or even who she was normally. "No, it's fine. I just needed a minute to adjust. I'm sure it's going to be an amazing experience. Will you pick a few things out for us to try? I think I'd like to get a small steak, just so I have something familiar," Viv replied. She figured that having something familiar to fall back on would make trying any weird-looking new dishes better since she would have a backup plan. If they didn't eat it all, she could always bring it home and they could have it for lunch or something.

"That sounds perfect. If it gets to be too much, we can close our table off or leave," he told her sincerely. He wanted this to be a good experience for her, slowly introducing her to the nonhuman side. It was going to be a big enough shock if they visited Netherworld and he wanted to make it as easy as possible for her.

Viv nodded, trying to keep her eyes on him. Now that she knew it was the nonhuman side, she kind of wanted to take another look, but at the same time she didn't want to offend anyone.

Mac smiled. "You can look around, just don't stare. Same as with a human restaurant."

Viv tried her best to casually look around. She didn't want to offend anyone or embarrass Mac. Were those...

"Mac, are those tentacles?" she asked quietly.

He followed her line of sight. "Yup. There are several types of shifters that have them, generally water-based ones."

She glanced away quickly when she saw a tentacle slide under the table to rest between their partner's legs. In the far corner was a Bigfoot-looking creature.

"Bigfoot?"

"There's sasquatch and yeti shifters. There's a spell in here that allows them to be shifted but if a human were to walk by, they would see only their human forms. The manager generally catches them before they make it this far back though."

"So you could eat in your demon form here?" she asked curiously.

Mac nodded.

"I don't think I've seen you fully shifted," Viv said.

"No, not yet. This booth isn't quite big enough for me to fully shift," Mac replied, an apology in his tone. "I could always show you at home, if you wanted," he offered.

"I think I do," Viv answered.

Their server came over and Mac ordered a bottle of wine, a steak and side salad for her. He then proceeded to order in a different language, she assumed from the nonhuman menu.

"How many languages do you know?" she asked.

"A few. I grew up speaking Netherkin and Entiretium since I was near my uncle's work a lot. To be an Enforcer, you need to be fluent in Entiretium and one other common human language. I grew up speaking English since it's widely used. Those three I'm fluent in. I do pretty well in Spanish and French, I know enough of German and Italian to get around. Arabic, just a few key phrases. I have a really hard time in Mandarin, so I only know a few curse words. Most nonhumans will know Entiretium. It's the universal language."

"Do the angels, the Arlysium side, have their own language?" Viv asked.

"They mostly use Entiretium. I'm not entirely sure how the demons came to have their own language; I guess we just wanted to be different," Mac said with a grin.

Their server returned with their wine and a few dishes she didn't recognize. The smells were strange too. Not unpleasant, but strange, not something she was used to. Some of the dishes had covers and she wondered if that was Mac's doing or if they came that way normally.

Mac waited until their wine was poured and it was only the two of them before rearranging the plates. "Okay. I got a few different things, not just Netherworld food. If you don't like something, it's not a big deal. Some things have spices and flavors you won't be used to. Some are going to look weird, but I double-checked that they are all safe for humans to eat. There are a few things that aren't, so don't order unless D or I are with you.

"This is a vegetable, kind of like a combination of an asparagus and a carrot," he said, placing a small piece on her plate.

Viv stared at it. It was blue. Not a dark color that might shimmer blue in a certain light, but a bright cobalt blue. This definitely wasn't a natural food color found in their world. She watched as Mac enthusiastically ate his. She ate a bite, slowly chewing, trying to figure out what it was. It was the texture of steamed carrots, with a hint of that sweetness but there were tones of asparagus and...cabbage maybe? It was also saltier. Viv couldn't decide how she felt about it; she didn't hate it, but it wasn't something she would necessarily order again.

"What do you think?" Mac asked.

"It's okay," she said slowly. "It's not bad, a little salty, but I didn't hate it."

"It's a sea vegetable, which tends to be a little saltier naturally. Okay, next one," Mac said, putting something new on her plate. "This was one of my favorites as a kid. I still like them when I go back home."

Viv stared down at it. It looked like a human heart, only much tinier, about the size of a quarter. It was bright red too. This was a favorite? Viv felt like gagging, but held it in.

"Mac. Please tell me this isn't a heart. I'm going to have to draw the line at that: no hearts, eyes, or brains, please. I don't think I'm that adventurous."

"What? No! No, it's a fruit. I guess it does look like a heart. I never really paid attention before. Uncle has a bunch of these trees growing in his backyard. It's not meat, I promise. I wouldn't order any organs without asking you first," Mac reassured her.

Viv closed her eyes and picked up the fruit. "I just eat it whole?"

"Yup, it's all edible," Mac replied.

She sniffed it. It didn't smell like meat, not that she thought Mac would lie to her, but her brain thought for sure that something that looked like that would smell differently. There were hints of citrus. Viv popped it into her mouth, noting the texture was like a crisp apple, but the flavor was like a cross between a kiwi and an orange. If she ignored how it looked, she enjoyed it.

"If I eat it with my eyes closed, I like it," she joked. "My brain is rebelling at eating it when I can see it," she said.

"I can understand that," Mac replied. "Ready for the next one?"

Viv nodded.

"This one is a warm dish. I grew up on this. It's like…I guess a goulash is the closest description. There's meat, no organs though, noodles, our version of a tomato sauce, and spices," Mac explained.

It looked tasty. The sauce was a deep red, with chunks of meat, what she assumed were vegetables, and small bits of noodles. Taking a spoonful, she gently blew the steam away. Her first bite had flavors bursting against her tongue.

It reminded her of a beef stew or goulash, but the savory notes were much stronger. There were hints of things that reminded her of when she used Cajun seasoning in her dishes. It was delicious and she happily scooped up another bite.

"That was delicious," she said when her bowl was empty. "I would gladly eat that again."

"I'll get the ingredients next time I go back home and I'll make dinner one night for everyone. I'm sure D would like to have it again."

"I'd love that. Thomas would like this too," she said.

"I'm glad you liked it. It's like a comfort food, I think. Makes you feel all warm and cozy. This next one looks weird, but I promise it's okay to eat and it won't be what you expected. Do you want to see it first or try a bite with your eyes closed?" Mac asked.

"No organs?" She clarified.

"No organs, no bugs, nothing weird," he promised.

"I'll try with my eyes closed then," she said, shutting her eyes. She heard some dishes moving around, a fork scraping against the dish.

"Okay, open up and I'll feed you a bite," Mac said.

Viv braced herself for anything from bitter to slimy. She wasn't sure what it was going to be, but it felt and tasted a bit like pasta. With a meat of some kind, like chicken or turkey. There was a sauce, creamy, a little like an alfredo but a smidge spicier. She swallowed, feeling a lingering heat in the back of her throat.

"That one was spicier," she said, opening her eyes. "I couldn't really tell what it was. Pasta? With a meat like chicken and a sauce?"

Mac uncovered a dish. Viv just stared. She had eaten that? It was a good thing she hadn't looked at it. The "pasta" looked like huge worms. The "meat" looked like eyeballs.

"No organs?"

"Nope, just looks weird when it's cooked. This is actually a vegetarian dish. The noodles are made with a traditional pasta press. The round balls are a vegetable that is often used as an alternative to meat given its flavor."

"Maybe breading and frying them would help them look less like eyeballs," Viv said faintly. She didn't want to be a wuss about trying other culture's foods, but she thought that was about the end of her adventurousness for today. Little steps, right?

Mac tilted his head, studying the food. "I guess they do. I never really thought about it, having grown up with it. I never understood why they would keep using that pasta press; they look like worms. You could make them in any other shape, but then it wouldn't be traditional." He shrugged.

He pulled the dishes off to the side, just in time for her steak and salad to come out. He had ordered a steak as well, not wanting her to feel bad if she didn't want to try any of the nonhuman dishes. She did pretty well, he thought. He felt a little bad that he hadn't realized the vegetable and the fruit looked like body parts. He had grown up with them and that was just how they looked. He was planning on ordering a cheesecake for dessert, so it would end the meal on a familiar happy note.

Mac was also eager to get home and show off his demon side. He had been trying to take things slow, letting them get to know each other better. He thought she was much more comfortable with him now, especially after she had seen some of his demon traits pop out the other night.

30

They had finished dinner, the chef coming over to see how they had liked everything. Viv had been happy to meet him, he was very charismatic. She looked forward to going to eat there again. When they got home, Mac had made sure she still wanted to see his demon form. After she reassured him, he said he was going to get changed and he'd be right back. Viv kicked her heels off while she waited. She didn't know if she should change as well, but figured he was changing so he could shift better. He'd probably tear the suit otherwise; it had been made to perfectly fit his human form. There was a knock on her doorframe, Mac standing there in a gray pair of sweatpants. Yum. She didn't think he was wearing any underwear underneath. He was also shirtless, allowing her to see his tight abs and the black bands around his biceps. He had a few that trailed down the back of his arm, stopping at the forearm. She really needed to ask him what those ones were for.

"I'll go as slow as I can and you can tell me to stop at any time, okay?" he asked.

Viv nodded and he took a few steps back.

His skin darkened, making him look tan, his height increasing by several inches, the muscles increasing in size too. He looked much bulkier in this form, but still agile, if that made sense. Which she figured made him good at his job. A pair of horns protruded from the front of his hairline near his forehead, curling more like a ram's than the straighter curve of D's. Even his hair grew a bit longer. His hands had black claws at the end of his fingertips instead of nails. His forearms were sculpted; she never thought of forearms as particularly sexy, but these were doing it for her. She remembered his penis had gotten larger the one time he had partially shifted in front of her and wondered if that was the biggest he got or if he was even larger when fully shifted. She could see the flames licking in his dark eyes. He gave a shudder and a pair of massive black and red wings shot from his back. They were smooth, more like leather, not feathered like she expected. His tail curled around his leg, black with those dark red swirls to match his wings. When she walked closer, she could see his horns were pure black.

"Okay so far?" he asked, a faint hint of fangs showing. He stayed still, letting her walk around him. His tail itched to grab her and pull her close.

Viv nodded, taking him in. His tail was curled around his leg, but she could see the tip flipping much like a cat's tail. "Does your tail always do that?" she asked.

"Um. No. It just really wants to touch you right now," Mac admitted. He didn't want to trigger any memories with his tail, so he was keeping it under control.

"Can I touch it or is it sensitive?" Viv asked, curious. She wanted to get used to it. It was part of Mac, and from what Thomas told her demons quite often used them in sex. She didn't want him to have to keep a part of him locked away.

"Yes to both. It can be sensitive, not as much as other places, but still sensitive," Mac replied. He slowly unwound his tail away from his leg, letting it hang behind him. He held his breath as Viv tentatively reached out, pausing right before she touched it. His would look a little different than D's and that bitch's because every tail, wings, and even horns varied. Just like with humans, they all had the same parts, but they were all slightly different. The whorl patterns on wings and tails could be very prominent or not there at all, horns could be straight, short, tall, or curly. Some were all black, some were red, some were a mix. Tail length, pattern, and even tip design varied. Some like D had a more pointed arrow-like tip, although his had rounded corners, and some were sleek like a cat's. He held still, letting Viv decide what to do. Her hand lightly touched his tail, tracing the patterns on it. He had a lot of similar markings to his uncle, marking them as family. It was just genetics as to which parent you took after for those types of things, and he had taken after his dad, who had been similarly marked to his uncle.

Mac let out a small moan as he felt her hands wrap around his tail, sliding it through her palms. She reached the tip and focused on learning the feel of it. "It's not sharp," she said.

"No. Mine is more streamlined than D's."

Letting go of his tail, she moved to stand behind him, running her hands up his back, fondling the base of his wings. The joints here were sensitive, and he involuntarily humped the air.

"These seem quite sensitive," she said, mischief in her voice. She let one hand slide around to the front of his chest, playing with his nipple before sliding down to tease at the waistband of his pants. Viv couldn't wait to play with Mac, to find what made him tick. Slipping her hand under the waistband, she reached for his cock. It was a bit larger in demon form, which was saying something since he was quite large in human form, but it had ridges and bumps now. Viv loosely gripped him, stroking his cock slowly. Once she had a good rhythm going, she stroked the base of his wings. A groan fell from his lips, his hips thrusting into her hand.

"Viv, I'm not going to last long," he said, clenching his teeth against his rising orgasm. The combination of her hands and the fact that she was touching him in this form had brought it on fast.

She let go of his wing, but kept the hand on his dick, just barely stroking it. She walked to stand in front of him, sliding his sweatpants down, gasping when she saw his demon cock. It had stayed the same skin color as the rest of him, but there were red swirls around it, lighter in color than his wings, but a similar pattern. The head was jutting out of his foreskin. He had gained almost two inches in length and an inch in width. He had ridges along the top and sides of his shaft, with bumps lining the bottom all the way to his balls. His Prince Albert piercing was still there and she wondered what it would feel like on her tongue. She went to kneel in front of him, but realized she wouldn't be able to comfortably reach his cock with his additional height. Viv took his hand and led him over to the bed, gently pushing him to sit down. She worked his pants the rest of the way off, noticing he was hairless in this form. How weird, and cool, was that? Viv knelt between his legs, one hand wrapping around the base of his shaft, giving him a slow stroke as she got comfortable. There was no way she would be able to fit all of him in her mouth, but she was going to give it her best shot.

Viv stuck her tongue out, licking a stripe from the base of his shaft to the tip. She ran her tongue around the barbells of his piercing. In the back of her mind, she wondered how it didn't rip through his skin when he changed forms, his penis larger than in human form. Maybe it magically shifted too? She'd have to ask him when her mouth wasn't about to be full. She looked up at him, finding him watching, hands clenched in the covers. Viv slowly sank her mouth over his dick, taking him as deep as she could until she hit her gag reflex. The girth stretched her mouth as wide as it could go, the ridges and bumps feeling a little strange against her tongue. They were firm, but had some give to them, much like the texture on her dildo.

Bobbing her head up and down, she tried to match the rhythm with her hand. She slid the other one down to cup his balls. It was a different sensation with them being completely hairless. It only took a couple of minutes before she felt his balls draw up and her mouth was filled with his cum. She swallowed quickly, realizing he didn't have a bad taste, a little smokey, a little salty, but not too bitter.

Mac panted for breath, a little ashamed of how quickly he had come. He normally had a lot more staying power than that. But now it was his turn to pleasure his mate. Grabbing her under her arms, he leaned back, tucking his wings in and pulling her with him. When her body was plastered against his, he gently pulled her head down for a kiss, his tongue thrusting deep into her mouth, twisting along her tongue. His hands slid under her dress, cupping her cheeks. He felt a small panty in the way and wanted to see what she had on.

Viv gasped as he rolled them, his arms keeping her safe. He held his body slightly off hers, resting his elbows on either side of her head. Mac bent down, taking her mouth in another kiss before sitting up, straddling her body. He slowly slid her dress up past her waist, groaning in delight when he saw the little thong she was wearing. The pale pink looked amazing against her skin. He sat back, giving her enough room to sit up so he could pull the dress off. Her pert breasts were held in a matching pink bra, though this had some lace detail to it. Mac reached around and unsnapped her bra, tossing it off to the side with her dress. She was perfect, her nipples a darker pink, already hard. He would guess she was around a nice B cup, perfect hand-sized in this form, not quite small enough to fit all the way in his mouth. Cupping her head with one hand, being careful of his nails, he leaned down to kiss her.

She gently bit his lower lip, pulling his tongue into her mouth, teasing him with light strokes. She gasped as he lightly ran a claw against her breast, across the nipple. They were sharp enough to cut, but he was being so delicate that she barely felt any pressure.

Mac pulled back, gently pushing her to lie down. "It's my turn to taste you," his voice rumbled.

Viv wondered if it was possible to orgasm from just hearing his voice like this. It was deeper, rougher, the sound moving through her body. Mac slid the underwear down her legs, climbing off the bed so he could spread her legs and step between them. He knelt on the floor in front of her, bending his head to breathe her in.

"You smell so good, love," he said, his warm breath teasing her lips. His hands slid up her thighs, his thumbs pulling her lips apart exposing her cunt and clit to his view. "Gorgeous," he said, leaning down to take a lick. Viv almost jackknifed with how good that one touch felt. Her hands grabbed his head, urging him to lick her again. His tongue swirled around her clit, just the way she liked it. He must have been paying attention when he watched her masturbate, she thought. Oh god, that was amazing, his fingers sliding into her body, filling her. As he began to thrust gently, he pressed upward and found her G-spot. His hand sped up, thrusting harder and faster, those fingers finding her zone every time, his tongue pressing to her clit, applying just the right amount of pressure. Her climax ripped through her, leaving her body limp.

Viv panted, enjoying the high she was feeling. Mac came up to lie next to her, his big hand resting on her stomach as he lay on his side facing her.

After a few minutes, Mac spoke again. "Did Thomas tell you how demons mate?"

Viv shook her head. "I don't think so."

"There's a vow we say, then we have sex. There's a blood exchange; it can be a bite, or I can just cut the skin and I can lick it, same for you. I need to mark you during climax."

"We both have to exchange blood?" Viv asked, trying to clarify it.

"Yes. Normally I'd bite you, but I can make a small cut if you'd rather do that. I'll cut my chest or arm, whatever's closest and you lick it. It doesn't have to be a lot, just a few drops."

"How do you mark me?" That was the part that sounded the worst to her.

"When you're climaxing, I need to say a quick incantation and place my hand where you want your mark. I'm not entirely sure what it feels like, but I don't think it hurts much. Then you get a black tattoo-looking mark, similar to what Thomas has on his arm."

Viv thought about where she could have it. With her work, she kind of wanted it in a harder to see spot. Thomas' showed with shorter sleeves.

"Arms are traditional, but I was thinking your thigh, higher up on the outside. It would be hidden under everything but a bathing suit, so it wouldn't cause any problems at work. Or back of the shoulder, but it might show with certain dresses. Or your wrist. You could hide it under a watch at work," Mac suggested. The possessive part of him wanted it to be where everyone could see it, but he also knew that she might want it a little more toned down for work purposes.

"I hate to hide it. I'm proud to be your mate. Can we do the wristband one, that way I can show it off when I'm not at work?" Viv asked.

"That sounds perfect," he said, leaning to give her a kiss. As her hands tangled in his hair, brushing his horns, his dick stirred, poking her in the hip.

"Already?" Viv asked, laughing.

"It's a bit sensitive near the horns," Mac told her. He slid a hand down her body, cupping her vulva waiting to see if she was ready for more.

Viv spread her legs, inviting him to touch. Mac slid a finger slowly into her, her body still wet from her earlier arousal. It didn't take much around Mac, he was sweet and his body was a work of art. He knew just how to touch her.

"Can we do it now?" Viv asked on a gasp as he slid another finger in, thrusting deep.

"Are you sure?" Mac asked, not wanting her to regret anything or feel rushed. "There's no hurry," he reminded her.

"I'm ready."

31

Mac's eyes flared bright with flames at her words, bending to take her in a possessive kiss as he held her hands above her head.

"We're doing this in human form for our first time. I don't want to hurt you," he said, his teeth clenched. He was worried his tail might come out to play and didn't know if she was ready for that or not. It would be easier on her body in his human form anyway, he hadn't stretched her enough for his demon one.

Viv watched as between one second and the next, his body returned to the one she was used to. The flames still shown bright in his eyes, his demon taking part in this as well. Mac slid between her legs, the head of his cock pressing just at her entrance.

"Repeat the words I say," he ordered, his voice hoarse with need. "Viv, you are my mate. I give to your keeping my body, heart, mind, and soul. I bind us together forevermore."

"Mac, you are my mate. I give to your keeping my body, heart, mind, and soul. I bind us together forevermore," Viv repeated. She let out a scream as Mac surged forward, impaling her on his dick.

"Oh god. So full, so good. Move, please. Move. Move, Mac!" she ordered, her heels digging into his back, urging him on.

Mac slowly drew back, the barbells pressing into her walls, pressing against that magic spot. "Yes, yes, yes," she chanted as he did it again. This was like nothing she had ever felt before. He supported his body weight with one hand next to her head, his hips pistoning into her, her body welcoming him. He felt like he was made just for her, the width of his penis filling her, the length bigger than anything she had ever played with before. His free hand came to play with her breasts, gently pinching the nipples, making sure to get each one. Mac leaned down, his mouth finding hers, his tongue plunging into her body like his dick was down below.

"Bite or cut, love?" he asked, gasping, his fangs dropping down.

Viv tilted her head to the side. "Bite." She wanted to have the full experience with Mac. A small scream escaped at the sharp pain of his teeth cutting through her skin, but it soon faded as a warmth spread throughout her. The heat rushed to her cunt, increasing her arousal. Mac shifted one hand to his demon claws, cutting his chest. Viv surged up, licking the blood. The angle change sent her climax rushing through her.

"Mac!" she screamed.

He grabbed her left wrist, chanting as a heat engulfed her arm. It felt like a bad sunburn. But it was all forgotten as she heard him shout her name, filling her with his cum.

Mac collapsed over his mate. He could feel her soul now and it was a beautiful thing. They were now tied together and she would live a very long time. He gently pulled out, running to the bathroom to clean her up. No one wanted to change the sheets right now. He also grabbed the healing cream he had brought from home for the mate mark. Sometimes it could be tender afterward.

Viv was lying on her side, looking at her wrist. "It's pretty," she said.

Mac finished cleaning up before looking closer. It was thin enough to be hidden under her watchband. The black swirls had an almost flowery feel, and he was filled with an intense possessive satisfaction to see Mate of Mac written on her skin.

"I brought some cream to put on it. It will help it feel better. Is it very sore?"

"Not really; it feels like a strong sunburn," Viv replied, watching as he gently rubbed it all around her wrist. "Did you get one?"

"I did, see?" Mac pointed to his arm, where a new band had appeared proclaiming him to be Viv's mate. He was surprised to see that some of the swirl work in Viv's had shown up on his as well. It was nice that they matched, he thought.

"You know what this means?" Viv asked.

"What?"

"I can go meet your uncle and hear all the embarrassing stories about you as a kid," she said gleefully.

"That's true. Maybe near Christmas? Netherworld doesn't celebrate it, but it would be fun to still get together as a family. I think D and Thomas were talking about seeing his family too."

"I think they were going for Christmas Eve, leaving Christmas Day at our house with the four of us. Maybe we can go down for a few days? Meet with your uncle, see your house, maybe hang out there with D and Thomas?"

"That sounds like a great plan," Mac said, grabbing his phone. "I'll send a quick text to Uncle and to D, making sure they're both open those days. I think Uncle will rearrange as much as he can so he can meet you. He probably won't be able to get away from work completely, but he'll at least be able to rearrange things to make sure he spends some time with us."

"Sounds good," Viv replied, snuggling into his body to keep warm. Mac reached out with one hand, the other still typing on his phone, and pulled the blanket over her. She rested her head on his chest, arm over his stomach, her leg sandwiched between his. The warmth of his body drew her into sleep.

Viv woke, finding Mac curled around her. She felt like donuts this morning and thought she'd run out and grab some for everyone. She had enough time. Carefully sliding out from under Mac's arm, she grabbed a quick shower and left him a note by his phone.

Walking into the kitchen she saw Thomas leaning against the wall by the coffee maker.

"I'm going to run out for donuts. I was going to bring some back for everyone. Will you and D still be here?" she asked, grabbing her keys.

"I have a late start today, so I will be for sure. I think D should be unless he gets a call. Let me grab my shoes and

I'll go with you. We can get some coffee too. The coffeepot is taking forever today," he complained.

"I'll be out in the car getting it warmed up," she said, pulling on her coat. It was days like this that she was jealous of Mac's heated seats. At least the garage kept the weather off it. That was definitely one thing she didn't miss about the apartment, parking outside and scraping her car off in the winter.

Thomas jumped in a minute later and they headed to her favorite donut place. Luckily it wasn't far and they also had great coffee.

"How's school going? Have the kids hit the crazy Christmas mode yet?" Viv asked. With only a few weeks between Thanksgiving and Christmas breaks, depending on how the holidays fell, she knew the kids historically got really revved up before Christmas.

"It's been okay, but now we're on a week and a half countdown, so stuff's going to get nuts. You remember how it is, hoping there's less homework, waiting to see if you get snow and can go sledding, eager to see what presents you got."

"I do. I remember the last couple of days before break being a time waster, lots of movies and cookies, maybe a book or gift exchange," Viv said.

They pulled into the parking lot. They got out of the car; it was easier that way to see what they had still available if they went into the store. They were pretty early though, so she thought they would still have a good selection, although they were getting close to the morning rush hour. Placing their order, Viv reached out to pay, her coat and shirt sleeves riding up and showing her new mate mark.

"Cool ink," the cashier told her.

"Thanks," Viv replied with a smile.

Thomas gasped and grabbed her wrist. "When did this happen?"

"I'll tell you about it later," Viv said. If she said last night, the cashier would wonder how it was so well healed since they had tats themselves. Normal tattoos didn't heal that quickly.

"I can't wait," Thomas said with a look.

They moved off to the side to wait for the coffees to be made and the donuts packaged. It was pretty crowded, the early morning workers grabbing their breakfast. They called Viv's name and they grabbed their donuts and the drink carrier.

As soon as they were in the car, Thomas turned to her. "Now dish. When did that happen?"

"Last night," Viv said, her cheeks heating.

"And how was it?" Thomas asked, smirking.

"Good. Amazing. Ten out of ten, would recommend," Viv laughed.

"Any tail action?"

"Thomas! No. Not yet. Maybe one day. I did touch it though, so I don't think I'll be scared of it, but who knows," she said with a shrug. She could feel her face heating. "Did you get a chance to talk to D about Christmas? Mac sent him a message."

"Yes, I did and we already talked to D's parents as well. They'd love to meet you officially. I mean there was a brief introduction at the engagement, but it's not like you guys really got to know each other well. And don't try to change the subject. Give me, I want to see it better," Thomas demanded, holding out his hand.

Viv sighed but gave him her arm.

"It's so pretty! Does Mac's match?"

"It does, his doesn't have as many swirls, but there's a few. His is on his arm with the other bands."

"I think yours is perfect, you can wear a bracelet or your watch to work and no one would know it's there and then you can show it off later."

"That was my thought too." Viv grinned.

Neither one of them paid much attention to the person walking by staring into their windows.

32

Viv looked at the note, all the blood draining from her face.

You shouldn't have accepted him as your mate. Now his sins will be wrought upon you.

"Ma'am. Are you alright? Was I wrong to give it to you? The man just said to give it to the woman librarian. I'm so sorry." The boy scrambled for his phone. "Should I call 911?"

"No. No, it's not anything wrong you did. He isn't a nice person though, so if you see him again, you need to stay away from him, okay?" Viv said, trying not to spook the child. It wasn't his fault some asshole used him to get a message through the library's wards.

She grabbed her phone; she called Thomas and then Liam. Thomas hadn't gotten any messages at work. Liam promised to come get the note. She wanted to call Mac, but she was going to wait until Liam and her boss arrived. She would wait until she was on the way home to call Mac. She knew he was on a job and didn't want to distract him, especially if this note had anything to do with it.

Liam came in, maybe ten minutes later. He must have sped on his way over, his partner coming in behind him.

"Thank you for coming, I wasn't sure who else to call. Mac is out on a case, and I didn't want to disturb him if he's in the middle of something," Viv said.

"Can you tell us what happened? I'm Gina, I'm not sure if you remember me or not," she said, holding out her hand to shake.

She vaguely remembered seeing both of them at the hospital when they came to check on her and assure her the fifth man had been caught as well, but so much of that time was a feverish blur. "It's nice to meet you again," Viv replied, shaking her hand. "Mac put wards over the library, the parking lot, and my car. We have them at the house too. I don't know if this person has been trying to get to me before and couldn't because of the wards, but they sent a child in with the note."

"Is the kid still here?" Gina asked.

Viv nodded. "He's over at that table, red beanie hat. I don't know his name, but he's in here a lot after school. His mom should be here in a few minutes to pick him up."

"I'll go see if he can call his mom so I have permission to talk to him. I want to get a description of the man while it's still pretty fresh," Gina said before walking over and crouching down to the boy's height. Viv kept an eye on them, not wanting him to be frightened.

"Do you have the note? I can try to grab fingerprints off it, see if it hits anything in either of the databases."

Viv handed over the note and the envelope. She did not want to keep it and was happy to get it away from her.

"Did you let Mac know?" he asked, sealing it in a plastic evidence bag.

"I will. I was going to wait until I was on my way

home," Viv replied. Liam gave her a look. "I promise I will let him know! He's been tracking someone they think is a serial killer and I don't want to distract him if he's in the middle of something."

"Fair enough. Let D know at the very least so he can be more aware. Did Thomas get anything?" Liam asked.

"No, I called him, but he didn't get anything. I don't think it has to do with the kidnapping, I think it's one of Mac's other cases," Viv answered. She watched as Gina handed the phone back to the boy, pulling out a pad of paper, taking notes as the boy answered. It looked like she might be sketching as well.

"I can work through the human and nonhuman channels, so I want you to call me if something else comes up," Liam said, bringing her attention back to him.

"Do you think he'll send something else?" Viv asked, worried.

"I don't know. But if you get any calls, messages, anything that seems weird, you call me. Here's Gina's number too, if for some reason you can't get ahold of me. Sometimes I don't get great reception if I'm in certain parts of Arlysium or Netherworld. Gina stays back in the human world while I'm there, so we don't miss anything important. Call her if you can't get me, okay?"

"I will, thanks."

Gina came over, a rough sketch in her hand.

"He had a decent memory," she said, holding out the sketch. "Do you recognize this guy?"

Viv looked at the paper, trying to think back to everyone she had run into lately, coffee shop, grocery store, post office. She shook her head slowly. "I don't think so. He doesn't look familiar."

"Okay. It's probably not a perfect fit, but it might be

close. I'll see if we can grab any video footage from the surrounding areas. He's tall, but of course that's coming from a child, so I'm not sure how tall. Blond hair, brown eyes. They could be hazel, kids often just say brown. No scars or tattoos that he could see. White guy. I know it's not the best, but it's better than we had to start with. I'll let you know if we find anything on the video," Gina promised.

"Thank you both," Viv said, breathing a sigh of relief. Just knowing that someone would be looking into it made her feel better.

She pushed it to the back of her head, other than apologizing to the mother when she rushed in to pick up her son. Viv immersed herself in work for the rest of the day. As she walked to her car, she kept her car keys in her hands, eyes looking all around. She didn't see anyone loitering outside the library's grounds. Getting in her car, she locked the doors and buckled in before taking out her phone to send a text to Mac. She figured it wouldn't distract him as much as a phone call and he could call when he was free.

Hey. Someone delivered a threatening note to work today. Liam took it and is looking into it. I hope you're being safe. Love you.

Viv hit send before smacking herself. She hadn't said 'I love you' to him in person yet.

Her phone rang right away, the screen showing Mac's image on the caller id.

"Hello," she answered.

"What kind of note?" he asked right away, anger and fear in his voice.

"It said something along the lines of I shouldn't have taken you as my mate and that your sins would be wrought upon me."

"Shit. I have a serial killer leaving notes with old-fashioned words like wrought. Any visuals?"

"He gave the note to a boy to bring in. He gave a description to Gina and she made a rough sketch. Blond hair, brown eyes, no visible scars or tattoos. Gina said kids often say brown for hazel or brown, they don't really differentiate. While the boy said he was tall, Gina wasn't sure exactly what that would be. She's looking for video footage from the surrounding areas trying to see if she can find someone who matches the description. I didn't recognize the sketch, but if it was just someone I passed on the street, I don't think I would remember them. He was average looking," Viv told him.

"I'm coming home tonight," Mac said.

"You don't have to," Viv protested. "The case is important and if it's the same guy, you'll solve two cases at once."

"I need to hold you tonight," Mac told her. "I ran into a dead-end today anyway, so a break overnight will be good. I'll grab dinner for everyone on the way home."

"I can't wait to see you. I could use a hug," Viv admitted.

"By the way, I love you too," Mac said, laughter in his voice.

"It just slipped out, what a horrible way to tell you the first time. I do love you though," she said.

"I know. You wouldn't have accepted me as your mate if you didn't," Mac replied. "I'll see you tonight. I need to wrap a few things up before I can come home."

"Be safe," Viv said.

She felt better after having talked to Mac. She missed him in their bed. This case had kept him out late or leaving early, he hadn't spent an entire night with her in days. Maybe they could have some sexy times tonight, she thought with a grin. She had an almost sheer black dress with slits up to her hips. It was really more lingerie but was cut like a dress. That should get his attention. She loved having a plan.

33

"Hi, I have a delivery for a Viv?" a person in a brown uniform said as they stepped up to the desk, holding a box from a local florist.

"I'll take it," Viv said. Maybe Mac had sent her something, she thought with a smile. He had been away a lot lately with work. He promised he had someone who would cover any of his open cases from December twenty-first through December twenty-sixth. They were planning on being in Netherworld from the twenty-first to the twenty-fourth. Christmas Day would be spent at their house, just the four of them.

Carefully opening the box, she saw a bunch of white lilies, which she thought was a little weird. They were popular at Easter and funerals. Picking up the note, she started to read. Dropping the note, she called for the delivery driver to wait.

"Sir! Wait please. Did you see who wrote the note or sent the delivery?" she asked, heart pounding.

"No, sorry. I just deliver. The front desk might

remember though. You can call and see," the man said before leaving.

Viv sighed and picked up the phone to call Liam again. Poor guy was going to hate seeing her number. She needed to get him and Gina something for Christmas as a thank-you. Maybe Mac would have some ideas.

"Liam here," his deep voice answered.

"It's Viv. I am so sorry to bother you again. There was a flower delivery today and another note. Delivery driver said he didn't know who sent it, but maybe the front desk would."

"Can you take a picture of it, including the store information on the box and send it to me? We'll stop by the store and question the cashier and see if they have any video footage. After that we'll stop by and grab the flowers and note. Don't let anyone else touch it."

"Thanks. I'm sorry to be causing you so much extra work," Viv apologized.

"Not your fault," Liam reassured her. "It's people being assholes that are making us have extra work. It seems to ramp up near the holidays. We're going to be in the area looking into something else anyway. I'd stick to the library grounds from now on though. This is the second delivery in as many days, so he might be ramping up. At least in the library you're safe."

"I will," Viv promised. She took several pictures of the box, the flowers, and the note and sent them off to Liam. She sent them to Mac as well, letting him know that she had talked to Liam about it. Mac was convinced it was related to one of his open cases and was working hard trying to hunt the person down. He had made her promise to keep him in the loop.

'Do you think you can stand against me? You're just

human.' The note hadn't been signed but was clearly written by a nonhuman. That paired with the funeral flowers, made her think it was more of a death threat.

Viv was determined to finish out her shift. The library was protected. Plus, she didn't want to take more time off work. Her boss had been very understanding when she had been abducted and then had time off for recovery. He hadn't raised a fuss over her taking time off to see out-of-town family for Christmas either.

"Deep breaths, Viv," a voice instructed. She hadn't even realized she was hyperventilating. She hadn't had a panic attack in so long, she thought sadly. She dropped her head low, concentrating on her breathing, slow inhale, slow exhale, counting to ten, then to twenty. She felt her pulse slow down to normal, her breathing coming a little steadier.

"Are you okay?" Beth, the part-time shelver, asked.

"Yeah, just a tiny panic attack. Thanks for stepping in," Viv said. Everyone at the library knew she had been abducted and injured. In the beginning they had all made a point to check in with her several times a day, but it had slowed as she adjusted back to work. It had been nice of them. She was just grateful that Beth had been there to pull her out of it today. She hadn't even realized she was sliding into a panic attack.

"Is everything okay?"

Viv nodded. "Just something with the case," she fibbed. She couldn't very well tell her that another nonhuman might be targeting her because of her boyfriend's work.

"Are those funeral flowers?" Beth asked, eyeing the box. When Viv nodded, she got an angry look on her face. "Someone sent those to you?"

"Just a few minutes ago," Viv said.

"Do I need to call the cops? I can call Ted if you need to leave?" Beth offered.

"No, I'm fine here. Being home alone would just be worse," Viv admitted. "I did call the police officer taking care of the case. He's on his way to get the flowers and talk to the floral shop."

"Okay. Call if you need anything. I'm here until three o'clock," Beth said.

"Thank you," Viv replied, touched. She had a good group of people here.

Viv vigorously rubbed her face, shaking out her arms. She sent a quick text message to her therapist, asking if she could get an appointment soon. She had been only going two or three times a month lately, but thought she probably needed to talk to her more frequently with all this going on. Especially if the panic attacks were coming back.

There was a surge around three o'clock when several schools got out. She walked around making sure there weren't any kids trying to do things behind the back rows, helped a few find references for homework, and directed the tutoring kids to the conference rooms. Of course, that's when Liam came in. She tried to finish with the kids as quickly as possible, while still helping them find what they needed.

"Hey Liam. Sorry for making you wait. It's always busy after school."

"No problem. I think it's great that they have someplace to go, especially if they can get help with homework and stuff. Did anything else happen today?" he asked.

"No, it was just the flowers and the note. Here," Viv said, handing it over.

She watched as Liam took a subtle sniff.

"Anything?" she asked.

Liam shook his head. "Too many scents here to tell. I'll dust this one for prints too, see if he left any behind this time. The other note was clean. The cameras were a bust, he either evaded them, or had his head positioned perfectly not to be seen. The only thing we did get was that he is tall, probably about six foot. We're trying to see if the footage is any better near the florist, but my hunch is that he's too smart to let his face be caught on camera.

"Mac reached out and let me know about his case. I've heard about it. This guy's been active for years, but he always metes it out far enough between that no one put the cases together. For some reason, maybe just because he thought he could, it ratcheted up this year. He's already had four kills this year alone. He's rumored to have hundreds under his belt. You need to stay alert and if you go out, keep Mac or D with you. Otherwise stick to your warded areas. I know Mac will catch him and I'll help in any way. Call me or Gina if anything seems off, okay?"

Viv nodded. "Thanks, Liam."

As she got off work, she called Thomas. "Hey, I was feeling like pizza tonight. Are you and D going to be home?"

"Yeah, and pizza sounds great. I'll place the order so you can get home faster. When you get home you can tell me what happened. And don't tell me nothing. I can hear it in your voice and pizza is one of your comfort foods."

"Stupid best friend instincts," Viv muttered under her breath.

"I heard that," Thomas said.

"I know. Fine. I'll tell you when I get home. Get the wine ready."

"Where's Mac then?" Thomas demanded. "That's twice this psycho has targeted you because of him and he's not even here."

"That's not fair, Thomas. He's trying to hunt down leads. He's working with Liam and Bert too. He comes home, it's just at weird hours. Sometimes he comes to the library and sleeps in the shadows to stay near me when he can. It's not his fault this guy is targeting me."

"It's because Mac is hunting him," Thomas pointed out.

"Because he's killing people. Do you want him to just be allowed to kill whoever he wants?" Viv asked, getting angry now.

Thomas just huffed. D was smartly staying out of it, washing dishes in the kitchen. By hand. One at a time.

"Did you blame D when we were kidnapped? When we were tortured and I was almost raped? Because of his work. Did you blame him? Huh?" Viv snapped, regretting the harsh words almost instantly, but she was tired of Thomas placing the blame on Mac. They had already been arguing about this for several minutes.

Thomas looked at her, his face stricken. He slowly shook his head.

"And neither did I. Mac and D help protect everyone. That's their job. Even if Mac dropped the case and gave it to someone else, who's to say that the guy would leave me alone? I could gain a stalker from someone coming into the library, who's to say that a killer hasn't come in before? Is it my fault then because I did my job? No. Just like it wasn't D's fault, and this isn't Mac's fault. It's the assholes who cause the problems, it's their fault," Viv said, running out of steam.

She stood up, taking her wine glass into the kitchen. "I'm sorry, D. I was mad, but I never thought it was your fault," she said softly, standing next to him.

"I know. Part of my job is being able to tell lies. We're okay, I promise. I think maybe it might be how he needed to hear it. You and I know it's not Mac's fault, and I think Thomas does too, but Mac is an easier target to blame than some mystery person," D said, wrapping her up in a hug. "Do you need me to call Mac?"

Viv shook her head. She knew he was on the other side of the country right now, looking through the physical evidence of some of the earlier cold cases left in this guy's wake. "I'm okay. I'm just going to go to bed," she said, hugging him back. "I love ya, big guy. You're the best."

Viv walked past Thomas, still mad at him but not wanting to argue anymore. "Love ya, T. Night."

34

Viv woke up the next day, dragging, her eyes feeling like they had been attacked by sandpaper. She had a hard time sleeping last night. Every creak the house made, every time the furnace turned on, woke her up. She knew the house was warded and no one could get her here, but her base brain apparently didn't get the memo. Grabbing a shower made her feel a little more human, Viv snorted at the thought. She pulled her hair into a messy bun and called it done. She needed a big influx of caffeine to make it through the day. Mac hadn't come home last night, which probably also caused her to not sleep well. She had gotten used to his heat in bed in a very short time and had a hard time sleeping when he wasn't there.

Walking out into the kitchen, she saw Thomas waiting for her, a cup of coffee and a travel mug ready to go.

"I'm sorry," he said. "I know it's not Mac's fault, but I'm scared for you. D gave me the nicest lecture last night." He sniffed.

"I'm sorry too. I lost my temper. I never, ever thought it was D's fault."

"I know. Now give me a hug so we can make up," Thomas demanded, opening his arms and making grabby hands.

"I hate it when we fight," Viv said, grabbing Thomas in a tight hug.

"I made you a coffee for here and one for work. Both have your favorite peppermint mocha creamer in it. Your bagel's almost done."

"Thank you. I love you, you know that?"

"I do. Just like you know I love you. Promise you'll call me, D, Liam, Mac, anyone, if something seems weird," Thomas demanded.

"I will. I'm safe on library grounds, in my car, and here. I'm just going to go to work and home until it's over. I don't want to take any unnecessary risks. I figured we can get the groceries or food delivered and the wards won't let anything unsafe through."

"That sounds like a good plan," Thomas agreed.

Viv ate her bagel, leaning against the counter, her hip resting next to Thomas'. She really did hate when they argued.

"Thank you for breakfast. I better go or I'll be late," Viv said, giving him a kiss on the cheek.

She kept checking her mirrors, seeing if anyone followed her from home, but she didn't notice anything unusual. She also figured the guy would want to stay away from the protective demons that lived in their house. Pulling into work, she breathed a sigh of relief to be under an additional ward.

Walking in, she turned on the lights, getting the computers woken up and everything ready for the library to open. It would be a good day, she said to herself. If she said it enough, she might believe it. Midmorning, she felt her shadows return and turned down the lights near the help desk, creating shadows closer to her for Mac to hide in. She felt a brush against her skin and popped in an earbud. It was times like this that she really wished telepathy was a thing, but Mac said that wasn't one of his powers. There were very few people who had that gift, according to D and Mac.

"I missed you," she said softly. If anyone noticed her talking to herself, the earbud would make them think she was on the phone. Not the most professional response, but she also didn't know a better way to talk to her shadowy boyfriend. After the last couple of days, she didn't care what it looked like either, she really needed to talk to him and be near him.

"Are you okay?" she asked. There was a light touch on her right arm, signaling yes. "I'm glad." She paused but figured D or Liam had already told him. "There were lilies and a note delivered yesterday. Liam collected them. Thomas and I got in a stupid fight, but we made up this morning. I'm going to stick to the house and work," she promised.

She felt her legs being embraced in a hug. "Why don't you grab some sleep? I know you must be exhausted. I can keep the lights dimmer so you can sleep behind the desk with me." Another touch to her right arm made her smile. "I love you, sleep tight." Viv smiled as she felt a brush against her lower back, their signal for "love you." She could work like this, knowing her mate was close. Just feeling him in the same space made her feel calmer and safer.

It was after lunch in the middle of the afternoon when the phone rang again. Viv answered her standard response. "Thank you for calling the library, how may I help you?"

A male voice chuckled. The sound sent shivers down her body, her hand reaching back into her shadows, trying to wake Mac. She felt the shadows draw closer, wrapping around her.

"You and your blasted mate can both die," the voice said. "But he's harder to kill. You're much easier, just a puny little human. Do you know how many of those I've killed?" he asked, glee and fond memory in his voice.

Looking down, she saw Mac text Liam. *Killer on phone to Viv at library. See if can trace.* She knew Mac wanted to rush outside and see if he was there, but she was grateful that he had stayed with her.

"No, and I don't particularly want to," she said, trying to keep him on the line to give Liam the best chance of tracking the call. "I'm sturdier than I look."

"Oh, I've heard all about how you survived an attack from a few of us. That demoness was beautiful to watch in action. Did she show you her barbed tail attachment? That was a particular favorite of mine to observe. It was an amazing piece of equipment. The person she impaled would scream and cry, it would rip them up so good, blood would just start pouring from them sometimes. She accidently killed one or two when she got a little too enthusiastic. Some of the others with her were amateurs, but she was the real deal. I was sorry to hear she was gone. It just means the rest of us need to up our game to fill the void left behind. She and her mate used to make the most delicious videos. Hmm, those were good times. I bet you looked delightful as they held you for her. I wish I could have seen it. Umm," he moaned into the phone, the rhythmic sound of skin on skin making it clear he was jerking off to the memories.

Viv felt like vomiting. At least they hadn't recorded her;

Mac and Liam's teams had torn apart the house and the building and found nothing like that.

"You can tell the lovely detective trying to trace this call, that he's out of time. I'll be going, and I'm not close by."

Viv slowly hung up the phone. She grabbed her cellphone and typed a message to Liam. *He hung up. Knew you were trying to trace it.*

Mac wrapped himself around her, the shadows probably looking odd if anyone looked behind the desk, but she couldn't bring herself to care at the moment. She needed the comfort, to know that he was there for her.

"Are you able to stay home tonight?" Viv asked softly. She didn't want to demand he stay home, especially if there was a chance he could stop the guy now, but she needed to feel him in bed next to her. She felt the touch on her right arm and felt some of the tension in her body relax. Maybe she could get a full night's sleep tonight.

A patron came to the desk, asking for help finding something, helping distract Viv from the phone call. She had never been more grateful for the after-school rush. It kept her busy until closing, Mac shadowing her into the break room, where he finally took his solid form.

"Hey, love," he said, grabbing her in a tight hug. "Are you okay?"

"Not really, but I'm okay because you're here. I had a hard time sleeping last night without you."

"I'm sorry. We thought we had a solid lead. He's been at this a long time and has left fake trails and solid-looking leads everywhere. Some of them are part of his crimes, but they're scattered about. It's like finding a needle in a haystack," Mac said. He was beyond frustrated with the case and now the asshole was targeting his mate and Mac couldn't find him to keep her safe. It was eating at him. He had lots of help on this case, and no one was having much luck. "Let's go home. Eat some dinner, snuggle, and go to bed," he suggested. He was exhausted and he knew Viv was as well.

Viv nodded, holding him a bit longer before letting go and stepping back to grab her coat and purse from her locker. Mac followed her out, watching around the area, using all his senses to see if they were being watched. It seemed quiet out for now.

Thomas and D weren't home yet, so Viv just heated up some frozen soup that she had made earlier in the month. She set the other container to thaw in the fridge in case they wanted some when they came home. She just wasn't in the mood to create a big meal, or even throw together something simple. She knew Mac had to be weary and exhausted. The case had been taking him all over the place. Luckily, he had been many places during his life and knew people everywhere, so he could open a portal most of the time. The ones where he couldn't, he had been porting to a nearby town or airport and renting a car and driving the rest of the way. It sounded horrible.

As the soup heated in the microwave, they changed into pajamas. Viv wanted to be comfortable and warm after today. They ate in relative silence, but Mac placed his toes over hers, keeping them in contact the whole time. She got a ding from Thomas, the text message saying he and D were going to go see a movie, if they wanted to go. She told them to have fun, but they were probably just going to go to bed.

Carrying the dishes to the sink, she rinsed them off and stuck them in the dishwasher to run later. She let out an undignified squeak when Mac swept her up into a bridal carry and brought her into the bedroom. He laid her on the bed, his hand resting lightly on her waistband, his eyes asking if she wanted more. Viv pulled her top off, giving him her answer. Mac carefully removed her pants before taking his own clothes off. He crawled between her legs, kissing her gently as he slid into her body. It was slow and sweet, something they both needed. As their orgasms faded, Mac drew the covers over them. Viv leaned over and grabbed her pajamas off the floor, putting them on before snuggling in. It was awfully cold to sleep naked right now.

Curling up against Mac's warmth, she fell asleep, his arms holding her tight.

Viv strained against the cuffs, her body spread eagle. The men surrounding her, their penises out and aroused at her suffering. She heard them laughing, taunting her. A whip here, a sting there, biting. When she started to fade, a sharp smack to her face brought her back.

"Hold her down. It's my turn now," the female said. Viv couldn't see much, but she knew this was going to hurt. Hands held her body open, despite her attempts to close her legs, to keep them out. She felt the barbs cut into her skin. This time there was no saving her. The metal-tipped tail shoved its way inside impaling her body. She screamed as she felt her body being shredded by the thrusts, her blood spilling onto the floor. The tail pulled out, whipping across her body, leaving traces of her own blood everywhere. The big guy was suddenly back, forcing his cock into her broken body as the others held her mouth open for theirs, others jerking off on her, kicking her ribs, shoving their fingers into any hole they could find, even the ones left by the bites.

"Viv! Viv! Wake up. Dammit, wake up!" a harsh male voice ordered. She knew that voice though. That voice was safe. Someone was shaking her, and then a gentle kiss pressed to her forehead. That didn't make sense. No one kissed her here. No one was gentle.

"It's not real, Viv. Come on, come back. I'll make us sundaes."

Sundaes? She frowned. Thomas wasn't here, D had rescued him. There was no food, no water, certainly no ice cream. She whimpered as she saw the men getting ready to change position, the scorpion tail coming toward her.

"NOW, VIV!" the first voice, the safe voice demanded.

She felt a grabbing sensation along her mate bond to Mac. It was like he was reeling her to him. She felt her eyelids flutter as she got closer and closer to him.

"That's it, that's my girl. Come on, you can do it," she heard Thomas say in his teacher voice.

She felt like she was in quicksand, but she clawed her way to being awake. She could feel her harsh breathing and the tears tracking down her face. Mac was leaning over her, his face the first thing she saw. A sob escaped as she pulled his head down to her, burying her face in his shoulder, breathing in his scent, letting it wash over her and anchor her in the now.

"It's okay. It was a dream, it's not real," he murmured over and over. He wrapped his arms around her, pulling her body into his, and then sitting up, putting her in his lap. Thomas walked over, tears in his eyes as well. He wrapped his arms around her and Mac, holding her tightly. He pressed a kiss to her head before letting go.

"I'm going to go get those sundaes ready. Maybe some Irish coffee too," he said, his voice thick with emotion.

Viv nodded, squeezing his hand before she let go. The door shut behind him.

"Do I need to call your therapist?" Mac asked softly. He'd pay any amount of emergency fee there was to get her help tonight if she needed it.

Viv shook her head. "I'll call her in the morning." She rested there, head on his shoulder, arms wrapped around him. She could hear his heart still racing. "I was back in the building. But this time she got the chance to finish. The first big guy, the one who left, he was there and went next. They held my mouth open and forced their fingers everywhere," she said, tears falling again, her breath hiccupping.

Mac held her tighter. "Okay. Let's do that exercise, see if that helps." He wasn't sure what else to do but didn't want to let her go. She was clinging to him like he was her only lifeline. It had been like this during the really bad nightmares right after the kidnapping as well. Her therapist had taught him how to do this exercise.

"Five things you can see?" he asked.

Viv opened her eyes. "You, the picture frame of Thomas and me at graduation, my rose, the comforter, my dresser."

"Good. Four things you can touch."

"You," Viv said, rubbing his back with one hand before moving it. "The bedspread, your pillow, the side table," she added as she stretched her arm out.

"Three things you can hear?"

Viv listened. "Your heart," she said with a faint smile. "The furnace, Thomas in the kitchen."

"That's awesome. How about two things you can smell?"

"You. Sweat." She needed a shower. Eww.

"You're doing so good. One more. One thing you can taste."

Viv leaned up, giving Mac a kiss. Nothing passionate, no tongues involved, just a press of her lips to his. She licked her lips as she pulled away. "You."

"How do you feel now?" Mac asked.

"A little better, not like I'm stuck in the dream."

"Let's try one more. Breathe in for five seconds. Now hold it. Good. Slowly let it out. One more time. In. Hold it. Let it out," Mac said, breathing with her.

Viv concentrated on her breathing, feeling the last of the dream fall away. "Okay. I think I'm ready to go out. Do you think I can grab a quick shower first? I feel gross."

"I'll go let Thomas know you'll be a couple minutes. I love you," he said, pressing a kiss to her forehead.

"Thank you," Viv said, breathing him in one more time.

She didn't even wait for the water to get really hot; it was warm, but not her normal temperature. She just wanted to wash the grossness of the night off as quickly as possible. She ran the soap over her body, scrubbing her hair roughly with shampoo. Viv paused, reminding herself that it wasn't real, that most of the dream hadn't happened, the stalker/serial killer's words just bringing back old fears. She still slid her hand to her vagina, making sure there were no rips. Taking a deep breath, she felt around her anus, breathing a sigh of relief when the hole was still small, no tearing, no bleeding present, no large scars that would have been left behind by the dreamed attack. Stupid brain. The real attack had been bad enough, she didn't need her brain to make it even worse.

She quickly dried off, pulling on new clothes, and left her bedroom to surround herself with her friends, her family. And gorge herself on sugar.

35

Viv opened the envelope, dread in her heart. There was a feeling of evil to it. Sliding open the flap, she tilted the envelope, not wanting to reach inside. Photos of dead people spilled out. Some of the photos were clearly old, they were in black and white but were yellowed and a little grainy. Some were polaroids. Others were more vibrant, newer. There were men, women, even a few children. All of them horribly, painfully dead.

Don't worry. These are some of my copies. I still have all my originals. I can't wait to add you to my collection, the note that fell out with the photographs read.

Viv picked up the phone.

"I'm on my way," Liam said in lieu of a greeting, hanging up quickly.

She used a ruler and gently pushed the photographs back into the envelope. She would let Liam look through them all. Maybe she needed to start wearing gloves when she opened or accepted mail, she vaguely thought. Not that they had had much luck pulling prints or fibers from anything so far. The guy was smart, she admitted. But maybe he didn't use to be so smart; some of these pictures were very old. Maybe they would get lucky and find something on one of them.

It took about fifteen minutes before Liam and Gina ran in. Viv nodded to the envelope.

"It's pictures this time. They're rather graphic," she warned. Both to prepare them, but also to let them know to be careful not to let the library patrons see. Gina nodded, pulling on a pair of gloves and laying out a plastic sheet. Liam pulled some on as well, but let Gina touch the envelope.

"Any other incidences today?" he asked.

Viv shook her head. "No. Not even a phone call. Every call has been normal. The delivery driver dropped this off a few minutes ago. There's a note inside with the pictures. Some of them look quite old, others are clearly newer," Viv said. She fell quiet, letting them look through each one, flipping them over, looking for notes, blood, pieces of hair, anything that might be an additional clue. She noticed they kept everything over the plastic, probably to collect anything that might fall off.

Gina sighed and slid the photographs back in the envelope, sealing it in an evidence bag. She slid the plastic sheet and their gloves into another one. "Nothing obvious I can see, other than this guy is sick. There's no pattern, nothing that I can see that ties them all together other than the assumption that they're all human. We don't even have a lot of bodies to do DNA tests to confirm that. At least the photographs will give us a chance to try to close some old missing persons reports. I'll send copies over to cold cases and the FBI, see if they can get started on them."

"I have a patrol car passing by the library and your neighborhood, day and night," Liam told her.

Viv nodded, not sure what else to say. The cops were mostly human and wouldn't stand a chance against him, but there were a few nonhumans like Liam and Gina on the force, so maybe he had assigned one of them. "Thank you."

Viv drove past the library, slowing down to turn into the parking lot. It looked like something was on the sidewalk near the parking lot entrance. It was still a little dark out, making it hard to see and she wasn't dumb enough to get out of her car to look at it. She pulled inside the lot but parked close to the entrance. It had looked like an animal, and she wanted to make sure it wasn't hurt. She would stay on the warded side of the property but could at least call animal control if it needed help.

As she walked closer, there was a strong smell and she had a feeling about what she would find. She gagged, holding a hand in front of her mouth when she saw the poor animal. She thought it was a cat, but it was so mangled and torn apart that it was hard to tell. The head was sitting a few feet away from its body, the spinal cord still attached. It was like someone had ripped it out. Viv sobbed, knowing it was the stalker/serial killer.

Pulling out her phone, she called Liam.

"Hello?" his groggy voice answered.

"There's a... I don't know. A cat maybe. It's been killed in front of the library," Viv told him, tears still running down her face.

"Viv, I'm sorry a cat died, but that's not really my jurisdiction," Liam said gently, still sounding half-asleep.

"This one is. It's been mutilated and it was left close to the parking lot entrance on the way I turn into the lot. I think it's a message from the killer."

"Are you outside the ward?" Liam asked, sounding much more alert.

"No. I'm on the safe side. People are going to start coming in soon. What should I do? Should I go out and try to clean it up?"

"No! That's what he wants you to do, to leave the safety of the property. Gina lives close by and runs in the morning. Let me see if I can reach her. Do not leave the property. Do you hear me?" Liam asked, sounding like he was pulling open dresser drawers.

"I'm not dumb, Liam," she pointed out.

"I know. But he's trying to find your weakness. One of us will be there soon."

Viv looked at the phone. She had maybe fifteen minutes before her regulars appeared. She didn't want to leave and have someone see it or even have the killer clean it up before Gina or Liam could get there.

"Viv!" she heard a voice shout a minute or two later. Looking down the street, she saw Gina in workout clothes running toward her. She was sweaty, clearly having already been on a run. Viv waved, letting her know she heard.

"What do we got?" Gina asked as she came closer.

"Dead cat, but I don't think anything normal killed it. I'm going to have patrons coming in soon and wasn't sure what to do."

"Liam's on his way, but it might take him a while depending on if he hits traffic. Do you have anything in your trunk we can cover it with until he gets here?" Gina asked.

"I have a tarp. It's still in the package," Viv offered.

"Can I have it? I'll buy you a new one," Gina said.

Viv nodded, running to her car to grab it. She also grabbed a pair of latex gloves from her first aid kit. Rushing back to Gina, she handed her the gloves first. "I had these in the first aid kit, if you need them."

"These are great, thank you." Gina pulled them on. Using the flashlight on her phone, she looked at the scene. There was blood and pieces of fur and guts everywhere in a six-foot area. "Shit," Gina muttered as she crouched down to look at the head.

"What?" Viv asked.

"There's a homemade collar; it's a piece of string with one of those plastic square key tags on it. The kind you can label to tell your keys apart?"

Viv nodded, her stomach sinking. She had a feeling what Gina was going to say next.

"It says Viv."

"Did you get my gift this morning?" the raspy voice asked.

Viv regretted answering the phone, but it was part of her job description.

She didn't answer, just waited for the asshole to say something else. She pressed the record and trace button that Liam had set up for her.

"Don't worry. I left your mate one too. This one was an old one I was keeping around, but figured she'd be better used this way. I'm afraid he's going to be too busy to come help you."

"I have plenty of help," she told him, trying to keep her voice from wavering. "I still don't understand what you consider the sin of what he's doing. He's trying to help people and stop them from being harmed."

He chuckled. "Is that what he told you? You poor naïve idiot. He just likes feeling important and feared. Not unlike me. I love the fear in their eyes. His sin is not embracing who he is, letting his darkness come forth, from trying to hold the rest of us back from our destinies."

"His destiny is to stop monsters like you," Viv countered. "He loves protecting and making people feel safe. Everyone has the potential for darkness; even if he has some, he controls his. Maybe you should give that a try," Viv snarked back. Stupid! she scolded herself. Don't antagonize the crazy.

"Nah," he drawled. "I'm good. I like what I do. I'll see ya later. By the way, I think you need more sleep. It looks like you're getting bags under your eyes."

Viv stood holding the phone, the dial tone sounding in her ear. She blindly reached out and shut off the machine. She knew the recording was going to be sent directly to Mac and to Liam, as would any location information. He must have been watching to see if she stopped to look at the poor animal he left behind. Viv knew he was already gone, but she still walked over and looked out the window. Liam was there, an official-looking tent covering the area where the poor animal was. It was big enough to have a person or two inside it, but Liam was on the outside of it at the moment. She saw him look up from his phone, searching the area. He must have gotten the recording. He might not have even been that close, she realized. He could have been using binoculars or seen her somewhere else on her route in to work. Maybe he even had a camera facing the library.

Seconds later, he turned and ran toward the library, shouting something at Gina over his shoulder. Liam rushed over to the desk, his hair a mess, his eyes shadowed. "What's wrong?" Viv said.

"Just got a text from Mac. He had another tip called in and went to investigate. This one panned out. The killer has clearly been leading them on a scavenger hunt, and finally gave them something to keep them busy. I don't know if it's a ploy to keep Mac away, or if he's getting bored and wants to make it more challenging for himself. Mac sent me an update of what he has so far.

"It's bad. It looks like one of his kill rooms, but why he would let us see it, I don't know. To gloat? It hasn't been used in a while, so it's not from his more recent victims, but he left the body there. It wasn't particularly protected with the windows being busted out and a leak in the roof, which means it's going to be a mess trying to identify and collect evidence. They're cautiously optimistic that he might have left something behind; she had something under one fingernail. There are pictures everywhere of what he did, how he stalked her. I have increased patrols and I'm going to give you an escort home, just to be on the safe side. He's never allowed evidence to be found before, so I'm not sure why he's had such a change in his pattern, but I don't trust it," Liam said.

Viv nodded, glad her shift was almost over. They closed early today and she was off tomorrow. Thank god. She had received a call, a delivery, or sometimes both, every day this week. She was ready for a break. The house would keep him away and the wards wouldn't let anything harmful through. Unlike at the library, she would have D there to run interference with the mail.

36

"I've got the bastard," Mac said as soon as Bert picked up the phone.

"I'll come to you and we can tell the team where to meet us. We're bringing him straight to Netherworld?" Bert asked.

"Yup, to Lucifer's stage," Mac replied. Technically it was in Netherworld, but they were skipping processing.

"Making a statement?" Bert asked. When Mac grunted a confirmation, he said, "I'll stand with you. Arlysium doesn't want any of our families targeted any more than you. The higher-ups have already confirmed they'll back any statement you or Lucifer make. I'm coming over now," he said, disconnecting their call.

Seconds later, Mac watched as a portal opened in his work office.

"What'd you find?" Bert said.

"I started going over the clues again, looking over anything that they might have in common. I still have no idea how or why he's picking the people he is, but they're all killed somewhere other than their homes. We're assuming somewhere far away from other people, since we haven't found police calls for disturbances or noise complaints. The site he gave us was bought and paid for before the killing. However, it's never changed names on the deed and someone is paying taxes on it. That was a bit of a dead end, as it's a trust type of thing, but the trust is also paying on a few other properties. I sent a few Enforcers to check them out and found similar kill sites, but no bodies lying out. They think there are several buried nearby and are bringing in the techs to search."

"How did you get access to the trust details?" Bert asked.

"We have a hacker on staff," Mac said simply. It wasn't quite legal by the human standards, but he had a lot more leeway as a nonhuman Enforcer. He would do whatever it took to keep his mate safe.

"We should really get one of those on ours," Bert said. "Okay, so you found a few more properties, but how did you get to him?"

"He called Viv after he sent the pictures. Part of it was bragging, part threatening. He mentioned something though, that the demoness and her Shadow mate used to make videos. I found a subscription service they created. It has evidence of rapes, tortures, and murders. People would subscribe and then tune in to watch. If they couldn't watch live, it was kept on the server. It was well protected, but our hacker finally managed to get in. She was able to track one of the payments back to the trust.

"Once we found the connection, we tried to find the server. Eventually our hacker found an office space. It was completely empty except for the servers. As she went through them, she found hidden files. The subscription service was supposed to be anonymous, but as we know, nothing is anonymous anymore. Oh, the general public and even an investigation probably wouldn't be able to connect people to the service, but the demoness kept her own collection of data on her subscribers. Maybe as a form of insurance of her own, blackmail? I'm not sure, but every customer had a folder. The folders had bank accounts, where they had homes, what they did for a living, which videos they watched, which videos they had submitted ideas for."

"Holy shit," Bert said excitedly.

Mac understood. They could potentially close a bunch of missing persons cases based on the victims in the videos. The folders would allow them to get these people off the streets. The ones who had requested certain types of videos, the ones who had paid to have a certain video made were guaranteed a spot in the Netherworld's punishment levels. The demoness had been smart, he'd give her that. She had made sure that the sign-up form clearly stated these were real events, someone would be kidnapped, raped, tortured, and/or killed. If someone submitted an idea or requested a certain type of video, then they were accomplices to murder, essentially hiring them to do it for them. Everyone had to sign off on it when they created their account, so no one could claim that they thought it was fake.

"Our hacker found the folder that linked to the trust. Our guy has two additional properties that aren't linked to the trust. I have Enforcer teams on standby with a witch to perform a containment spell. I thought we could have both our teams meet here, combine them and send them out to each house. You and I each go to one," Mac suggested.

Bert nodded. "Sounds good. I know it's technically 'our'

case, but it's your mate he's been harassing. Which house do you feel he's at? You should be there to grab him."

"I have a feeling he's here," Mac said, pointing at a nondescript house on the fringes of an almost abandoned town.

"You take that one then. Call and we can port to you if needed. If he's at mine, I'll give a holler."

Mac gave a short nod. It was almost over, he could tell. His demon was raging, eager to destroy the person who had brought the nightmares back into his mate's life.

It took them about an hour to gather the teams, brief them, and get suited up for a raid. He had no delusions that the guy would come quietly.

Mac wrapped the special cuffs around the man's wrists, relieved that they had finally caught him. Mac's instincts had been right and the man had been sleeping in the house he had chosen when his team stormed the house. After binding his legs as well, Mac had called Bert to let him know he had him and was taking him to Netherworld. Bert said he would meet him there. They were now standing on Lucifer's stage, their teams surrounding them. It was time to make it clear that their families were off limits.

"You're a coward picking on those weaker than you. I happened to find some of the videos you liked to watch, as well as some of the pictures you left behind of your own kills. I thought you might like to experience some of those for yourself," Mac whispered as he leaned down next to the trussed-up man. "And you're right. I do have darkness inside me, and I'll use that to protect the people I care about. The biggest one being my mate. You really should have left her alone. We still would have caught you, but you probably would have skipped this part of your punishment."

Mac made a gesture and another Enforcer brought out a few tools, while another pulled the tarp off the machinery. "This was made just for you," Mac told him. "You really made a dumb mistake," he said, tilting his wrist so that the man could see the mark. "Did you really not realize my mate was his too by definition?" As the man's eyes widened and he struggled in fear, Mac tutted at him. "It's too late now. You really pissed off Lucifer going after one of his. He'll get to you in a minute, but you're mine for now."

Lucifer took a step forward.

"Anyone who bears my mark is mine. That means their mates and their families are mine. To come after them is to come after me. And that will not be tolerated."

God ported in, standing next to Lucifer. "The Enforcers protect. Their jobs are to stop those who do not follow our laws, who would expose us to humans, who upset the balance. We will not tolerate their families or mates being targeted. If you have a fight with them, it's with them. They understand the risks. But mates and families are off limits. Otherwise, you will face us directly. This message will be sent to anyone registered under nonhuman status. There will be no leniency given to anyone violating this." God gave Lucifer a pat on the back before porting out. He really didn't like seeing blood, if Mac remembered correctly. And this was going to get messy.

Mac took a step back, taking off his watch, and placing it with his wallet and keys in a waiting basket. He typed out a quick group message to Viv, D, and Thomas. *Got him. I'm safe. Bringing him to Netherworld. Will be home late. Love you,*

V. He quickly sent another one to Liam, although he was careful with his wording since it was to Liam's work phone. *Found and arrested. He won't be killing anyone else. Bringing him in under my jurisdiction. Will send paperwork over later.* They had a system where their hacker would input documents into the FBI database, making it seem like it was a federal arrest. A commendation letter praising Liam and Gina would be sent as well. They deserved it with all the extra work they did trying to keep Viv safe. At least this way, Liam's supervisors would give him a little bit of breathing room for a couple of days.

Mac placed his phone in the basket as well. He let his demon form come forth, walking over to the killer. He hoisted him over his shoulder, walking over to the machine. Bert stepped up, helping strap him in. A metal band went around his forehead, connected to a long thin wire. A few words were spoken, causing the wire to fuse to his spine, keeping his body straight. His hands were cuffed at the wrists and attached to the head gear, leaving his torso completely open and exposed. The head gear connected to a ball socket on one end of the machine. They snapped thick metal cuffs around his ankles. These were connected to a block that kept his legs apart by several inches. The block had a hole through the middle, although the end by his feet had a long hollow metal pole welded around the hole. This piece would connect to the machine.

The man was hoisted up by several Enforcers, his body held aloft as the head gear was hooked to the machine, followed by sliding the metal tube into position. "This next part, I thought you would appreciate," Mac said. "I heard you really admired the demoness' barbed tail attachment." He moved to the end of the machine, turning it on. The hydraulics pushed a hidden smaller pole out through the pipe. The man couldn't escape, his legs held in place by the cuff, the wire fused to his spine stopping him from sagging or squirming away. The screams of the man could be heard around the gag as the barbed-covered pole pushed its way inside his body. "Oh. Did you not like it when it's done to you?" Mac asked, feigning surprise. "You really won't like this next part."

Mac locked away his conscience for now, letting all his rage, fear, anger, and darkness come out. There was a fine line between punishment and revenge and he knew he was stepping over it, obliterating it. But he would do anything to keep his family safe and if making a statement like this would show not to mess with his, then so be it.

Mac stood under the showers in the locker room for the Enforcers. He had been coated in blood. He let the hot water loosen the sore and stiff muscles. The man had finally died under Lucifer's hand. Mac wasn't sure if his soul would be destroyed or sent to eternal torment. The last bit had been the messiest and the stuff that could haunt nightmares. First, the killer had been flayed, as the machine had been basically a giant spit roast. They had added a rotating blade that popped up from the side, much like an apple peeler. When that was done, there was a separate pedal to open the pit underneath, allowing the flames out. Bert had pressed that one. The entire area could hear the screams, despite the gag, as newly uncovered nerve endings had been exposed to heat and eventually burned off. There had been a few other techniques they had employed based on the man's own preferences to torture others, but eventually

Mac's heart felt heavy and he stepped back to allow Lucifer to take over. If the man thought Mac was bad, he wasn't in any way prepared for Lucifer. He hadn't been appointed to his position because he was weak.

Mac knew it had to be done or others would think they could come after their mates to coerce Enforcers to leave them alone, but even with all his rage and need for revenge, it still hadn't brought him any joy. A sense of closure maybe. A small sense of peace that he had helped protect his mate. Dressing in new clothes after burning his blood-soaked ones, he grabbed the basket with his personal items and headed to his office. He shut the door, turning on his heaviest bass-filled metal and rock music playlist. He sat in his chair, leaning his head back and closing his eyes, letting the beat flow through him. Focusing on his breathing, he worked on getting to a state where he could portal home. He didn't want to come home to Viv with blood on his body and his mind still a mess.

A knock on the door brought his head up, a freshly showered Bert standing on the other side. Mac waved him in.

"You doing okay?" Bert asked. They had become closer over the last couple of cases and Mac was happy to call him a friend now, not just a coworker.

Mac shrugged. "I know we needed to send a message and I think it did that. And he was right; I do have a bit of darkness in me. Otherwise there's no way I would have done that, much less helped come up with some of it."

Bert nodded. "I think everyone has the potential to fall into darkness. Most would want revenge for what happened to Viv if it was their mate. There are very few, like extremely few, who don't have any darkness in them. She's not even my mate, but I wanted to hurt him for what he had done to a mate of a friend. I think this will send a message that no matter which office we work for, what type of nonhuman we are, we'll band together to protect our own. You should go home. See Viv, lie next to her in bed, know she's safe. I'll see you later. I want an invite to dinner for this goulash I hear you make," Bert said with a smile, opening a portal to his own home and stepping through.

Mac let the music wash over him for a few more minutes, easing his body back into a state of calm. He had no idea why heavy bass helped, but it did. He clicked the music off, standing up and stretching. He was about to open a portal when Lucifer walked in.

"It's done. God and I also sent out the message to all nonhumans. I don't anticipate something like this again. At least I hope not. Bring her to see me soon," he added.

"We're coming down in a few days for Christmas," Mac replied, reminding him.

"I forgot that it was so soon," Lucifer admitted. "I'll see you then." He gave Mac a squeeze on his shoulder and walked back out.

Mac took a deep breath, making sure his energy was close to normal and opened a portal home.

Mac found his family huddled in the living room, the fireplace on, empty coffee cups on the table. Viv and Thomas huddled next to each other under a blanket, asleep. D came out of the kitchen.

"They couldn't stay awake any longer, but insisted on staying up until you got home," he said softly. "How did it go?"

Mac pointed to the kitchen and they walked back, keeping their steps light. He kept an ear open for Viv, making sure he could hear if she woke up. He didn't want her to hear anything too graphic.

"We found him in one of those two properties. He had trophies and memorabilia about his kills all over his house. There were scrapbooks dedicated to each one; where he found them, their schedules, all typical stalker-type stuff. Then he drew out how he wanted the kills to go. Some of the books had pages of rants and crossed-out drawings when it didn't go his way. There were a few where it seems the person got away. There was plenty of evidence to convict him," Mac said, keeping his voice low. "He tried to run for it, clearly not expecting us to find him, but the witch did great with the containment spell. We got him bound and brought him to Netherworld."

"How do you feel now?" D asked. Mac had kept him up to date on the case and he had been aware of what the punishment was going to entail.

Mac was silent for a moment. "I'm okay. I think it did what we wanted, getting the message out that you don't mess with the mates or families. I do worry that he may have been right when he said I had darkness in me and the potential to be a monster," he admitted.

"He was wrong," Viv said firmly, somehow sneaking up on him. "I don't think monsters can love. Whatever you did, you did it because you love. To keep others safe. He did what he did for his own pleasure and wants."

"What if I did it for revenge?" Mac asked softly.

"For the ones you love," she pointed out. "I don't need or want to know the details, but I know whatever you did it was to try to protect others."

"I don't know that I'm as good as you're making me out to be," Mac warned.

"No one is all good. I think you're perfect for me, so stop being mean to yourself," Viv ordered, wrapping her arms around his waist.

"Wha' happened? Mac's home?" A bleary-eyed Thomas stumbled over to join them. "Is it done? Viv's safe?"

"She's safe," Mac promised. "We found the person who was behind it. He was brought in front of Lucifer and we made an example of him. Lucifer said the nonhumans clearly didn't get the message earlier, but there was no mistaking the message this time. Viv and our family are off limits. I don't think something like this will happen again."

"Good. I'm glad you're home and safe," Thomas said. "Let's go to bed," he said, grabbing D's hand and pulling him down their hallway.

"Come on," Viv said, pulling Mac to their room. "I need to hold you."

"I got a shower before I came home," Mac told her, wanting her to know that he wasn't coming to their bed with any trace of the killer on him.

"Good, then you can get right in bed," Viv replied.

Mac stripped as soon as he crossed the threshold, wanting to hold his mate in his arms. He didn't tell her that he would do it all over again, capturing and torturing a man to make a point to leave her alone. He would do it a thousand times over if it meant keeping her safe. If that made him a monster, so be it. He'd have no regrets.

Viv snuggled back into Mac's arms, happy to have him home. She had told him the truth last night. She didn't believe he was a monster. He worked hard to protect people, especially those who couldn't defend themselves. She also knew that whatever had gone down last night had to be especially gruesome and harsh to make an impression on nonhumans. They lived for so long and had seen so much, that it was probably easy for them to get jaded. To get past that would require something extreme. She really didn't want to know, not because she thought it would change her opinion of her mate, but because she already had enough horrible images in her head. Her nightmares didn't need more fuel.

"What should we do today?" Mac asked, holding her tighter.

"We really need to get the Christmas presents wrapped. We're supposed to go to Netherworld in three days for our visit. I need to look through everything and make sure we have presents for everyone too. I didn't get much done over the past week. I think I got the gifts finished with online shopping, but I was very distracted and need to make sure I didn't forget anyone. Can you help me pick something out for Bert, Liam, and Gina? I know I have them left. I thought it could be delivered to their homes since I don't think we'll see them before we leave. Maybe we can have them all over around New Year's? As like a thank you dinner, or something, or is that silly?" Viv asked.

"I think that sounds perfect. Bert was angling for an invite to dinner for the demon goulash. I know of a few things they might like for Christmas, and I have their addresses. We can online shop today and get those out, and then wrap the presents we have for everyone else. Do you think we can wrap out in the living room, or do you want to do it in your reading room?" Mac asked.

"Let me grab out D's and Thomas' gifts and I'll wrap those later. We'll do the rest in the living room; Thomas will probably want to hang out anyway. He's been worried."

"I'll throw some sweatpants on and go make blueberry

pancakes and bacon," Mac suggested. "Why don't you grab a shower and the gifts? Breakfast should be ready by then."

"You're going to spoil us," she said, pressing a kiss to his lips. She held his face between her hands. "I love you. Thank you for watching over us."

"I love you too. Always. Forever," Mac promised.

37

Mac brought Viv to his house to stay for their mini vacation in Netherworld. They would go visit his uncle, but he wanted to make sure they had alone time as well. Viv's nightmares had been popping up again with the stalker behavior of the serial killer he had been hunting. He didn't think she wanted Uncle to hear her if she had any while they were here. Mac was hoping that the nightmares would stop again now that the man had been caught and punished.

Plus, he didn't want his uncle to be able to overhear them having sex. They were staying in tonight, letting Viv adjust to being in Netherworld. It took a minute to adjust to the sky and the different sensations. Thomas had been here a few times now and would have a much easier time. Thomas and D were coming over for dinner tonight. Tomorrow he and Viv would be going to his uncle's house for introductions. He was nervous about having his mate and only blood family meet, but he knew his uncle would love her. He just hoped Viv could see past his uncle's job and see him for the man, well demon, he was.

He was planning on making the goulash dish she had liked at the restaurant. It was a good comforting dish. He had a take-and-bake loaf of bread as well. His uncle had made sure his house was stocked before they had arrived. Viv was changing into sweatpants and a t-shirt, wanting to be comfortable. It's not like Thomas or D cared what she was wearing.

He got the stew started, setting it to simmer. He pulled out some vegetables that he brought from the human world and started making a salad. When he finished tossing the salad, he went to check on Viv since she hadn't come back out from the bedroom. He found her curled on the bed, fast asleep. He left the light on but pulled a blanket over her. She hadn't been sleeping well, so it was a good thing she was taking a nap. He searched through his sock drawer, finding the box his uncle had promised would be there. Opening it, he smiled. He couldn't wait to give it to her.

A few hours later, there was a knock on the door. Thomas and D came in carrying dessert and a few bottles of wine.

"Let me get Viv. She fell asleep. Can you watch the bread for me? It's close to done," Mac said.

"It smells great," Thomas told him, already heading to the kitchen.

Mac went to his bedroom, making sure to make noise. "Viv? Thomas and D are here," he said approaching the bed.

"Hm. Already? Are they early?" she blinked up at him.

Mac smiled. She was adorable when she was sleepy. "Nope, you fell asleep. Dinner's about ready."

"I'm sorry. I didn't mean to fall asleep," she said, climbing out of the bed.

Mac gave her a kiss. "You needed the sleep. Now we can have some fun with our friends."

Viv nodded and they walked out to the kitchen. D was already setting the table; he had been over enough times that he knew where everything was. Thomas was taking the bread out of the oven and stirring the goulash.

"You made my favorite," Viv said with a smile.

"Yup. There's bread and salad to go with it."

"And dessert and wine!" Thomas added, coming over to give Viv a hug.

"You look better," he said, looking her over.

"I guess I needed some more sleep," Viv admitted. She did feel much better, ready to celebrate with her family.

Dinner was amazing and there weren't any leftovers. She needed to wait a bit to eat the dessert, which Thomas informed her tasted like a cannoli, but in a layered pie. He got the recipe from D's mom the last time they had visited and he assured Viv it was delicious.

"Do you guys want to play some games while we wait for dessert?" Mac asked.

"Sure, what kind of games?" Thomas replied.

"I've got board games and card games, but they're demon versions," Mac said.

"Do you still have Three You're Out?" D asked.

"I think so, let me go look," Mac replied, pulling himself out of the couch.

"What's that?" Thomas asked as Mac left the room.

"It's a dice game. We used to play it a lot when we were kids," he heard D respond. He opened the closet, digging through the mess of games. He tended to just shove them someplace when he was done with them. He finally found it; the box held together by tape, the corners having long since broken apart.

Mac gingerly unpacked the box, spreading the faded and taped-together map out on the table.

"The goal of the game is to make it around Netherworld without getting eaten. If you roll a three, you get tossed into the ocean where you're eaten."

"By those gnarly fish we saw," Thomas grumbled.

"I told you, you're too big for them to eat," D said, laughing.

"We need to go on a trip," Thomas told Viv. "Then you'll see and can agree with me."

"Has D taken you to Smoke, that restaurant I told you about?"

Thomas shook his head.

"You go there and try some of the food in the nonhuman room, and I'll go with you to the ocean. Make sure you have D with you to order the food that is human-safe though."

"I will," Thomas promised.

"You guys ready to play?" D asked, eager. This had been his favorite game growing up, which explained why Mac's copy was so worn. They had played it a lot.

Thomas proved to be very adept at the game, winning three out of five rounds. Viv got up, stretching.

"I'm going to make some coffee. Does everyone want some?" she asked.

After a round of yeses, she went to the kitchen to get the coffeepot started. Thomas followed, pulling out the cannoli pie. "This is a cute house. I'm so glad they're close together. We can still walk to see each other if we're here at the same time," he said.

"I know! I was worried they would be far apart," Viv replied. D didn't live on the same street as Mac, but he did live within a ten-minute walk. "I love you, you know that?" she asked her best friend, laying her head on his shoulder.

"I love you too. I'm so glad Mac got his head out of his

ass, and you gave him a second chance. We'll have hundreds and hundreds of years together. It's perfect that our mates are best friends too," Thomas said happily, wrapping his arms around her in a hug.

"Are you excited to finally meet his uncle?" he asked, letting go to slice the pie.

"I am, but nervous too. He helped raise Mac and it's his only blood family left."

"He'll love you," Thomas reassured her.

The coffeepot gurgled its last drops and Viv focused on getting a tray of drinks made up. Thomas finished plating the pie slices and left the kitchen, making a squeaking sound at the doorway. Viv turned but didn't see anything.

"You okay?" she asked, worried.

"Yup. Just a hiccup-sneeze combo. I'll take the coffees. Can you grab napkins? I forgot to bring them," Thomas said, taking the tray out of her hands.

Viv shook her head at her suddenly empty hands but turned around and grabbed napkins from the pantry. She started walking back into the living room, but stopped as soon as she crossed the threshold. Mac was there, kneeling on one knee, a small box in his hands. Was this...? Viv felt her eyes start to tear up. Thomas already had his phone out, standing off to the side. She was a little amused at the thought that she was getting proposed to while wearing some of her oldest clothing.

"Viv, you make my life complete. You are joy and laughter, love and acceptance. I was a complete ass and almost lost this, but you gave me another chance. I know you already accepted me as your mate, but I would love if you would accept me as your husband too," Mac said, holding the ring out to her.

"Yes! Of course, yes. I would love to be your wife," she

said, dropping to her knees in front of him, napkins falling to the ground as she ignored the ring and grabbed his face with both hands, pulling him in for a kiss. Mac pulled her close, wrapping one hand in her hair, thrusting his tongue deep.

She pulled back when she heard Thomas cheering. Mac slid the ring on her finger. It was like nothing she had ever seen before. The silver band gleamed and the diamond looked like it had a tiny flame inside it.

"It's a Netherworld hellfire diamond," Mac explained. "It's been spelled so that a regular human won't see the flame, so you don't have to worry about it at work or anything."

"Let me see! Congratulations," Thomas said, coming over to give them both a hug. "It's perfect, good job," he told Mac with a smile. "Maybe we can do a double wedding?" he asked Viv hopefully.

"I would love that. That would be perfect," she replied.

Mac held Viv's hand as they walked to his uncle's. It appeared to be just down the street, but in reality, his uncle owned all of this property. The other houses were for his main guards. When they weren't on shift guarding him, they had their own places to go to, to live with their families if they had any. Even if he himself didn't get separation of home and work, he understood the importance of it for his people. Mac could have moved farther away, but he liked being close to his uncle.

He knocked on the front door, not sure if his uncle had any visitors today. Sometimes people would pop in on official business. He could sense a few guards around the property and the house, but they must have been hiding in the shadows. Probably trying to give Viv space and not overwhelm her.

The front door opened, and his uncle stepped out. He had chosen to appear in his human form, which wasn't too unlike Mac's. They were both tall and muscular, pitch-black hair. His uncle's was longer, pulled back in a man bun, which Mac loved to tease him about. Mac had dark eyes, whereas his uncle had bright blue. Even their demon forms showed their family resemblance.

"Welcome. I am so pleased to meet you," his uncle said, holding out a hand.

"Viv, this is Lucifer," Mac introduced them.

"Nice to meet you, sir," she said, shaking his hand. He could feel her nervousness.

"None of this sir stuff. You're family. I'm just glad Mac got his head out of his ass and decided to man up and be the mate you deserve."

"Uncle Luc," Mac groaned.

"Uncle? Your uncle is *the* Lucifer? And you didn't think to tell me before now?" Viv asked incredulously. She smacked the back of her hand to his chest. "Dumbass," she muttered.

He probably should have mentioned that they were going to his *uncle's* house before they left, he thought. He had just assumed that she knew; almost everyone he worked with knew they were related.

Lucifer laughed. "He really is," he agreed. "Come on. Let me show you around. I hear you like libraries."

Mac trailed after them, watching as his uncle won over his mate as he brought her over to the family side of the house. They could be trouble together if they ganged up on him. But man, he was happy. He couldn't wait to see it.

"...then there was the one time, he stripped completely naked and ran down the street with the pack of dogs. He had decided he wanted to be a dog too," his uncle was telling his mate. Maybe he should have been paying more attention to their conversation.

"I was four, Uncle. And I'm pretty sure you and dad had egged me on," Mac defended himself.

His uncle shrugged, a huge grin on his face, not denying anything.

"Did anyone get pictures?" Viv asked, laughing.

"No, but I'm sure I have some other ones around here somewhere."

Mac was convinced that he could find any embarrassing pictures lying about before his uncle could. Luckily, she was distracted as soon as they entered the library, her happy gasp filling the air. It was quite the room, with a rolling ladder along the main floor, and a spiral staircase leading to the second floor, which was part library and part seating area. It had been Mac's favorite room of the house growing up. You could sink into one of the plush chairs or couches, or curl up in the window seat.

"This is amazing! You have a rolling ladder and a spiral staircase! Are you kidding me?"

Mac watched in amazement as his mate ran around the room like a kid on those Christmas shows, all excited and hyped up on sugar. She flitted around the room, stopping to look at random things, awing over some of the pictures of Mac when he was little.

"I think she likes your library, Uncle Luc," Mac said dryly.

"Good, it's an easy way to get her to like me," his uncle joked.

Mac could hear the nerves in his voice though. Uncle really wanted Viv to like him.

"I like you already because you took care of Mac. You loved and raised him to be an amazing person, so you must be an amazing person as well," Viv said, coming over to wrap his uncle in a hug.

His uncle's face was shocked, his eyes wide and he didn't hug back right away. Viv held on though, and Lucifer's arms wrapped around her gently. Mac couldn't remember anyone but him giving his uncle a hug. People just didn't hug Lucifer, ruler over the Netherworld. Mac grinned, seeing the shock turn to happiness, his uncle's eyes looking suspiciously wet.

38

Mac had been in his demon form more often since they were in Netherworld, Viv thought. Not that she minded, she found both of his forms sexy. Right now, he was relaxing in his oversized plush chair, reading a book. They were meeting with Thomas and D at D's parents' later, but they had a couple of hours until then. Viv felt her arousal grow as she watched Mac absently wet his lips. She loved seeing the little hint of fangs, and she couldn't wait to play with his horns again. She thought she might be ready for his tail. Thomas raved about it and she wanted to experience tail play herself.

Walking over, she dropped into his lap, gently moving the book out of the way.

"Hey, love. What's up?" Mac asked.

Viv leaned over and kissed him, sliding her tongue against his lips, asking to be let in. When Mac opened his mouth, she slid her tongue in, twining it against his. Mac's hands grasped her hips, holding her tight. Viv ground down, rubbing her butt against his growing erection. Mac stood, carrying her into the bedroom. The living room windows' blinds were open and he didn't want anyone to see his mate naked. "What do you want, love?"

"I want you," Viv said. "Just like this."

Mac paused. "Are you sure?" He was bigger in this form and he didn't want to hurt her.

"I'm sure. I thought maybe..." Her face turned bright red and she didn't finish the sentence, but she did reach out to run a hand down his tail.

Oh! Mac thought, surprised. A rush of lust shot through him, his demon side eager to claim his mate in this form and to share everything with her. He leaned down, taking her mouth in a possessive kiss, desperate to sink into her body.

Viv gasped as he tossed her on the bed. She bounced once before watching him prowl toward her. His eyes were glowing, the flames in them bright, a sure sign of his heightened emotion. His tail was lashing behind him and she felt herself grow wetter as she imagined what it might feel like inside her.

"Strip," he ordered, his voice gravelly. He was cupping the front of his pants, the bulge visible.

Sitting up, Viv took off the shirt and bra first, her breasts bared for his pleasure. Mac growled, leaping onto the bed. Literally leaped. He was crouched in front of her with one jump, his eyes focused on her face, one hand reaching out to trail a claw gently down the slope of her breast. Viv watched as her nipple hardened under the touch, gasping as he cupped a breast, leaning down to gently suck on the nub, his fangs careful not to pierce her skin. Her hands reached out, grabbing the base of his horns, rubbing the sensitive skin there. Mac groaned, gently pushing her to lie back.

He ran his nose down her chest, pressing kisses along

the way. Reaching her waist, he unbuckled her belt, unbuttoning and unzipping her pants. Viv placed her feet on the bed, lifting her hips to help him get her jeans off. He took her underwear off at the same time, leaning down to smell her.

"You always smell so good, love. Like home," Mac said, trailing a finger down her mons, teasing her slit. He lay between her thighs, running his tongue against her skin, her lips were plump, eager to have him lick between their folds. He slowly licked, teasing her by darting his tongue in to touch her clit. When she started writhing on the bed, he finally slid his tongue between her lips, circling her clit, sending shocks of pleasure through her. Mac slid a finger into her body, thrusting slowly, his tongue loving on her clit, circling it and then lapping at it. Viv tilted her hips upward, helping his finger find the best spot. As he added a second finger, his teeth glanced over her clit, causing a whole bunch of sensations to run through her. "Again," she demanded, pushing his head down. Mac chuckled as his lips touched her body, sending the vibrations through her. As he added a third finger and then a fourth, she was ready for him to fill her. "In me," she pleaded. She needed to feel him inside, filling her. She needed it more than air at this point.

Mac slid his cock into her heat, Viv throwing her head back as her body stretched around his. Oh god, he felt so good, she was so full. He gave a few small thrusts, sending sparks of electricity along her veins. "Yes, more," she demanded. Mac rested on his knees, holding his weight up by his elbows. Viv took a deep breath, smelling him. She was surrounded by him, his arms on either side of her head, his body over hers, his body in hers. She could feel the rasp of his dick against her walls, dragging along the sensitive skin, causing all her nerve endings to flare in pleasure.

Viv wrapped her legs around his waist, keeping him deep inside her. Mac leaned back, sitting and resting on his heels. His wings flared out, helping him keep balance as he held her torso away from his chest, their only connection point at their waists and arms. Viv grabbed his arms but trusted him not to let her fall. She felt suspended in the air, his cock holding her up. She cried out as he thrust into her, his massive dick rubbing against her passage, causing pleasure to shoot through her. Oh gods. This was like nothing she had ever experienced before. The ridges along the top of his penis rubbing over her G-spot, the bumps along the bottom stimulating the rest of her sensitive tissue, the barbells almost overstimulating her. Her whole body clenched as her orgasm screamed through her when his tail snuck in between their bodies, pressing on her clit. Her body was racked with shivers as he played her body, keeping her arousal high even though she had just orgasmed.

"Again, Viv. Come for me again before I fill you," Mac demanded.

Her head tossed back and forth. "Please, Mac," she pleaded, not knowing what she wanted.

"Do you trust me?" he asked.

"Yes!" Viv screamed at him, desperate to come, the intensity of what he was doing almost too much. She needed a push of some sort and she didn't know what.

Mac pulled his tail away, grabbing a bottle of lube from the nightstand, squirting some on the tip of his tail.

"Trust me," he said as his tail moved behind her.

Viv gasped as she felt it circle her hole, someplace no one had gone before. The skin was so sensitive there, her body was ramping closer toward climaxing, but it still wasn't enough. "Now," Mac said, his tail sliding into her ass. Viv stiffened as there was a brief pinch of pain, the tail stretching her hole. Mac slowly moved his tail, letting her get used to the feel. She was so full, stuffed in both holes. Viv screamed as he suddenly started thrusting his hips, driving his thick length into her cunt, the tail thrusting into her ass. The dual sensations were too much and her orgasm burst through her, sending lightening pulses of pleasure throughout her entire body. She felt his dick swell, the base thickening even more.

"Mac?" she asked, her voice hoarse.

"It's my knot," he grunted, gently forcing it deeper into her body. "You can take me, love. You were made for me."

As the knot locked them into place, Mac demanded, "One more for me."

Viv couldn't breathe as the tail thrust into her ass, his hips thrusting in short bursts with the limited motion the knot would allow. She could feel it tugging at her entrance. Her mind blacked out as the ridges on his dick vibrated, pulsing against her G-spot. When he scraped his teeth against her neck, taking a bite, her body trembled, every muscle shaking under the force of her orgasm. Everything went black as her body was swept away in pleasure.

Viv slowly woke up, her body sore, but in a good way. Her lower half a little tender, but there were still traces of pleasure shivering through her. Opening her eyes, she saw a concerned Mac leaning over her.

"Are you okay?" he demanded.

"Hmm. That was amazing," Viv said as she stretched.

"I wasn't too rough?"

"No, that was perfect. I don't think I've ever come that hard," she said.

"Come on, let's get you into the bath so you can soak. I have it all ready." Mac picked her up, carrying her to the bathroom.

"Mac. Look at me. I'm fine. It was wonderful. I can't wait to do it again," she said honestly. The ass play had been a surprise, but she had enjoyed that too. She had never wanted to try ass sex before, but if it was like today, she could see the appeal. Not every day, but sometimes.

Mac lowered her gently into the warm water, already with scented oils in it. He still didn't look at her as he gently washed her. Viv grabbed his arm.

"What's the matter?"

"I don't know. I have these urges and I don't want to hurt you. I've never had this before."

"What urges?"

"I want to take your ass, fill you with cum and plug you with my tail before I fuck your pussy so full of my seed that I breed you," he said harshly.

"Oh god," Viv said faintly, her vagina instantly getting wet, feeling heavy with arousal.

"Please," she begged, feeling desperate for what he was describing.

"I don't want to hurt you; I was rougher than I wanted to be," Mac said through gritted teeth, scenting her arousal even through the water. Viv sat up on her knees, her breasts glistening with the oiled water.

"Then fuck me partially shifted. Please Mac, I needed it.

I don't know what's going on, but I'm so hot, please. I need you."

Mac growled, grabbing her from the tub and striding back to the bedroom. Getting locked together in the bathtub would not be comfortable, he had the basic instinct to realize. He put her on her hands and knees on the bed, his body shrinking down to his half-shifted size. He was still bigger, but not full-demon big in this form. He maintained his tail, wings, and horns though. He made use of his tail, stretching her open, his fingers playing with her ass, sliding in with his tail, scissoring her open. His other hand slid around to her clit, circling it the way she liked.

Bending down, he licked a strip over her furled hole, hearing her gasp but her hips pressed back, seeking more. Mac grinned, eating her ass as he stretched her open with his tail and fingers. He slicked his dick with lube, holding her cheeks open. "Relax and push out," he ordered as the head of his cock slowly breached her.

Viv whimpered, the sharp bite of pain back, but his tail came around to play with her clit, the pain and pleasure merging in her brain. She held her body up by her elbows, her ass tilted in the air as Mac slowly thrust, letting her get used to his size.

"I'm okay," she reassured him.

Mac's tail slid into her cunt, thrusting until she was moaning, her hips rocking back and forth, seeking more pleasure. His hands gripped her waist tightly, holding her in place as he pounded into her ass, tail thrusting into her cunt. Mac grunted as she felt warmth fill her, which was a bit of a weird sensation. Mac gently pushed her shoulders down to the bed, pulling his dick out. She whined in protest as the tail pulled out of her vagina. Her walls clenching around him, trying to keep him in.

Seconds later, her ass was full again, the tail plugging her, keeping Mac's cum there. She looked behind her, seeing him clean his dick off before dragging her hips back. He pressed a gentle kiss between her shoulder blades before slamming his dick home. Viv screamed, his cock filling her, rubbing along the already super sensitive tissue. She wondered briefly if you could die from too much pleasure. The tail didn't move, just kept her full and plugged, but it added an extra feel of tightness, pressing against his dick through her walls. She wondered if he could feel it as well.

"Mine," he growled, voice deep, flames burning bright in his eyes.

"Yours," she agreed as she felt his knot swell. Mac leaned over her back, biting the back of her neck. Viv screamed as her orgasm was pulled out of her, her body collapsing on the bed. Mac's body followed, blanketing her as he continued to thrust, causing the comforter to rub up against her clit.

"Mac," she pleaded.

"Mine," he uttered, biting her again.

Viv growled back, "Mine," before turning her head and biting his forearm, drawing blood. She swallowed it, her body giving one last weak attempt at a climax. The world went black as she smiled.

39

"Viv. Please love, wake up," she heard Mac begging.

"Hey," she said drowsily, struggling to open her eyes.

"Oh thank gods," Mac said.

Viv opened her eyes all the way, staring at her mate. His eyes looked suspiciously shiny, although no tears fell.

"What's the matter?" she asked.

"You passed out again. I am so sorry. We're sticking to human sex," he muttered, gathering her to his chest.

Viv let herself snuggle for a second, while taking stock of her body. She was sore, but it was the soreness of really good aerobatic sex, not the pain of something being wrong. Placing a hand on his chest, she pushed back enough to look at his face. "We are not sticking to human sex," she said with a frown. "It was intense. I'm not hurt, just a little sore. Which considering I've never had anal before today or taken a dick that big before, is to be expected. It was amazing. I'm not saying we're going to do that every day, but we will be having sex again in your demon form, even tail sex. It was the best sex I've ever had," she told him.

Mac grinned, his demon almost purring in happiness. He could feel the smug smile on his face but didn't think there was much he could do about it. Best sex. Go him. "You still should have a hot bath so you can soak. I have some healing cream we'll use after the bath, just to make me feel better that I didn't hurt you," he added as she started to protest.

"Fine, but you're coming in the bath with me. There's enough room."

Mac got the bath refilled; grateful he had an on-demand hot water heater. Once it was deep enough, he carried Viv to the tub, carefully stepping in and lowering them both into the water. Viv sighed, leaning her head back against his shoulder as her body relaxed into the heat.

Mac let them soak until his alarm went off. Getting them out of the tub was tricky as Viv had fallen asleep. "Viv, wake up, love. We need to get ready to go to D's parents'," Mac murmured. He used his toes to pull the plug, letting the water out. Viv grumbled but stood up. He grabbed a towel and wrapped her up, quickly drying himself off. He grabbed the small glass container of the healing cream, urging Viv to lie on the bed.

Viv sat but kept the towel around her. "I can do it," she said, embarrassed for some reason.

Mac shook his head. "Please, love. I had my tongue in your ass, putting some cream there isn't a big deal. Let me take care of you," he asked.

Viv leaned back, parting the towel, and spreading her legs.

Mac looked over his mate quickly, seeing a few bruises from where his fingers had gripped her hips. He spread a little bit over those.

"Bruises," he explained, ashamed of himself for losing control like that.

"Nope. You don't get to be embarrassed or feel bad either," Viv told him. "Best sex ever, remember? I wouldn't change a thing."

Mac nodded, accepting her words as truth. It helped that he could feel it along the mate bond. Her openings were a little tender looking, but she had been right. They weren't injured, just had a good pounding. He still applied a light layer of cream, hoping to ease the soreness. When she sat back up, he applied a little to the bite marks at the back of her neck.

They got dressed, Mac opening a portal to D's parents' house. This had been his second home growing up, just like his uncle's was D's. He opened the front door, calling out "I'm here!" as he went inside.

The group converged on them, covering them in hugs and kisses.

"Welcome," D's mom exclaimed, enveloping Viv in a hug. "I'm so glad to meet you properly. D has told me all sorts of wonderful things about you and I'm so happy Mac has found his mate. Mac's like my other son; feel free to call me Ma like the boys do. I'm so happy to finally have a girl in the family!"

Mac and Viv were headed to his uncle's to visit for a couple of hours before everyone else came over. Luc wanted a chance to give Viv her puppy and let it bond to her before there were other distractions.

Christmas Eve was going to be so much fun, Mac

thought gleefully as he helped grab the bags of presents. He was beyond excited to see Viv's reaction to her present from his uncle. D, Thomas, and D's parents were coming for dinner, after having their own family get together earlier in the day. For the nonhumans getting together today, it wasn't a religious celebration but a celebration of family and bonds. He could fully get behind the spirit of love and togetherness of the holiday, even if he knew the truth behind all the trappings of the religions, not just Christianity. There were pluses and negatives to them all.

"Are you sure we shouldn't bring anything with us? Not even a bottle of wine? I feel weird going and not bringing something for a host gift," Viv said.

"If it makes you feel better, go grab one of the bottles of red that I have on the bottom shelf. It's Uncle's favorite," Mac replied. He didn't understand tradition of hostess gifts and the need to bring something, but he also didn't want his mate to feel upset. He was going to be smart and let her do what she wanted.

Viv waved to some of the families that were out on the street as they walked to Lucifer's.

"Do you guys have holidays you celebrate?" she asked.

"As demons or nonhumans in general?"

"Either. Both," she said.

"There are a couple. In general, we don't have a lot. Most of your religious holidays are simply another day for us. There's a Creation Day and the Day of Restructuring. Respectfully, when it's believed intelligent life began and when the Netherworld and Arlysium sections were formed," Mac said.

"Do you do anything to celebrate?" Viv asked, not wanting to miss any traditions he might have.

"Not really. Uncle and I usually get together on the

anniversary of my parents' deaths and our birthdays. Otherwise, we don't have a lot of traditions. I see him more than that of course, but those are the days we always make a point of seeing each other."

Lucifer was waiting for them in front of the house. Mac swore that man was almost bouncing on his toes in excitement.

"Hello! Happy gift day!" he shouted.

Viv laughed but stepped into his hug. "Hello, Uncle Luc. We brought you a bottle of wine; Mac says it's your favorite."

"Thank you," he said, ushering them inside the house. Mac placed the gifts in the family room, following them into the kitchen and placing the wine on the counter.

"I have some food for appetizers and a roast in the oven for dinner. Are you hungry, thirsty? Or can we do presents now?"

Mac shook his head. No one who saw his uncle right now would believe that he was the stoic, scarily lethal, ruler of the Netherworld. He was downright giddy.

Viv looked at Mac in confusion. She had no idea why he was so excited after all. "We can do presents now," she said slowly.

"Yes!" Lucifer cheered. "Let's do yours first. We have to go outside though."

"What's going on?" Viv whispered to Mac as they followed Lucifer outside.

"You'll see," Mac replied.

His uncle led them over to the kennels where they could hear the puppies.

"The dogs are here?" Viv asked excitedly. She knew he had Hellhounds but hadn't seen them yet.

"Yes. The last Hellhound litter is weaned and fully

trained. They're a good batch. Some of them are joining the Enforcers."

"Can I see them?"

"Of course," Lucifer said, leading them the rest of the way to the kennels. "Wait here and I'll let them out. Just a minute, I'm coming," he shouted to the excited yips.

"Did you always have dogs around growing up?" Viv asked.

Mac nodded. "Uncle breeds them and most of them work as guard dogs or with the Enforcers. There were always dogs and/or puppies around. I even had one that followed me to school and watched over me there."

His uncle came back with the mother and father, the puppies following. They had gotten so big! Still not as big as a fully grown adult, but they were almost to Viv's waist. Braedon, the adult male, could look eye to eye with Viv.

"Pups, this is Viv. She's Mac's mate. She's ours," his uncle said, a bit of his power leaking into the words, letting the dogs know that Viv was family, theirs to protect.

He watched as the pup they had chosen for Viv tilted his head, sniffing the air. He glanced at Lucifer who nodded in return. The pup came up to Viv whining, looking for pets. Viv looked down and Mac swore he could see the hearts in her eyes.

"Oh, look at you! You are adorable. May I pet you?" She held a hand out to sniff.

The pup shoved his head under her hand as a response, making Viv laugh. Viv scratched between his ears, running a hand down the length of his back. "You're so soft," she said, pressing a kiss to the top of his head. The other pups started moving in closer, also wanting pets. Her pup stayed next to her, but his brothers and sisters were loving the attention.

"They're so cute," Viv said. "And you train them all by yourself?" she asked Lucifer.

"I do. That way all the commands are the same and they know I'm the leader of the pack. I'll teach you before you go back home, but Mac knows them all as well. This guy here," Lucifer patted the pup, "is your Christmas gift. He's been fully trained in protection, as well as being house trained. I have the vaccination records you'll need for the human authorities. He's also listed as a service animal so he can go with you wherever you need him to. I can't have my niece running around unprotected, can I?

"I'd also like to offer to add my mark to your demon band. My mark is known to all nonhumans and to mess with what is mine is to die. A horrible painful death. I'd like to add my protection, if you're willing."

Viv looked at Mac, who nodded, showing her his mark on his inner wrist.

"Yes, thank you," Viv replied, holding out her arm. There was a slight inhale when the mark took hold, Mac remembered it feeling like touching a hot stove. Her pup whined, pressing his body against hers. When his uncle let go of her wrist, his mark was woven into the lines, not disrupting the decoration of the demon mark, but like it had been part of the design all along. The words Mate of Mac were still along the top of her wrist, the new marking from Lucifer on the underside like Mac's. Her pup licked her arm quickly.

"Oh!" Viv said softly.

"Hellhounds have a healing property in their saliva. They can't heal everything, but it works wonders on minor and some medium-sized wounds," Lucifer said.

One of the other pups brought over a ball, dropping it at Viv's feet. She laughed and picked it up, throwing it for the pack. As Viv played with the puppies, Lucifer pulled Mac away. "How is everything going? Is she okay after the stalker incident? I wanted to ask earlier but didn't want to bring it up in front of her if she was doing better and risk making it worse. I made sure he was also trained to help during panic attacks and when she has nightmares, just in case."

"Yeah, she's talking with her therapist more and it's been getting better. Uncle Luc, I need to ask you something," Mac said, his face turning red.

"Anything."

"So, um. We had sex while here, but it was way more intense than at Earth. I'm worried I'm going to hurt her. I don't have these urges at home."

His uncle looked at him sharply. "In demon form?"

When Mac nodded, Lucifer sighed. "Your dad said he had already had the birds and bees talk with you, so I didn't go over it again. And for that I apologize. I should have made sure you knew everything. It only happens with mates, so you wouldn't have had it happen before. When you're in demon form, especially when you're in Netherworld, your native home, and your mate is fertile or close to fertile, your base instincts will be to breed. There are several signs; increased arousal, more possessive, maybe rougher sex, wanting to breed them, plug them with your cum inside, biting. Your mate will have similar effects."

"You're saying I could have impregnated her?" Mac asked, shocked. The sudden image of Viv carrying his child was arousing though.

"Maybe. If it was just the once, try keeping to your human form while here to keep the impulses down or wait until you're back on Earth to have sex. Or wear a condom."

"Yeah," Mac replied, still in shock. He definitely did not remember having this conversation with his dad.

"Hello?" a voice called out from the side of the house.

"We're in the back," Lucifer called out. "There's no pressure, but I would make an awesome great-uncle," he said quietly to Mac, grinning.

"You totally would," Mac replied, giving his uncle a quick one-armed hug before walking over to the gate to let the rest of their family in.

"Hello, Lucifer. It's so nice to see you again," D's mom said, coming in with her arms full of food and presents.

"Let me grab the door for you," Lucifer said, rushing over to open the back door. D's dad followed with even more things in his arms.

"Ma might have gone a little overboard," D said, laughing.

"Might have?" Mac asked incredulously. He had never seen so many gifts in one place before.

"Thomas, come meet the puppies! Guess what? This one gets to come home with us! Isn't he amazing?" Viv called out.

Mac had already talked to D and Thomas about the dog, and he knew there were a few toys under the tree at home for him. He didn't want to bring an animal into their home without checking with them first. Luckily, Thomas had also been wanting a dog.

"They're adorable! And huge!" Thomas exclaimed. The pups crowded around him, looking for attention. Thomas laughed, the sound light and happy, as he used both hands to pet each pup.

"Oh, Viv. He's going to be awesome. I can't wait to take him for walks with you. Do you think he can have a Pup

Cup when we get coffee? What are you going to name him, or does he already have a name?"

Viv looked at Mac. "Uncle was waiting for you to pick one. He'd nicknamed him Faolán, which is 'little wolf' in Gaelic. He's not a wolf, but that's what he was using," Mac said, shrugging.

"Say it again?" Viv asked.

"It's spelled F-a-o-l-a-n, with a fada over the second A. You pronounce it, I believe, fwail-awn."

Viv looked at Thomas, both of them muttering it under their breath. Thomas shrugged in answer to some look Viv gave him. "It's different. There probably won't be anyone else calling it out," Viv pointed out.

"True."

"I like it. Let's keep it," Viv said. "Faolán, my not so little pup," she said, kissing his snoot. Viv laughed, wiping her nose as she got a kiss in return.

"Dinner time!" D's mom called out.

They all trooped back inside, Viv's pup following them while the rest lay down to take a nap in the sun.

Mac stuffed himself with food, listening to the stories D's parents and his uncle told about their childhood. Viv and Thomas were laughing so hard they had tears in their eyes. The gift exchange was just the cherry on top, as the saying went. He had a wonderful night and he couldn't wait for tomorrow's relaxing day at home with more delicious food and gifts. Life was wonderful. A year ago, he never would have imagined this scene. Today, he would do anything to protect it.

EPILOGUE

"Push!" Mac encouraged.

"You push! I'm tired," Viv snapped back. It had been a long labor and she was exhausted. She could hear the nurses murmuring in the background that if it went on for too much longer they would be doing a C-section. She had been told the baby was big and it might be difficult for her, but she had been optimistic that she could do a vaginal delivery, one with an epidural and pain meds. Her pregnancy had been closely watched by both Mac, Thomas, and the doctors. There had been no issues from the scorpion poisoning from her abduction. She had felt so relieved.

Now she was in the labor and delivery ward at the nonhuman hospital with D, Thomas, and Lucifer waiting in the waiting room.

"I want to try one more thing before we decide to do a C-section. I have a cream I can apply, it's magical in nature. It's a type of muscle relaxer but it should also potentially help you not rip."

"Will it hurt the baby?"

"No, it was designed just for labor and delivery, especially for large babies."

Viv nodded. "Let's try it."

The doctor nodded, reaching for a shimmering tub. "This is going to feel really weird, kind of tingly from what I've been told. It's going to help open your channel more than your body would naturally. Everything will go back to normal once it wears off, so don't worry about that. If this doesn't work, we're going to have to go to surgery. Your body can't take much more of this and the baby will be getting tired too."

Mac held her hand, watching as the doctor shoved her whole hand up Viv's vagina. He winced, but Viv didn't seem to feel it.

After a minute, Viv started to wiggle. "Oh, that's weird," she panted through a contraction.

The doctor leaned down, checking her progress. "Okay, next contraction you're going to push. Start and stop when I tell you."

Mac watched Viv's stomach tighten again, the muscles rock hard under his hand.

"Push. Now, Viv! Go, go, go, keep pushing. And stop."

Viv's head dropped back to rest on the bed, her forehead sweaty. Mac leaned down to give her a kiss. "You're amazing. You've got this. Let's meet our baby, huh? After this you can have a huge milkshake and a slice of peanut butter pie." Once she had arrived at the hospital she hadn't been allowed to eat and it had been almost a full day since then.

"Here we go again. Get ready, Viv. Push!"

Mac watched in the mirror behind the doctor. He thought he saw the start of dark hair and tiny little horn nubs. "Keep pushing! I can see the head coming, go go go!" the doctor ordered.

He winced as he saw the state of his mate's vagina. He didn't know it could stretch that big and he was grateful for the cream the doctor had used because he didn't think it would have been possible otherwise. She was tiny and the baby clearly was not.

"Okay, Viv. I think one more will get the head out. Then we'll stop and wait for the next one. You're almost there," the doctor encouraged her.

Mac felt her stomach turn rock hard again. "Now!" the doctor shouted.

His mate pushed with everything she had, the dark-haired head popping out. "Stop, get your breath. Okay, one more Viv. Give me everything you have, let's get this baby out!"

Viv took a deep breath, pushing, her neck and face straining. There was a rush of baby and fluids. Mac watched as the doctor cleaned the baby's face off, getting them to cry out. Oh gods, look at what they had made, he thought in awe.

"Congratulations guys. He looks healthy and perfect. Let's get him cleaned off and measured and you can hold him. Dad, why don't you stay with him while I get Viv cleaned up."

Mac looked at his love, getting her nod. He followed, watching as they gave him goop over his eyes, measured his length and weight. He turned around to look at Viv and almost threw up when he saw the placenta fall out into a metal bowl. Those looked like their mixing bowls at home. They needed new ones, he decided. Maybe cheerful colors in a porcelain or ceramic. Not shiny metal. The doctor was checking to make sure it was all discharged and ended up putting a stitch or two down there. Mac was glad the epidural was still working. The doctor was applying a healing cream to Viv's vagina, especially over the stitches, so it should be healed up by tomorrow. He felt sorry for humans who gave birth and had to wait to heal.

He followed as the nurses brought his son back over to Viv, laying him down on her chest, wrapping a blanket over them.

"He was a big one," the doctor said, coming to stand next to him. "Part of the problem was his size, part was that he was shifted, making him a little bigger. We'll have to see what he's like when he switches to human form. He should do that in the next day or so. When you guys have the next one, we'll know to start the cream earlier. If it looks like they're shifted, we might induce a little early to try to keep their size down too. She's a trooper. Congratulations, his stats are perfect. We're running a blood test to make sure nothing weird shows up with her history, but I'm not antici- pating anything. Other than the size, which I think we can attribute to your own size and him shifting, which also can happen in demon births, everything was normal.

"Do you want the rest of the family in now or do you want some alone time?"

"You can let them in," Viv said. She had a hospital gown on again and a blanket over her legs and up to her waist.

The trio came in, D's parents having told them they would wait until they were home and would bring meals. Thomas' parents were dog sitting at their house. Thomas took one side of Viv's bed, Lucifer the other.

"He looks just like you did when you were that age," Lucifer said softly. He gasped when the baby opened his eyes at the sound of his voice. "Well, except for those blue eyes. Those are all your mate. Congratulations. He's perfect."

"He's adorable, Viv. Look at what you made," Thomas

crooned at the baby, who grabbed hold of his passing finger.

Lucifer leaned down, giving them both a kiss. "I have to go, but may I?" he asked, gesturing toward the baby's wrist. Viv nodded and Mac grabbed the healing salve out of his pocket. At the first whimper, Mac swiped on the cream, letting the baby settle back down. He now had Lucifer's mark, protecting him from the world. D and Thomas had also received theirs in the months since Christmas. "Congratulations. He's amazing. I wish I could stay, but work calls me back," he said sadly.

"We'll be there to visit soon," Viv promised. Mac had been surprised that his uncle had left Netherworld at all. This was the only time since his parents' death that he could remember it happening. They had even had their double wedding in Netherworld so that he could attend. They had later had a ceremony on Earth so Thomas' parents could be there.

"You guys ready to leave and head home?" the doctor asked with a smile as she knocked on their door the next morning. "Everything looks good, just come follow up in a week or so, sooner if something feels off, but you look great. We got the lab results back. Hunter is perfectly normal. Except for one thing, and it's not bad. It looks like he carries an anti-venom to scorpions. It's built into his DNA, so he'll be immune to any normal or shifter stings from what we can tell. Now, don't go getting him a pet scorpion and test it, but that's the only thing that showed up. Go home, relax, and congratulations again," she said, giving Viv a hug before leaving the room.

Mac had already packed their bag. He helped Viv stand up and then handed over their son before opening a portal. His uncle had given him a bit more power, allowing him to portal multiple people at a time. It would come in handy with kids. Wrapping an arm around her waist, Mac guided Viv home where Faolán was waiting on the other side anxiously. Thomas and D were there as well, D's parents keeping Thomas' busy in the kitchen so they could port in undetected. Luckily, Hunter had shifted to his human form this morning.

Viv bent down, showing the baby to Faolán. "This is your little brother. Isn't he cute? You guys will have such fun together," she told him. The pup sniffed the baby and gave him a gentle lick. "Good boy," Viv praised him. She walked over to the couch, easing herself down, before adjusting the baby to be held with one hand. She rubbed the pup's ears with the other.

Thomas sat next to her, quietly talking. D bumped Mac's shoulder with a grin. "We may have bought a few more toys," he admitted. "They're in the nursery. Faolán has some too. I'm going to help Ma in the kitchen. Why don't you sit and rest?"

Mac sat in one of the recliners, his eyes heavy. He had sat up all night watching over his family and it was catching up to him now. As sleep stole over him, he smiled, hearing the sounds of his family.

NOTE FROM THE AUTHOR

Thank you for reading *Demon's Mate*! If you enjoyed the story, please consider leaving a review. Reviews, no matter how short, are invaluable to independent authors. They help with visibility, encouraging other readers to give the book a try. Even a simple star rating is amazing. Thank you for taking the time if you leave one. It means so much to me!

ABOUT THE AUTHOR

I have loved reading since I was a child. I also enjoy baking, photography, and seeing new things. The world is a crazy place; sometimes escaping into a great book is the only way I can truly relax. Happily ever after romances are my favorite type of book, so my stories will end with an HEA, even if the road is a little bumpy getting there. I currently reside in the Midwest with my family.

If you sign up for my newsletter, you will get a free short story from the Nightwood Clan series! *Christmas with the Nightwood Clan* is a glimpse into the Clan's first Christmas together and takes place during the Christmas in *A Hairy Situation*.

You can find me here:

HarperDakota.com
HarperDakota.com/newsletter
Harper's Readers Group
facebook.com/AuthorHarperDakota
instagram.com/harperdakotaauthor

ALSO BY THE AUTHOR

NIGHTWOOD CLAN

Bite Me Again

A Hairy Situation

Pointed Love

Forged In Love

Linked In History

Hoarded Secrets

Warded Bonds (Coming Soon)

The Nightwood Clan's Favorite Recipes (Nightwood Clan series companion)

STANDALONE

Demon's Mate